Circle Back
Around

Kyle Hunter

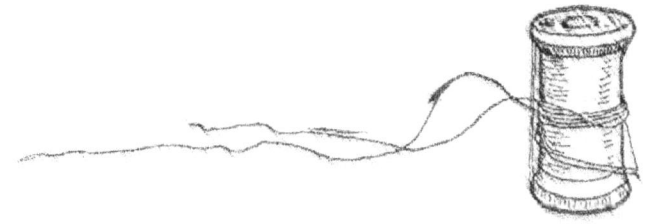

Monceau Publishing

P. O. Box 30981
Raleigh, NC 27622
www.Kyle-Hunter.com

Cover design by Erika Alyana Sañga Duran.

Thread graphic from Creative Commons.

ISBN 978-1-7322682-2-7

Acknowledgements

My thanks to Dr. James Watson from North Carolina State University and Copland Fabrics for their helpful information regarding textile mills in North Carolina.

Circle Back Around

Chapter One

Hailey Anderson closed her office door and collapsed into her cool leather desk chair. She would have savored a leisurely lunch hour instead of a frenzied rush of errands in the July heat of North Carolina. But lately, that was typical, amidst the pressures of her family's textile mill. She sat motionless, allowing herself five minutes to close her eyes and relax her shoulders. Cool air poured with a rattle from a vent in the corner of her office and its icy flow chilled her neck, drying the beads of perspiration.

The phone jangled into the quiet. Her eyes flew open and she glanced at the phone. An inside line. "This is Hailey."

"Did you see the paper today?" The breathless whisper came from Lenore, her longtime secretary.

Hailey leaned back in her chair and peered through the space between the vertical blinds to the area where mill administration was corralled. Her eyes met the worried gaze of Lenore, who clutched the phone to her ear.

"Not yet, Lenore. I haven't had a chance. Bad news, I guess?"

"Another mill is closing. Pristine. It's one of the oldest in North Carolina. They're falling like dominos."

"I knew they were struggling. That's a shame." Hailey swallowed and fingered the loose thread dangling from her skirt.

Her hands were moist and tension needled her stomach. "But we're not closing, Lenore. Don't worry."

"Are you sure? Even Cannon, as big as they were. And other mills our size, one right after the other. Why would we be any different?" Panic laced each word.

Hailey bit her lip. How to comfort the woman while her own insides were in similar turmoil? She struggled to think of words that would be reassuring, convincing when, to even her ears, they sounded hollow.

"Just because another mill has closed doesn't mean that we will. People still need fabrics and clothes, don't they, now?"

A long pause hung on the line. "I guess so. Still, that doesn't guarantee . . . I'm sorry, Hailey. I know you and your dad are doing the best you can. I—I just don't know what I'd do if I lost this job. You know, with Jerry out of work and all . . ."

"I know, it's hard. But we're trying to be proactive and creative so we don't join the statistics. Be assured of that."

"Thanks." Lenore's voice lost its edge, but its usual cheerfulness was still missing. "Sorry to bother you."

"No, you haven't bothered me. I'll take a look at that article. Maybe it'll give me some ideas."

Hailey hung up the phone and stared at the newspaper, perched on the edge of her overfilled desk. It taunted her like a cobra about to strike. If only she *could* be proactive and creative. Paul Anderson, her father and owner of the mill, was anything *but*. He seemed to be hunkering down for the final and tragic defeat of Anderson Mill.

If Anderson closed its doors, she'd have to find a new job, like everyone else who worked here. Yet for her, it was more than a job. Even as a child, she'd wandered in and out of the various buildings—the carding department, where the raw wool was cleaned, the spinning room with hundreds of dancing vertical spools, the weaving area with rows of noisy looms—asking dozens of questions about what went on there. Everyone in town knew the Anderson family and their mill. They'd employed hundreds of the residents of Larkspur, North Carolina for four generations. For Hailey, many of those employees had names, faces, histories. And she was part of them, yet felt responsible for them at the same time. Like a good parent.

She pulled the newspaper closer to read the headline and the first few sentences, then shook her head. It had happened again, this time, to a neighboring mill whose owner she'd known for years. She leaned back in her chair and sighed. Her gaze panned the small office, a dingy square closed in by colorless walls. The drawing table, spread with designs and fabric samples, dominated the room. Against the wall her desk grimly shouldered her stacks of unfinished work and her computer, which broadcast bad news almost daily.

A tall window behind her desk overlooked a swatch of land with tall grasses and a few dumpsters, a dreary scene that matched her current life, except for one detail. During most of the day she could hear the faint rumble of dozens of looms one floor below, churning an endless, comforting heartbeat into the quiet.

Hailey glanced back at the newspaper, hesitant. Might be worth a try. She rose and took the paper in one hand. After launching a determined glance at Lenore's frightened one, she strode down the hall toward the presidential office, her mind churning out words and phrases as she went. Maybe she'd luck out and Dad would be receptive.

"Hey, Dad," she ventured as she crossed the threshold of his office. A pleasant smile might pave the way.

Her father swung his chair around and motioned to her with one finger, pulling the phone closer to his ear. Fatigue painted his pale blue eyes, which were surrounded by creases she hadn't noticed before. His gaunt face no longer resembled the ruddy Scotsman he was when she was a child. Every day bad news and criticism rained down on him, yet he only dug deeper into his favorite strategy of "wait and see". Only she was pretty sure he'd wait until there was nothing left to see.

"Yes, Hailey." He let out a gut-deep sigh as he set the telephone back on the cradle, his weary eyes on her.

For a split-second Hailey was more worried about him than frustrated. His withered frame no longer filled the executive chair. She reminded herself why she was there and rallied her arguments.

"Dad, did you hear about Pristine?" She placed the paper onto his desk, with a twinge of guilt for dumping more bad news on her beleaguered father. Yet, he had to see facts. The headline, an ugly black gash, read "Another Mill Falls in Forsythe County." She watched his face as he glanced down at the paper. His frown deepened as bushy white eyebrows furrowed, but he didn't speak.

"It has me worried. We need to be more proactive." Despite wanting to stay calm and professional, she added, "*Please*, let's do something new before we have to lay people off. I know you don't want to do that."

Paul Anderson's gaze hardened on his youngest daughter. That stare used to freeze her in her tracks when she was a child. She knew what he'd say next.

"Hailey, my drama queen, you always were emotional about the mill. We *are* taking action, and that's all you need to know."

She wouldn't let him off that easily, patronizing her as if she were still eight years old. "We have to plan a strategy. I'm afraid we'll shut down if we don't do something different. We—we lost another order to Pakistan, just this morning. The Owens account."

A flash of alarm slid across his face, but he pulled on a mask of calm just as quickly. Hailey schooled her voice, knowing it could easily burst out in staccato notes of panic, just like Lenore's had. *Calm, Hailey.*

"I'm asking you again to leave this to me. You are a designer. That's your role. It's not your job to save the mill. That's *my* job. I have lots of pressure on me. Now please, I have a meeting in ten minutes." He turned his chair slightly away as if to dismiss her. She saw only the shiny bald spot amidst wiry red-gray hair as he bowed his head toward his papers. Deflated, Hailey could only leave the office, as her eyes burned. She'd said what she had to say. But as usual, it hadn't made any impact on the elder Anderson. None.

She lowered her gaze, pretending to scan the newspaper she still clutched in her hands, as she passed Daniel Carlton, the assistant manager. The last thing she needed was for him to see tears in her eyes. He'd find some way to use it, sooner or later. Besides, she wasn't in the mood for greetings, especially his. All she wanted to do was wail. As she passed Lenore's desk she just shook her head then closed her office behind her.

Six years. She'd tried to make a difference at Anderson Mill for the past six years, tried to reverse the fast leak, and had failed. Whatever she said to her father about any subject—especially the mill—was like talking to the wind. An indifferent, chilly wind. It had always been that way, and it had always stung. An acute and all-too-familiar pain, yet it paled against the threat nearly engulfing her family's business. For some crazy reason she had deep roots in this factory, whose employees were closer to a surrogate family for her than her own family. It wasn't merely a job. If only she could make

9

a difference. If only she weren't fated to watch it slowly grind down and go the way so many other mills had gone in the last decade.

Growing up in a textile town, Hailey had always taken for granted the fact that these factories would always be part of her landscape. Textiles had once been the largest industry in North Carolina, but during the eighties and nineties, they rapidly lost their place. Hundreds of jobs vanished and would never return, having been replaced by foreign contracts and automation. The new millennium had shown improvements, but the mills weren't out of danger, even now in 2004. Hailey had watched the trend with interest, then mild panic, as she understood that it could happen to them, too. Especially with the current style of leadership. In response, she'd tried to court new clients on the side, bring suggestions to the presidential office. Nothing made a scratch.

When the long work day ended, Hailey wearily drove toward her townhouse a few miles from the mill. Her languid gaze painted across the familiar buildings . . . the town hall, the park in front of it where the city held an art festival in summer and placed a tall evergreen at Christmas, colorfully lit, towering in the center, gathering townspeople for caroling or New Year's Eve festivities.

On the diagonal corner sat The Scoop, a local ice cream parlor where she and her sister, Hope, went as children, escaping from their preoccupied parents on Saturday afternoons. They'd share secrets while enjoying one of twelve homemade flavors.

How she'd love to be able to sit down with Hope right then, pouring out her fears and anguish, since Hope had always been the one she'd turned to for family warmth. But Hope had never shared Hailey's attachment to Anderson Mill. She'd moved away to Colorado without a twinge for the family business, while Hailey was still anchored and rusting in place.

She could always talk to her best friend, Nina, whose calm manner usually put Hailey's frustrations into perspective. But Nina had recently gotten engaged to Justin. Hailey wouldn't dampen her friend's joy with her own struggles.

Hailey passed the post office, Hank's Auto Repair, the Ace Hardware store. So many memories from a lifetime in a small town that now hemmed her in, narrowing her possibilities, suffocating her.

Tears moistened her lashes and blurred her vision. It was bad enough that things didn't look good for Anderson Mill, in danger of joining all the bleak statistics of textile manufacturing in the previous decade. So many of Anderson's employees were like grandmothers and grandfathers to her. She'd known their children and their grandchildren, had watched them grow up. She saw the dread on their faces as they spoke to her of their fears. It squeezed her gut to see them tied in knots by day and likely losing sleep, as they wondered when they, too, would hear that their jobs were gone. For some, it was the only work they and their children had ever known. She could only guess what they would do.

Hailey pulled into the numbered space at her condominium complex and, with a deep sigh, left the air-conditioned sanctuary of her car. The sweet fragrance of fresh-cut grass wafted toward her. Up the street, her neighbor, Alex, was shoving something bulky into the dumpster. When the mass finally disappeared into the opening, he stepped back and turned in her direction. Seeing her, he lifted an arm in a static wave then sauntered away toward his condo.

Her hand raised in a weak response as she watched him, for too long. She hadn't seen Alex since the homeowners' meeting a couple of months earlier. That evening they'd had a minor debate, as she objected to the landscaping fees. She'd probably come across as stubborn and hot-tempered. She'd considered dropping by his house to apologize, not for her opinion, but for her tone. That gesture might have smoothed things out instead of reminding him to avoid her.

Hailey let out another long breath from a deep well inside as she locked the car. Friday afternoon. What would her weekend hold? Trying to stay cool and push away dark dread until Monday, when she'd have to face it all over again. She'd forgotten what it was like to feel any other way.

Chapter Two

A glance at her watch told Hailey she was only barely on schedule. It wouldn't do to set a bad example just because she was the boss' daughter. However, as she approached the dumpster near her condo, she struggled to keep three plastic bags in her grasp, slowing her pace so she could arrive at the same time as Alex.

"Hey, neighbor," she said with a friendly smile when he reached the dumpster.

His dark eyes met hers and an electric current bolted through her.

"Hi, Hailey." His glance fell to her three plastic bags. A half-smile quirked his lips. "You've got quite a trash collection there. It's not all that far to the dumpster, you know."

Now would be a perfect time to say something clever, but with her mind completely scrubbed of wit and reason, that was unlikely. So, she smiled and shrugged, and smoothed an unruly bunch of auburn curls over one shoulder. Standing next to him, she guessed his height topped hers by six inches or so. His raven-black hair curled slightly under his ears and crept a couple of inches down his neck. She'd known him casually for two years, and his presence always made her slightly breathless. And occasionally speechless.

"Thought you'd like to know the association did hire a new landscape company this month," he said without looking at her, while he pitched the bag overhead like a basketball into the yawning mouth of the dumpster.

"Oh, really? I didn't know. I guess that's good." Hailey sighed. Too bad he brought up *that* subject.

"Looks like your heated protests paid off." He smirked and looked down at her as he stepped back. She couldn't interpret his expression, which seemed an odd blend of ridicule and kindness. He turned away.

"Alex," she said. He stopped and shifted back to her, expectant. "I, um, I came across impatient at the meeting that day, but wanted you to know I'm not always like that." She shrugged one shoulder and added, "I almost stopped by to apologize." An olive branch of humility, despite her wordy babble.

He looked at her for a moment, as if considering what to say. "You should have." Then he grinned. "Have a good day."

She watched his broad back as he sauntered away. A wave of shame frothed up inside. What did he mean by that? She *ought* to have come by to apologize because she'd been obnoxious? Or, he would have enjoyed seeing her if she'd come by? Oh, why hadn't she acted on her good impulse? It could have helped their strained relationship. At the least, he'd know she regretted her fiery response at the meeting. At best, he might have invited her in to talk, and they could have gotten to know each other better. He'd have seen that she wasn't a hot-headed shrew, but a kind, fun-loving, sensitive—

Hailey frowned and trudged glumly back toward her car. No other way to see it. She'd blown it with him.

Nothing new on that count. Her success with men was the same as everything else in her life, in need of emergency resuscitation. Three years earlier her last boyfriend, Joel, moved to Boston for a new job, yanking away a love she'd thought would last forever. He'd said he loved her, wanted a future with her. But within a few months his promises and commitments frayed like a worn blanket then finally disappeared. Turns out she'd been easy to leave, easy to forget.

Since then, no one else had come close to igniting her emotions or interest. Until Alex. But Alex was still miles away, a stranger, even if he only lived on the next block. With him, there was nothing to hope for. She simply irritated and frustrated him.

Once back in her office the day's pressures flooded in and shoved out every other thought. At two in the afternoon she turned to her computer to see what some of the competition was doing. From one site to the next, she scanned services and offers. Some textile companies were sending yarn to Pakistan or India, then bringing woven fabric back for finishing. If they were doing that, it must be less expensive, even with transport and customs. Could be worth a try, if turnaround time wasn't too long.

Other companies were exploring high-tech fabrics, which heat and cool with body temperature. They were also experimenting with other industrial fibers, usually chemically based. Still others had specialized in Jacquard weaving, a highly-prized weave of French origin which required programmable heads for the designs. She'd love to bring Jacquard designs into Anderson Mill, but the equipment was prohibitively expensive, and would require specially-trained personnel. She'd have to think of something less pricey and more practical. Even with a bargain, her dad would probably balk and find reasons to refuse. Though some of their equipment had been modernized in the previous decade, daily methods of production remained the same.

What was he waiting for? Maybe Dad was planning to ride the wave until it dissolved into foam, then quietly retire and forget about Anderson Mill.

Hailey caught the pathway of her thoughts as guilt stabbed at her. The mill wasn't dying yet. And of course, her father wouldn't deliberately neglect measures that might save it simply because he was scheduled to retire soon. In fact, she'd never heard him speak of retirement and wondered if he even planned on it. He'd hang on until he was eighty or more. What else did he have? He'd been married to the business all those years, and was alienated, more or less, from his two daughters.

Hailey glanced at a framed photo of Hope and her daughter, Devon. Snow-covered peaks rose in the background of their smiling faces, flushed above colorful ski vests. Unlike Hailey, who had always been compliant and tried to please their father, Hope had gotten pregnant in high school. When her daughter, Devon, was three, Hope took a job in Denver, where she'd been ever since. It had left Hailey feeling orphaned. Two years later, their mother moved west as well.

Suddenly an intense longing to be there in Colorado with her sister and niece—or anyplace far away from the continual pressures of Anderson Mill—assailed her. As Hope had recently told her, she was long overdue for a visit.

She drew her eyes away from the photo and rocked gently in her chair. For now, she'd have to be solution-oriented and drag her thoughts back to the crisis at hand. She *must* make a difference at Anderson. Her eyes returned to the computer screen. Maybe she could research the projected costs of sending yarn to Pakistan and having it woven and sent back, or even buying the yarn itself there. If the numbers were convincing enough, perhaps her father would agree to a trial run. And if that worked, he might accept some of her other ideas.

What was she thinking? Had he ever been open to her ideas? Had she ever been able to make a real difference at Anderson Mill, and in her father's eyes? Yet she hadn't brought that one up yet. Might be worth a try.

She was out of her chair before she registered a small voice inside, urging her to have the figures in hand first. It was impulsive to approach him with vague ideas but no data to back it up, especially after their last conversation.

Hailey arrived at her father's office then hesitated in the hallway. *What am I thinking?* The words rang again in her skull, but she shook her head. His door was ajar. When she saw Daniel Carlton already in conversation with him, she hovered in the hall. Daniel glanced up at her, deadpan mask on his face, and continued pouring over the document with her father. Her father was scowling. Might not be a good time. Maybe she should come back later.

As she turned to leave, she noticed a photo on his credenza, the same framed photo of Hope and Devon on the ski slope. She'd never noticed it before, and it surprised her that he had it so centrally placed in his office. A melancholy ripple coursed through her for a moment, both for her dad and for herself. She swallowed it down.

Daniel stood up, took a file from the desk, and left the office. He brushed by her and murmured, "Next in line."

She frowned and glared after him. She didn't desire special treatment as the boss' daughter, but she wasn't one of the factory workers, either. She and Daniel were both managers. He'd been there five years, and she'd been there six. He'd always seemed coolly disdainful to her, and overly eager toward her father.

She peered into the office then stepped gingerly inside. "How is your day going, Dad?"

He looked up and a shadow of warmth flickered across his face.

She took heart.

"About the same as usual, I'm afraid," he said wearily. "I know you don't think I see what's going on around here, but I do. Keeps me up at night."

Hailey's eyes widened at his admission. She lowered herself into the chair beside his massive desk, still watching him. "I know you have a lot on you. I hope you know I just want to help. I'm not being critical. I'd like to help you brainstorm new ideas. We can offer new products, improve our website, making it more modern. Things like that. Just one thing at a time." She kept her voice soothing and low, unwilling to break the spell of the moment of vulnerability.

Her father's brow furrowed. "More modern? We don't actually need a website, but you insisted, so we got one. Lot of good it's done."

Hailey chafed at his comment but continued to speak calmly. "We *do* need a website, but not just a placeholder on the web. It should command respect, let people know that we're serious and have a good product. A bad-looking website is worse than none at all, in today's world. Ours is outdated-looking." She hadn't wanted to say anything oppositional at this point, but the website? Everything about it was tacky. "You should look at competitors' websites. Customers care about these things."

Paul Anderson sat back in his chair. The icebergs had returned to his eyes. "Serious customers won't care about it. Quality service and products are what they care about, and we give them that."

Hailey leaned forward. "What about people who aren't customers yet? We have to give them some impression before they take the first step, don't we? That's why companies invest in their sites, to make that good first impression. Even some of the Pakistani sites are pretty good."

18

"Oh, don't talk to me about Pakistanis. They're stealing our livelihood. They'd take it all if they could."

Hailey frowned. Her idea about sending raw yarn to Pakistan wasn't going to be well-received. "I'm just using that as an example, Dad. If the Pakistanis have good websites and they're our competition, shouldn't we outdo them? That's only one idea. We can offer higher end fabrics, or offer products in home fashion, for example. Upholstery, linens. Make them available in a catalog or maybe online for ordering. Online has been the growing trend for years now. We could try selling finished products desired by the general public."

"So, you think we should just jump on the bandwagon and become a retail store?"

A small sinking began inside Hailey, piercing the small balloon of optimism. She rallied her flagging boldness. "Yes, why not? We should see what our competitors are doing, and do as much or more. We could do that much, don't you think?"

But her father was already shaking his head, his mouth a frozen grimace. "Let's just go run out and do what everyone is doing. We've had a reliable product and service all these years. A reputation."

"But the market changes, Dad. Our reliability and products can be there until Doomsday, but if the public wants something else, we're done. We *have* to move with the market. That's what businesses do to stay alive. And better, they have to anticipate changes before they come, because when they come, it's often too late."

He lifted his head and met her eyes. "Do you think it's too late for us?"

She paused and shifted in her chair. "I—hope not. No, I don't think it's too late, but if we don't take action soon, maybe reorganize a little bit—"

"Are you talking layoffs?"

"No, not necessarily. If we can implement some changes that will utilize the current work force, no layoffs at all, unless they become necessary."

"Implement changes? You're talking about taking risks, Hailey. Huge, expensive risks, and we're running on thin ice as it is."

"Yes, I know. Or at least I have suspected as much. That's because it's late. It would have been good to try some changes sooner. But I don't think it's *too* late."

He stopped and eyed her in silence. Finally, he said, "Seems you don't approve of the way things have been run. Have you got some good ideas to give me, since you know so much?"

Her throat went dry. She'd expected passive dismissal, not bald opposition. Yet amidst sarcasm, he was asking for ideas. And some of her best ones now escaped her. She swallowed. "Well, like the ones I've mentioned. Improving the website. Offering products online. That'll take some organization, but it could pay off in the long run. Some companies are even working *with* the Pakistanis or Chinese, sending products there for some of the middle stage labor, then back here for finishing."

"What?" A mottled blotch of red appeared on his cheeks. "You propose working *with* them? They're taking our clients, will take our whole industry! I can't believe what I'm hearing."

"That's just an idea, Dad. Some companies are saving money that way. Here's another idea, we could cut some stages like spinning, and just do weaving, for instance. Or experiment with industrial fabrics."

"That'll take more chemists, who we can't afford to hire. But Pakistanis? Why don't we just move the mill to Karachi? Or bring them here?"

"Dad." She laid her hand on his forearm. "It's just one idea. I didn't mean to upset you. My point was that there are many things we can try. A lot of it can be outsourced. You don't have to hire anyone."

"I should let *you* try to run this mill. You'd understand. You make it sound like all you have to do is try a little of this, a little of that, like it's some kind of cake recipe. This mill has been in our family for generations, and all you want to do is sell out to the latest trend. We don't have to abase ourselves just to survive."

"It isn't abasing ourselves to use common sense business principles that everyone uses. Everyone but us." Hailey bit her lip. She hadn't meant to say it.

He eyed her again. "I have work to do. Go back to the design room. How many times do I have to tell you to stay in your department and manage your projects? Let me do my job. I hope we don't have this conversation again. I'm warning you, Hailey."

A chill ran through her. He hadn't talked to her like that since she was a teenager. And the warning had always worked like a charm. She'd been too frightened of Paul Anderson to find out what came after it.

Yet suddenly she wasn't frightened—of him or of the fate of the mill. "Don't worry, Dad," she said evenly as she stood up, though her heart pounded against her rib cage. "I won't bother you again about this, I promise. I don't want to stand by, paralyzed, while everything falls down around us. That would be too hard. So, I'm giving you my notice."

She turned to leave, but not before having the satisfaction of seeing his mouth drop open. The sharp, staccato sound of her father calling her name followed her down the carpeted hallway, but she didn't turn. She held a stiff smile on her lips even as tears cascaded down her cheeks.

Chapter Three

Hailey stood back from the small rented truck and stared at the last of her boxes neatly tucked inside. The lump in her throat throbbed up into her neck until even her jaws ached. She was leaving Larkspur, North Carolina. Where she'd been her entire life. Moving across the country.

She wouldn't cry. This change was the right thing to do. Six years at the mill, four of them in this neighborhood. Hailey shook her head. She simply had to move on.

"I think that should about do it." Hal, one of several of her church friends, wiped perspiration from his brow with one wrist while Steve swigged cold water from a bottle. For the previous two hours, Hailey's condo was emptied of life. Now it was only a shell ready for the next occupant, bearing no sign of the years she'd lived there, struggling to make a difference, and finally conceding defeat.

Of course, her father hadn't believed she would really quit. He'd thought she'd been piqued and would reconsider once she'd cooled down. He hadn't even tried to persuade her to stay, and that had only hardened her resolve to leave. For too many years, he'd taken her for granted, not heard her heart, not given her credit for having wisdom about anything. For too long she'd made no headway, no impact, though she'd certainly tried. It was time to turn to a new chapter, time to rebuild her confidence apart from the mill. Apart from Paul Anderson. Some things just weren't meant to be.

The previous month had sped by in a whirlwind, as Hailey sold and gave things away—furniture, clothing, even her car—said goodbyes, and made phone calls in preparation for her arrival at her new destination. Hope had been wild with joy at Hailey's decision to go west. She called and emailed frequently to tell Hailey about an apartment or a job possibility she thought might be suitable. Her mother, Tessa, was more reserved, but had also expressed gladness at having her younger daughter living close by for the first time in years. Finally, Hailey would have a real family. Finally, she'd matter to someone.

"Who is renting your condo?" Steve asked her.

"A young single mom. She'll be here soon to get the key, then I'm on my way."

"Denver, Colorado. That's quite a hike. You could stop along the way if you see anything interesting." Steve blocked the sun from his eyes with one hand.

Hailey swallowed against the rising emotion inside. Probably not. She'd be too eager to slam the door on her old life and begin the new one. Seeing Hope's face would sponge away any clingy regrets, all lingering misgivings.

Nothing would change at Anderson Mill. She was powerless to stop the inevitable, though it might take years. The mill employees she'd known all her life had hugged her fiercely and watched in sad bewilderment on her final day. Lenore had sniffled and clung to Hailey as she said goodbye. Hailey had closed her office door, sagging cardboard box cradled in her arms, and walked out of Anderson Mill for the last time.

"We'll miss you, Hailey," said Justin, Nina's fiancé, his blue eyes lacking their usual cheerfulness.

"I'll miss you guys, too. Thanks so much for your help today." Hailey stepped forward to give each of them a tight hug. Her eyes misted as she pulled back. When she came to Nina, she held down a sob, though Nina wept without embarrassment. Her dark hair wisped around reddened eyes. Hailey fiercely whispered, "You'll always be my best friend, nothing will change that. I'm going to miss you so much." She held Nina in a tight grasp for several seconds then pulled away. "I'll visit at some point, not sure when. For the wedding, for sure. As soon as you set the date, let me know."

Nina nodded, her cheeks wet with tears, her ruddy complexion a darker pink. "I really *am* happy for you," she mumbled, then laughed. "I know it doesn't look like it."

Hailey smiled as her tears also trickled from her eyes. After another tight, prolonged squeeze and a promise to call, she stood and watched while Justin and Nina drove away, along with the others. Several moments later, she paid and thanked her teenage helpers, who'd cleaned the condo after the boxes and furniture were carried out. Then they too drove away.

She stood alone in the grassy common area of the complex that had been her home for the last four years, breathing in the sudden calm. Not many of the residents were outside that day. Scattered gatherings of tall pines, maples and crape myrtles, leaning and whispering in the breeze, would be the only witnesses of her departure.

Hailey glanced around the grounds. No sign of Alex. She hadn't seen much of him in the last two weeks, though during a final encounter at the dumpster, she'd told him she was leaving. She thought he looked disappointed, but she'd never been good at reading his expressions. He had only wished her well and bestowed a killer smile before turning away. For the last time.

She shook her head and grimaced. No sense thinking about that. She was leaving for good, moving across the country to Colorado. There would have been no point for him to say anything else. Not that he was even thinking that way. Not that he'd ever tempt her to stay. No, it wasn't like that. If it were, maybe she wouldn't be leaving in a half-hour.

A wave of melancholy engulfed her otherwise confirmed sense of well-being. Then the crunch of tires on gravel yanked her from her reverie. She looked up. A yellow Mustang parked a few feet from where she stood and her new renter, Maggy, stepped out. "Hey, Hailey. Got here as soon as I could."

"Everything's ready for you." Hailey walked along the landscaped sidewalk to the condo with her new renter. "I'll just do the walk-through with you, and then it's all yours."

In a numbed state, Hailey walked the woman through each room of her former home. Every phrase she spoke echoed, and the scent of freshly scrubbed surfaces reminded her it wasn't hers anymore. Finally, she handed the keys to Maggy and gave her a sheet of paper. "Here's the information for the management company, should you have any repair needs or anything. I hope you enjoy living here."

Hailey trudged back to the truck, fished a different set of keys from her jeans pocket, and took a slow, departing look at her neighborhood.

಄   ಄   ಄

So, this is what it felt like to cross through seven states in a truck. Hailey blinked drowsy eyes and shifted to take pressure off of her rear-end, almost numb after several hours, her second day on the road. She only drove across corners of some states, while others seemed an endless stretch of land. Hope would have liked West Virginia, with its mountain passes and green leafy curtains everywhere. But she'd found her own slice of paradise there in Colorado, one Hailey would soon share, with sunshine most of the year, though no searing temperatures in summer, as she'd had in Larkspur.

Her phone rang and she reached for it on the passenger seat. "Hi, Hope."

"Just called for a status report. Where are you now?" Hope's cheerful voice filled the phone.

"Just passed Saint Louis." Hailey glanced around at the flat terrain and the ribbon of highway before her, which seemed to stretch to the edge of the earth.

"I can't talk long, but wanted to touch base. How does it feel to be away from the prison?"

Hailey laughed. "Great at this point, though it's still sinking in. I'll still worry about Anderson Mill. Nothing I can do now, though."

"As a general rule, I couldn't care less about the mill. It's no wonder Mom finally left Dad to come out here. The mill was always his mistress, and the three of us didn't matter much. We should all hate the mill."

Hailey winced at Hope's harsh words. "I don't hate it. It's always been such a part of me. But I just can't give it anything else. I've run dry."

"You gave it your life blood, practically. Now come out here and start living!" Hope broke into a giggle. "Remember the pact we made when we were young? That we'd always stay near each other?"

"You mean the pact you broke twelve years ago when you moved away?" Hailey kept her voice light, though Hope's decision to move had devastated her at the time. Hope had always been

Hailey's anchor during those years when their parents' preoccupation had left them both feeling like islands floating alone in the Anderson ocean.

"I left for the same reason you're leaving now, to escape it all. Now you can actually have a life. *And* keep our pact. I'm so glad you came to your senses, dear Sis."

Hailey couldn't suppress a smile. "Me too. I can't wait to see you all."

She hung up the phone and visualized wrapping her arms around Hope, knowing it wasn't a temporary visit, but a permanent move. For the first time in years Hailey would be a part of Hope's life. Holiday gatherings, shopping trips, vacations, sisterly talks over coffee—in person. She hadn't seen her niece grow up, but could gladly slip into Devon's teenage years before they were gone. Hailey treasured the chance to draw closer to her mother too, or at least try.

As an added benefit, Hailey would finally have the chance to try her design skills on her own, to test herself in the marketplace without the protection or the limitations of the mill around her. She could even one day work for herself as a freelance designer. She was free, finally free. Never before had her life been so exciting, so unpredictable.

In a sense, leaving Anderson Mill was like divorcing her past and the vast web of relationships she'd always taken for granted. For a fleeting moment she braced against a ripple of alarm. Who would she be in Colorado, without the lifelong identity of Anderson Mill? Was she escaping, taking the cowardly way out? She swallowed and pressed her lips together for a long moment. Then aloud she huffed, "What's wrong with escaping a hopeless situation? It's time for something new."

Now she could develop her *own* goals and lifestyle, instead of living in the shadow of the mill. She should have made this move sooner, instead of doggedly following a misguided dream of pleasing her father, or contributing to a factory. She knew that her motives were mixed. A legitimate desire to save the family business inextricably woven with her quest to rise above the sense of invisibility she'd felt all her life. It all seemed so pointless now. Well, better late than never.

Four days later, as Hailey and her rented truck crossed the state line into Colorado, she let out a whoop of celebration. On the last stretch of her journey she passed a blur of small towns as she bore down on her final destination. At last she saw them, appearing as a filmy smudge against the horizon. The Rocky Mountains. As she drove they emerged into focus, distinct, majestic, solid.

Hailey glanced at the clock on her dashboard. Within two hours she'd arrive at Hope's home in the western suburbs of Denver. Her mother lived in Boulder, a half-hour's drive further, but would be there to join the welcome party. Thoughts of Larkspur were left far behind. The future—new opportunities and a true family—lay before her, just beyond the mountains.

When the small brick ranch house came into view, Hailey let out a long sigh. Her shoulders and rear had been aching for hours. She wasn't sure she'd even be able to stand upright again, let alone walk, after nearly thirty hours in the truck. But she was there.

Before she could descend from the vehicle, Hope bounded out the front door and across the front yard. The sisters embraced tightly, squealing and laughing at the same time. "You're finally here! We already opened the wine, hope you don't mind."

Hailey grinned. "No problem. It feels so good to finally be here." She stood back from her sister, who resembled her very little.

Hope's straight dark hair, so unlike Hailey's unruly auburn ringlets, was pulled into a small ponytail. A modest-sized tattoo adorned one shoulder and an earthy-looking smock dress hung down over leggings. "You look so good, Hope. Fit and healthy. Have you lost weight?"

"I firmed up with so much hiking." Hope linked her arm through Hailey's. "We hiked all summer, whenever we had the weather and free time for it."

"Can't wait to do that with you guys." Hailey smiled and pleasure cascaded through her tired body.

They walked together up the brick path toward the house just as her mother, Tessa, emerged, arms outstretched. Her salt-and-pepper hair was pulled up in an elegant chignon and long earrings dangled nearly to her shoulders. "There's my girl," she called. Hailey went into her arms for a long hug then turned toward fifteen-year-old Devon, who had appeared beside her.

"Bet you're tired, Aunt Hailey." Her voice was muffled against Hailey's shoulder as they hugged.

"I sure am. Five days behind the wheel. Devon, you're taller than your mother now." Hailey was amazed at how her niece had changed since the previous Christmas when they'd all met in New York for the holidays. Devon grinned, displaying sparkling braces and flipped her straight blond-brown hair over one shoulder.

"How was your trip?" asked her mother after the four of them were settled in the living room with cool drinks.

"Uneventful, but long." Hailey sipped her iced tea, soothing her parched throat in a cool gush. "I was nervous at first, crossing the whole country by myself, but it was a straight shot."

"How's Daddy? Did he break down in tears when you left?" Hope asked, her voice laced with sarcasm.

Hailey squeezed her lips together. "No, he was still angry, I think, but didn't show it. You know old stoic Daddy."

"*Stubborn* stoic Daddy," supplied Hope with a snort.

"He was surprised until the end. He never thought I'd do it. I guess he thought I was bluffing."

"Frankly, I never thought you would either," Tessa murmured and took a sip of Merlot.

"You probably thought I'd chicken out. Well, I didn't." At times Hailey herself had wondered if she'd end up weakening. In the end, she knew that going back would solve nothing, and would earn her plenty of ridicule, if not from her father, then from herself.

"I'm very proud of you, dear," said her mother. "I guess you had your dose."

"I was overdue for some changes. I had hoped to contribute, but felt powerless—"

"Big surprise," muttered Hope. "Just because you're an Anderson doesn't mean that you need to sacrifice your happiness and your future on the altar of Anderson Mill. You're your own person too, you know."

Hailey nodded, her lips pressed tight. Her own person . . . She'd finally learn who that person was, hundreds of miles away from Anderson Mill. "True. But I still didn't want to see it flounder, like other mills in our area."

"Honey, that's the story all across the South, and for a couple of decades now. Especially in North Carolina." Tessa shook her head. "You gave it your best shot." She paused and looked

31

thoughtful. "Anderson has had its ups and downs over the generations. Though I have no more ties to Anderson Mill, it would make me sad to see it go down."

"Me too," murmured Devon, who had been quiet since entering the house. A grave silence followed as the women contemplated the fate of the mill.

Devon pulled herself up from where she'd sat cross-legged on the floor and flopped down next to Hailey on the couch, her arm touching Hailey's. She looked up at Hailey, hazel eyes shining. "I'm really glad you're here, Aunt Hailey. We're a family again."

To Hailey's surprise, tears sprang to her eyes. She blinked and slid her arms around Devon, squeezing tightly. "Yes. It's good to be a part of your lives. Life is too short to not be with the ones we love." Finally, she'd done it, left her cold, distant father and found the warm welcome of her true family clear across the country.

As she leaned back on the couch, a mental image fluttered unbidden into her mind, mocking her contentment . . . the gates of Anderson Mill chained from the outside, weeds growing up around them. She swallowed, aware of a heavy weight that suddenly formed inside her. But it was no longer her story, no longer her problem. At least that's what she told herself, as she fought to recapture the current moment.

Chapter Four

Hailey's computer screen glowed a cold stare. The popping sound from a small kitchen near her desk signaled the near completion of freshly-brewed coffee. Before she could rise to fill her cup, her extension rang.

The clipped and ever-cheerful voice of Patrick, her supervisor, chirped through the phone like a sparrow on caffeine. "Hailey, I need those designs for Faircliff by Tuesday. Can you make it happen?"

Hailey knew he wasn't pressuring her, but she still felt a ripple of irritation. She wished she could work for herself, at her own pace. Maybe someday soon. "Sure, Patrick. I can bring them by your office later today to see if I'm on track with what the client wants."

"Great, great. That works. I'll be here all afternoon."

After a month of searching and interviewing, Hailey had been grateful to find a job closely related to her previous experience, designing for a home textile distributor. The designs were done in-house, but all the work was sent overseas then shipped back for distribution. She'd once suggested a similar process to her father. It wasn't the ideal creative outlet, since she spent her days following the narrow parameters of the company's vision.

Hailey's desk was arranged in a large square with those of three other designers. Their phone calls filled the air with an indistinct web of conversation. Sunlight spilled through long windows, and beyond them, the gray outline of the mountain range rose up through white-trunked aspens, nearly bare of yellow leaves.

When she settled back at her desk with a steaming mug, she glanced at the clock. It would be three in the afternoon in Larkspur. A pang of guilt nudged at her. She hadn't spoken with her father since her arrival. She hadn't yet given him her new home number, and he'd never liked calling her on her cell phone. She was still his daughter. She jotted an email note to him and included her home phone number. If he wasn't still angry, he might call.

After the work day Hailey opened the door to her unfinished apartment. She flipped on the kitchen radio to give herself some company. A local sale announcement reverberated through the half-empty room. This weekend she'd finish outfitting her place to make it homey before Christmas. Since her arrival, much of her time had been taken searching for a job and housing.

She picked up the phone and quickly dialed Hope's number. "Hey, Hope, I guess you aren't home from work yet. Just wanted to see if you were free for lunch this weekend. I haven't seen you lately." Hailey squeezed her lips together. Shouldn't have said that last sentence. She didn't want to make Hope feel guilty for being too busy to get together.

Once Hailey had gotten settled and her mother and Hope returned to their jobs, Hailey was alone more than she had expected. Of course, that was normal, she understood that everyone had their own lives. Still, it left a hollow ache as she wondered if her craving for family would eventually be fulfilled. She didn't know if she'd truly solved anything by coming to Colorado, if she'd just escaped one disappointing family relationship for another.

After a heavy sigh Hailey settled onto the couch and opened a notepad to start a shopping list for the apartment. Pillows for the couch, a throw, some colorful vases for flowers, new curtains . . . She let her imagination lead her vision of the small room. A wooden picture frame leaned against the worn couch, which she'd borrowed from one of Hope's friends. The frame held a detailed felt-pen drawing of an iguana, sketched two years earlier from a photo Hailey had taken during a trip to Brazil. Despite flaky scales, horns, and other protrusions sprouting from its head, she'd been able to capture a wise, knowing look in its direct gaze.

How much time had passed since she'd taken up a pen or charcoal to draw anything? Life had been so pressured, but that wasn't the only reason. She'd almost begun believing art was frivolous, an implicit message she'd inferred from her parents, and from Joel as well. He'd called it her "cute hobby" and her parents never made many comments about her artistic creations one way or another. With time she sketched and painted less often, then not at all.

Well, that was about to change. Colorado should afford her endless scenic subjects for painting and drawing.

Against the wall leaned another sketch, one of the mill dating from 1875, still in bubble wrap. Guilt nudged her, but she forced herself to slip the visual reminder of Anderson Mill into the hall closet. As she closed the closet door with a satisfied smile, her phone rang. It took her several seconds to recognize her father's voice.

"Dad? You sound different. Are you okay?"

"Yes, about like usual, but real tired these days. I should slow down." Even his chuckle sounded fatigued. "Not sure how, though."

Hailey sank back onto the couch, touched by the change in his tone. He'd almost admitted human frailty and age. Maybe he'd become more flexible, more open since her departure.

"You sound tired, Dad," she said. "I think slowing down is a good idea. Can you give more responsibility to Daniel, or others? I would hate to see your health suffer." As much as she loathed suggesting that Daniel have more authority, it might make her dad's life easier.

"Oh, I'm alright. It's the weekend and I don't plan to go in tomorrow. I'll just rest, maybe play some golf. Haven't done that in years."

"I'm glad to hear that. You probably need something relaxing to do."

"So, how are you getting along out there?"

"I'm getting settled in. I found a job a couple of months ago, and that's been keeping me busy."

"Thanks for sending your number. I was sore for a while, but you're still my daughter."

Hailey smiled. Was this her father? Two years ago, he'd never have said such a thing. "Thanks, Dad. I appreciate it. I'm so glad you understood."

"Oh, I didn't say I understood. Walking out like that was typical Hailey, but it's okay. I figured it would happen sooner or later."

Hailey bristled, her previous compassion evaporated like mist. "What do you mean, 'typical Hailey?'" Irritation rang in her voice. "Do you know how many *years* I worked for you, without you hearing even one of my suggestions? Do you know how many times you put me down, as if I hadn't had a single good idea in my entire life?" Her voice had raised a few more decibels. *Calm down, Hailey. Don't give him a reason to call you impulsive or headstrong.* These were her father's favorite adjectives for her. And he knew how effectively they pushed her buttons.

"Now, don't be headstrong, Hailey. I only meant that you were aggravated and it seemed to be growing."

"Do you think I might have been a *reason* to be aggravated? I told you I didn't want to stand by and see the mill go down. That was one reason I left." Her voice softened. "Having no credibility was another. You never believed in me, Dad." Tears pushed against her eyelids and the cramp in her throat tightened

"Okay, I'm sorry I brought it up. Let's let the past be past. I hope you're happy out there. I'm still at the office now, but wanted to say hello and see how you were getting along."

Hailey's shoulders slumped. He hadn't even heard her plaintive cry, one she'd repeated her whole life. *You have never believed in me, Dad. You have never seen me.* A few hot tears slid down her cheeks. She had to be strong, at least until she hung up. "Okay, Dad. Thanks for calling. You take care of yourself, now."

Her heart was still throbbing when she hung up the phone. New tears joined the others that had fallen onto her T- shirt. He hadn't changed. He hadn't refuted her statement. Still the same stubborn, arrogant old man. How dare he call her to "keep in touch" and remind her of her impulsivity? *He'd* been rigid and blind, not her. Hadn't he?

"Thank you, God, for bringing me here," she shouted, her voice breaking. She jumped up off the couch to shake off her irritation. "His stubbornness doesn't touch me anymore. I'm in Colorado now."

And yet, the tears continued to fall.

 G3   G3   G3

The February sky brooded with gray jowls. The warmth of the coffee shop contrasted with the cool snap in the as Hailey pushed the glass door open and went out. It had snowed a dozen times since her arrival five months earlier. She loved watching the feathery flakes drift down in a dizzy, whimsical dance.

Hailey pulled her wool cap tighter over her thick curls and rewrapped her scarf, which Nina had made for her. She missed her friend. She wondered how soon she'd make the kind of friendships she'd had in Colorado. Here, even after five months, she still didn't have any history. If it weren't for Hope, she'd feel completely alone and invisible—still. On that count, not much had changed.

She swished away the dry, fluffy flakes from the front and back windows with a gloved hand. As she drove home flakes turned to dizzy flurries that pinged off of the windshield. In North Carolina the temperatures would have started creeping up into the fifties already, or even higher.

When she entered the familiar space of her apartment, a festival of pastels greeted her—pink and blue flowered cushions piled on a creamy yellow afghan, which disguised the bland brown of the borrowed couch beneath. Fresh daisies and carnations in pink, white, and lavender poured out of painted ceramic vases, echoing the same shades in the drapes. Her apartment was cozy and comfortable, but she knew she'd eventually need more space to start her business.

A thought buzzed into her mind like an unexpected bird landing on the windowsill. She ought to buy a house before starting her business. She knew she wanted to stay permanently in Colorado, despite the occasional feelings of being rootless and alone. Now might be the time to buy, since she'd have no problem getting a loan with a fulltime job, whereas it might be nearly impossible once she had a start-up business. One day she'd be able to transition to her own business with a few clients in the evenings or on weekends.

For a brief moment she wondered if it was too soon, if she was running again toward the fulfillment of some elusive rootedness. No, after all her years in apartments and condos, having a house would feel secure. Looking for one would certainly perk her out of her winter blues and homesickness. It would thrust her ahead on her plans for her new life.

Chapter Five

Hailey slowly strolled back through each room of the small ranch house for the second time, glancing down at the notes she'd taken. "Did you say that the windows are new?"

"Yes, they're only two years old. Double-paned." Todd, her real estate agent, stood in the bedroom doorway. "And with the gas heat, you're looking at low bills."

She nodded, taking another look at the closet space. The bedrooms were small, but would be plenty for her bedroom, an office, and a guest room.

In the living room, a wide path of sunlight poured from the picture window. She could glimpse a sliver of the mountains through the leafless branches of the towering aspen trees, stark white against a velvet blue sky. This was the third time she'd come to see the house, after visiting eleven others in the previous two weeks. This was the house. It would be ideal for her brand-new life.

Todd hovered nearby as Hailey imagined her pastel world in the living room. The small fenced back yard was enough to grow flowers and have a few friends over for a barbeque. A corner clump of yucca plants and Russian sage promised white and purple flowers in the spring.

Hailey's eyes rose to Todd's and found him gazing intently at her. He was handsome, no denying it, with startling blue eyes and curly, cropped hair. She'd spent hours with him over the past two weeks as he lined up homes for her to see almost daily. Heat rose to her face and she turned as if to examine a fixture.

Finally, she returned a smile to him. "Okay, I think I'm ready to make an offer."

Todd grinned, deep dimples carving into his jaws. "Great. We can go by my office now, if you have time, and draw up the paperwork. Once the closing is done, we can celebrate." He paused. "Maybe I can take you out to dinner?"

A small hum began inside her. How long had it been? "Sure, that would be nice."

As Hailey drove back to her apartment following the formalities at Todd's office, she grabbed her phone and left a short message for Hope. "I did it. I made an offer. Call me when you come home, or better still, come by, and I'll tell you all about it."

No turning back now. She'd bought herself a house. And might even have a date as well, though she wouldn't mention that to Hope until Todd followed through. She'd waited patiently over the last five months for the pieces of her life to come together. Now it seemed that they were, and quickly.

Hope had called, insisting on all the details. "I can't come tonight," she'd said, "but come over for coffee this weekend and you can tell me all about it." Thankfully, the new house was an easy drive from Hope's.

As Hailey was cleaning up the supper dishes the phone rang. She was surprised to hear her father's voice on the phone. "Hailey, it's your dad. Hope you're doing alright. Listen, I have something important to ask you and I need you to hear what it is and think about it for me."

Hailey sank down on her knees onto the couch. "Hi, Dad, is everything okay? Is the mill okay?"

"The mill is still open, if that's what you mean. We're plugging along." His voice had a slight edge of sarcasm, but slid into a quieter, humbler tone. "I haven't been feeling well lately. I never told you that when you were still here. I guess I was too focused on other problems to know how bad it is. I finally went to see my doctor about a month ago."

Hailey's throat went dry. "What is it? Are you okay?"

Her father cleared his throat. After a pause he said, "No, I'm not. I have a serious heart problem. I had a lot of pain in my chest and when I went to see a cardiologist, he told me I'd had two small heart attacks. I didn't even recognize them, just kept going. Doctor says I'm going to need an operation within a couple of months. Open heart surgery. A bypass."

Hailey gasped. She knew all those months her father seemed smaller and more frail. "When?"

"It's not scheduled yet. They're working all that out. Probably end of February or early March. They're keeping a close eye on me in the meantime."

"How long have you been sick?"

"It's been a little while now. I've been on nitroglycerine medication since last year. For the first attack, I thought it was just bad indigestion or something. Then the second one forced me to go see someone. Doc says I'm getting weaker all the time. He told me if I'd waited a month or two longer, I'd probably be dead. I'm headed for a big attack any day now."

"I—I don't know what to say. I'm sure the stress at the mill isn't helping matters. You'll have to slow down before something bad happens." Hailey's throat tightened and she struggled to swallow. Guilt for her frustration with her dad flooded her. She could have lost him.

"More than that. I have to stop. Doctor says I can't work for at least four months or even more after the operation."

"Four months! What will you do?"

"Well, that's why I'm calling. I'd like you to come back and run the mill. You know the mill better than anyone, and more importantly, you love the mill. You have a heart for it."

Hailey's mouth dropped open. She gripped the arm of the couch, struggling to breathe. "Wha—" His words slowly penetrated her fogbank of disbelief. He knew she had a heart for the mill? He'd noticed?

With a jolt she realized what he was asking. "And you want me to move *back*? Dad, I've only been out here for five months. I've settled here, I have a new life here, a job. And I put an offer on a house to buy, just *today*." It wasn't possible. He couldn't be asking this of her now. Not after everything that had happened between them.

"Is it too late? For the house, I mean."

"Um, no. I just made the offer and I haven't gotten a response, but they'll probably accept it. And I want to buy this house. I want to settle *here*."

"I'm just asking you to think about this. I know it's a pain to have to come back, after you went all the way out there. We parted on bad terms, and I'm sorry about that. But I'm confident that you'll do a good job. I haven't always told you that, but I'm sure of it. You're the best person to take my place."

"I don't know." Hailey stood up and paced across the room. She mopped perspiration from her forehead with her wrist. Suddenly she felt sick all over. "Hope will be so disappointed if I leave already. I just got here. I don't think—"

"Hailey, please don't answer now. Just sleep on it. Give it serious thought and I'll call you tomorrow. Doctor says I can't continue working right after the operation. He said four months was optimistic. It might be at least six, or possibly more. Depends on how I come through it."

"Then what, after six months? I go back to the design department?" Her dad was talking about a heart operation and she was concerned about her employment. Shame pricked at her. Yet if she made the effort to go back, what awaited her afterward?

"I'd like you to have a more central role if you want one, even when I'm ready to go back to work. All the ideas you talked about, you can try some of them." His voice sounded frail, broken.

"Okay, I'll think about it and we'll talk again. But brainstorm other options, because it's not a foregone conclusion that I'll say yes." Hailey shook her head and grimaced. She was stalling. There was no way. She should just tell him no and not leave him hanging.

"I know. I'll try to think of some other ideas too. We'll talk tomorrow."

Hailey hung up the phone as a muffled scream of frustration rose up from her throat. How could he ask this of her? How could he think she'd leave Hope, Devon, her mother, a mere five months later?

But if he were sick and kept working—and he surely would if there were no one to take over—he could have a heart attack and die, just like *his* father had. Could she let him do that?

Open heart surgery, not high blood pressure or cholesterol. He'd been ordered by his doctors to stop work for a minimum of six months.

Hailey could just imagine how devastated Hope would feel. But Dad's health was in jeopardy. If Hope knew he'd be in the hospital and that Hailey was going to run the mill in his place, maybe she'd understand.

The phone rang again. Hailey almost didn't answer it, but saw it was her father again. "Hailey, I wanted to be sure and tell you that you will be acting president, with full authority to do what you think is best. I won't have any strength to bother with the running of the mill for a good six months. It will be all yours. And another thing, I don't want Hope and your mother to know about the severity of my health problem. I'm not ready for them to know about the heart attacks. Let's wait it out. They'll just worry anyway."

"You don't want Hope to know you're having open-heart surgery? She's your daughter, Dad. She has a right to know."

"There are lesser operations. Let her think it's something like that. I'd just rather her not know the severity of it, not until later on. I have my own reasons. I'd like you to keep that to yourself."

"Seems it would draw you two closer if she knew. Mend some fences. What if, uh, I hate to say this, but what if you—if you don't make it? You'd never have the chance to work things out with her." Hailey's voice came out threaded on a whisper.

A long silence hung between them. "You have a point," he finally said. "Just tell her I have some health problems and will have an operation. And that the doctor told me to slow down. That should be enough at this stage."

Hailey grimaced. "If I say yes and decide to move back, Hope will *never* understand, if she doesn't know it's something serious."

45

"Please, Hailey. This will be enough for her to know."

Throughout the night Hailey hardly slept. Alternately she prayed for guidance and weighed the pros and cons. She'd been so happy to finally be there, to start over, to see Hope and her mother often. Finally, to have some semblance of a family. How could it be snatched away from her so quickly?

She knew well what kind of "family" awaited her in Larkspur— a cold father who accepted her less than the employees at the mill did. Hope would accuse her of being weak, wanting to please again, especially if she couldn't know the gravity of her father's condition. What would her father's privacy cost Hailey?

She'd possibly be saving her father's life by taking over the mill, so that he could recuperate without stress. He'd promised her a more prominent role with more authority. And in the short term she could try her ideas, possibly saving the mill and the jobs of all those dear people who counted on the Andersons.

But Hope—

And so it went throughout the night. The mill, her father, the surgery, Hope, her house, her new business that hadn't started yet. Not to mention the daunting task of repacking and returning across the country. Where would she live? Her condo was rented for the next six months. It wasn't possible he'd ask this of her. And yet . . .

She thought about the little house and the offer she'd made on it just that afternoon. It wasn't too late to back out. But she didn't want to back out. Oh, what should she do? Had God allowed the timing of her father's call *before* she bought the house? Did *He* want her to return to Larkspur?

Hailey prayed and dozed through the murky hours of the night, pleading for wisdom and clarity. Finally, around four in the morning, in utter exhaustion, she fell asleep.

Chapter Six

Hailey awoke the following morning, her eyelids scratching as though small sticks were wedged under them. A band of morning sun blazed from the window into her face. She buried her head deeper into the pillow.

Several groggy seconds later she remembered why she'd slept so poorly. Her father.

She sat upright like an over-wound spring. He couldn't ask her to come back. But could she leave him alone to be cut on and poked with needles, not even knowing if he would survive? She'd been proud of her own courage and boldness, cutting herself loose from a hopeless situation. She shouldn't dream of going back.

Hailey kicked off her covers and stumbled to the bathroom. After sloshing cool water on her face, she realized she wouldn't be able to function at the office that day. With no sleep and an impossibly difficult decision before her, she called in sick and brewed a strong pot of coffee. On the east coast, her father would likely be at the office, unless he'd already stopped working. *That* was difficult to imagine.

For an instant she saw herself sitting in his tall-back leather chair, controlling every aspect of the mill. That, too, was difficult to imagine, but she felt a stirring inside her, a flutter that began timidly then fanned outward. Acting president. He said she'd be acting president and could try her ideas. He was silently asking her to save the mill.

Hailey cradled the hot mug of coffee between her palms as she leaned her elbows on the kitchen table. Her father had insisted she was the best person for the job. He was likely as aware as she was that both Daniel and an outside president would charge brutally toward efficiency, disregarding the gentle people who'd made the mill function for decades.

She *cared*. Her father had said it himself. She cared about the mill's future and its employees. She could help bring it into the twenty-first century, save jobs, make it great again. All that with possibly saving her father's life.

And making him proud of her.

At ten o'clock the phone rang. Hailey tensed. She wasn't ready. She needed more time. Hearing Todd's voice, warm and familiar, she relaxed her shoulders.

"Hi, Hailey. I heard right back from the seller's agent. The sellers have a counter-offer for you. Do you have time now to talk?"

"Yes, I have a few minutes." She stood with the phone on one ear as she added coffee to her cup.

"Good. Of course, they refused the low offer we made, but they offered to change the roof, and keep the same price they'd set. They know the roof is ready for replacement pretty soon, so they'll do that instead of coming down on the price."

Hailey frowned. "That's the counter-offer?"

"Yes. You have a day or two to respond, so just think about it. No rush."

"Okay. I can't give you an answer now. Maybe by tonight or tomorrow."

"Just give me a call on my cell when you've decided. You're free to make another counter-offer, of course."

The roof hadn't seemed that bad when she'd been there. She'd offered twenty thousand below the asking price, but a roof that size would cost under six thousand. She couldn't accept the seller's counter-offer, but she couldn't even think about it. She needed first to know if she'd stay in Colorado.

A cloudless, cornflower-blue sky beckoned her through the living room window, along with unseasonably warm late-January temperatures. If she got out of the apartment and moved around, she could think more clearly.

Hailey slipped into jeans, a sweatshirt, and sneakers, and let herself out the front door. When the sun and breeze hit her face, she felt lighter. The sun blazed down, glinting off of the remaining patches of last week's snowfall like sparkling diamonds. The sky was such a bold blue against the spiky bare aspen branches, it hurt to gaze at them. If winter could be this majestic, what must spring be like? It wouldn't be long, just another month or so, when the thaw would begin and the landscape would burst into color. Would she even be there to see it?

Hope, Devon, and her mother. They pulled her toward staying. But she hadn't found friends, a church home, or a job she loved, and Todd was still a stranger. Yet she liked Colorado and had pictured herself living there long term. Moving back to Larkspur seemed like defeat, like pedaling backward. Like running back home.

But all of the puzzle pieces had changed places.

Maybe Hope would understand. Hailey shook her head. She wouldn't fool herself. Her departure would be painful, like a betrayal, especially after all the years they'd been separated, and finally fulfilling their pact of living near one another. Hope's prickly relationship with their dad would color her view on Hailey's return. She'd accuse Hailey of caving in to his pressure once again.

"Lord, please guide me through this." Her whispered words created clouds of vapor in the cold, still air.

By the time Hailey closed her apartment door behind her, her spirits had drooped, yet a glimmer of hope also huddled down in the darkness. She was being given a chance, one she'd always wanted, even without the added weight of her father's condition.

She'd see her friends again, go back to her church, which she missed. She could one day buy a house in one of the charming older neighborhoods, fix it up. She wouldn't have time to start her business, but she wouldn't need to. She'd *have* a business to run, one she already knew and loved.

Suddenly, the choice seemed clear. Exciting, painful, and clear.

"Dad, it's Hailey." Hailey's hand was moist with perspiration as she held the phone. "Are you at work?"

"I came home early."

Hailey's eyes widened with surprise. "Early? You *never* do that."

"I'm not the same as before, Hailey. I get tired before the day is over. I've started leaving at three every day. I do a little bit from home, if I can, but I can't do what I used to. I hope you'll come back."

"I've decided to come." Her voice was soft in the phone. She thought she heard him breathe a slight gasp. "It wasn't an easy decision, as you can imagine, but I'll be glad to do what I can."

He paused and cleared his throat. "I'm so glad, Hailey. I think you'll do a good job. And I really don't have anyone else. How soon can you get here?"

"I haven't thought that far ahead, but probably within a month. I have to give notice on my place and make arrangements. I'll need to find housing there, because I rented out my condo."

"I can look here, too. I'm sure we can find you something, even if it's just temporary. Then you can take your time to find someplace you really like."

The thought of looking for housing again, only this time in Larkspur, seemed surreal. "I don't know how I'm going to tell Hope. I'm seeing her for coffee at her house this Saturday, so I guess I'll tell her then."

"Remember what I asked you. No details."

"Yes, I remember." Dread at the thought of telling Hope invaded her. "Say a prayer for me," she told him impulsively, despite the fact that he wasn't necessarily a believer. "I hope I don't lose my sister over this."

"Always my drama queen." Her father chuckled. "It'll be okay. Especially later on when she realizes what you're doing.'"

Hailey paused. "What am I doing, Dad?"

"You're saving the mill, just like you've always wanted to."

Hailey couldn't suppress a smile. "Yes," she said slowly. "And maybe keeping you from killing yourself over it."

He laughed aloud. She couldn't remember ever making her father laugh—or laughing with him. "I hope I'm not even close to the truth," she added. "You take care of yourself, and do everything the doctor tells you. You just better be alive by the time I get there."

51

"Don't worry. Just come as soon as you can."

ಞ   ಞ   ಞ

Hope reached up toward the cupboard but instead grabbed the small step ladder she kept near the refrigerator. "I'm so short I have to use this for almost everything in my kitchen." She climbed the ladder and pulled two coffee mugs from the top shelf. "I save these mugs for special occasions. We're going to celebrate your new house."

Hailey was seated at the kitchen table, her heart pounding like a tympani drum, her hands slick with perspiration. How she would have loved for this moment to be one of sharing news, talking about the new house, how they'd spend time there, decorate, visit each other. It would be sister heaven to anticipate the future of shared moments. She'd lost sleep again the night before, running different openings through her mind. More than likely none of it would come out like she wanted, or be received as she hoped.

Finally, a steaming cup of dark roast coffee sat before her and Hope settled into the facing seat. "So, tell me about the house. Where is it? What did you negotiate?"

"Well . . ." Hailey moistened her lips and swallowed against a parched throat. Maybe talking about the house first would calm her, prepare her to tell Hope the news that weighed on her chest like a family of elephants.

"I won't be buying the house I told you about after all."

Hope's eyes widened. "They didn't accept your offer?"

"They gave me a counter-offer I couldn't accept. They didn't want to come down at all on the price, then offered to replace the roof."

"What was the difference?" Hope's dark eyes matched her coffee. She took a deep sip.

"About twenty thousand. A no-brainer."

"But you counter offered."

Hailey shook her head. "I, um, was going to but then got a surprising phone call." There, that opened it. Her heart accelerated to the point she thought she could hear it banging inside her rib cage.

"Really? From who?"

"Dad."

"What'd *he* want?" Hope's tone took on a surly edge.

"Well . . ." Hailey sipped her coffee, ignoring the burn tracing down her throat. "I hadn't heard from him in a while. He told me that he was having some health issues and had seen his doctor."

Hope's brow furrowed. "Is he okay?"

"His doctor told him he has to slow down. Not surprising at his age. You know he works all the time."

"Yes, I seem to remember *that*. So, he's okay?"

"For now, he's hanging in there, but his heart is getting weaker. He'll get worse if he doesn't do what the doctor said."

"Yeah, I guess that is surprising news. He and I aren't close, but I sure don't wish him any harm."

"Uh, that's not all he told me." This was the time. She needed to spit it out. With a deep sigh she threw herself ahead. "He has to cut back. That's what he meant by slowing down. He, um, asked me to consider coming back to help him run the mill."

"What? He wants you to come back?" Hope's eyes blazed with indignation. "I hope you told him where to go. In a daughterly way, of course."

"I've spent the last two days tormented, thinking seriously about it."

"You didn't!"

"When I left Larkspur, the mill was already struggling." Hailey spoke slower now, measuring each word with the gravity she knew they held. "It was in bad shape. Dad was working late a lot. It took a toll on him. I saw his health go down, even in the last year I was there." Hailey watched Hope's expression, hoping for a sign of understanding. "He wants me to take a central role, try some of the ideas he wouldn't let me try before."

"Don't tell me you're tempted, after all he's put you through. I can't believe he would think you'd even consider it."

"But I *have* considered it. It'll mean possibly saving the mill. And Dad—" Hailey took another sip of coffee to wet her mouth. "It may help him get better. Don't you see?"

Hope's face paled. Her mouth dropped open for an instant then shook her head vigorously. "No, I don't see. I can't believe it, you're considering this, aren't you? You've already decided to go."

"Yes," Hailey told her quietly. "You can't know how I hated telling you this. My heart is breaking—"

Hope sat forward in her chair. "What? Your heart is breaking because you're running back to that old man who used you and never had a nice thing to say for thirty years? What's wrong with you, Hailey? What about our pact? We're finally in the same place!" Her voice rang out sharply into the still kitchen.

Hailey winced.

Hope pushed back from the table, nearly spilling her coffee. "Well let me tell you something." Hope's voice cracked and her eyes reddened. "*My* heart is breaking." Tears squeezed out from her black-lashed eyes and left angry tracks on her face. "And Devon's heart will break. She had her aunt for what? Five whole months? Don't you think she wants to spend time with you?"

"I'm . . . I—"

"So does Mom. So do I." Hope spoke through her tears. "You're going to just let him take you away from me, just like that?"

Hailey stood and circled the table to stand beside her sister. She laid her hand on Hope's upper arm. "Hope, please try to understand. It may only be temporary. I can't say right now. I think, for all his faults, Dad needs me now." If only she could tell her how sick her father was. That he was going to have his chest cut open, that he might not make it. And that he wouldn't be able to run the mill for months afterwards. Hailey pressed her lips together.

"He wants to *use* you, as usual." Hope shrugged off Hailey's hand and narrowed her eyes at her. "What's this control he has over you? You go running back, like a pathetic puppet."

"I'm not a puppet." Hailey's voice was firmer now, though it still beseeched. "I decided this on my own. I won't be in the design department. I'll be *running* the mill, trying to save it. I'm sorry for the timing. I'm so sorry we didn't have more time together. I'm sad about that—"

"Yeah, I can really tell." Hope picked up their coffee mugs, walked to the sink, and dumped them out. "I guess you miss all the heat, the mistreatment, the pressure. Maybe you actually like that. Maybe it's too peaceful out here for you."

Tears streamed down Hailey's face as she pleaded with Hope. "I hope you'll understand one day." Her voice broke. She clutched the edge of the antique wooden table, fearing she'd fall as pain ripped through her insides and clenched her throat nearly closed. "There are certain things I can't explain to you right now. You'll simply have to trust me."

Hope had turned her back toward Hailey. Her shoulders shook as she sobbed, leaning over the sink. "I knew it." Her angry words slashed out like a whip, her back an impenetrable shield. "I knew it was too much to hope that we'd be close again one day."

Hailey swallowed and closed the gap between her and her sister's back. "We *are* close. That's why this is painful, because we're close." It seemed so ineffectual, so useless to speak. There was nothing to say. No words would make it better. "And we'll always be close, Hope. No matter where I am."

Hope didn't speak. Finally, she turned back to Hailey, her face shiny with tears. She shook her head and with a parting stare, turned and left the room. Hailey heard a door slam and then muffled crying.

Hailey let herself out the front door and slowly returned to her car, remembering the happy reunion five months earlier. Why had God even allowed her to move here? Maybe she'd made a mistake in coming. She leaned over the steering wheel against her arms, engulfed in sobs that never seemed to end.

In saving the mill, she might lose her sister.

Chapter Seven

The rented truck bounced and rattled as Hailey crossed an area of maintenance outside of Kansas City. It didn't seem possible that only a few months ago she'd driven these same roads. Now they were faded with winter wash, stripped corn and wheat fields to the earth's edge, hamlet-sized towns separated by town-sized stretches of empty land. The monotony of the landscape didn't lull Hailey into drowsiness. The near-constant burn of tears kept her wide awake, as did the discomfort of bouncing against the vinyl seat.

Pathetic puppet. Hailey couldn't block her sister's words, or the acute pain they caused, as they rang between her ears. Hope only knew of Hailey's past misery at the mill, not the opportunities that awaited her. She only hoped she wasn't heading to the same misplaced goal, the same quest to matter for her father.

Hailey scanned the flat horizon. The dusty highway miles seemed to mock her. *Here you are again. Figured we'd see you back here. Just couldn't be strong, could you?* Town after town, signpost after signpost. She'd been so sure. She thought God had led her there. Hailey shook her head, perplexed. When she missed the signals, she sure did it big. She wished she knew what God wanted, wished He'd tell her clearly. Maybe it would have required more faith to stay in Colorado. Maybe *returning* to North Carolina was the mistake. It was impossible to know, except perhaps with time. She'd left Larkspur with nothing to lose. Now she was doing the same thing. The story of her life.

Tired of introspection, Hailey grabbed her cell phone from the passenger seat and punched in Nina's number with one hand as she shifted her gaze back and forth from the road ahead of her. Nina would probably be home from work by now. They'd only spoken briefly when Hailey had told Nina the news of her return to Larkspur. "Hey, Nina. I'm sorry I haven't given you any updates in the last two weeks."

"I understand. I was so just happy that you're coming back, I didn't need any updates." Nina's cheerful voice soothed Hailey's bruised heart. "You must've had a truckload of things to do. When do you think you'll you get here?"

"I'm just outside of . . ." Hailey scanned the green highway sign, "Louisville. I should be there by Friday, dinnertime."

"I'll have a special welcome dinner for you."

"Thanks, Nina. Seeing you again makes it easier to come back." Hailey paused. "I just hope this is a good decision."

"Maybe if you hadn't left, your father would never have realized he needs you and values your involvement at the mill. Ever thought of that?"

"It's a high price to pay for me to find out," Hailey grumbled then added, "I do think coming back is the right thing to do. But I'll be honest, I feel like I've been spun through the washer. Sturdy cycle."

"I'm sure you do." Nina's voice softened. "It'll take you some time to get settled again. If you can help your dad and help the mill, don't you think it will be worth all of this? Hope will understand eventually."

58

"Not so sure about that." Hailey winced at the painful jab inside at the mention of Hope's name. She'd been cool and distant up to the point of Hailey's departure.

"I hope I can make an impact at the mill, if I can figure out what to do."

"You've been around it your whole life. Of course, you'll know."

"As a child. I hope it will come back to me." She hadn't let her thoughts wander that far.

"Were you able to get an apartment lined up?"

Hailey turned her blinker and eased toward the ramp to exit. It was about time to look for someplace to eat dinner. "You'll never believe, but my dad found me a rental in the same complex where my condo is."

Nina laughed. "I won't have to get directions to your new place, then."

Hailey smiled. A thin strand of comfort took root.

ଔ   ଔ   ଔ

"It's good to see you, Hailey." Jack Bower, supervisor of inspection and shipping at the mill, crinkled his weathered face into a map of lines as he smiled and encircled Hailey with a strong-armed hug. He'd just arrived at the townhouse, joining three other mill employees who'd volunteered their Saturday morning to help Hailey move in. He turned and shot up one hand in greeting to Charley and Rick, who were struggling to angle her mattress through the front door. They both nodded and smiled.

"And you too, Jack." Hailey noted he looked older than he had only a few months ago. "How has the year been, or should I even ask?"

"It's been kind of tense. Lots of bad news all around. I'm just glad you're back to give us a hand."

"I'll do the best I can. Not just for you all and the mill, but for my dad too."

"He's no worse, I hope," Jack said.

Hailey shook her head. "Not that I know of, except getting ready for his surgery next week. I'll go by and see him when we're finished here." In a way she dreaded seeing her father. His health had likely declined even more since she'd last seen him. She also secretly wondered what his attitude toward her would be, since she no longer needed to be persuaded.

"Keep us posted. He's in our prayers."

Hailey returned a grateful smile then bent to pick up a small box. It was heavy with her books, so she heaved it down on the dolly and reached for another one. The men took the bigger items while she and Vera carried anything that could fit in both arms. "Thanks for coming to help, Vera," she said. "Bet you were surprised to hear I'd come back."

"Sure was. Couldn't believe our good luck." Vera's ample smile displayed a few gaps and more warmth than most people Hailey knew. Her bleached hair contrasted with black and gray roots, all pulled back into a wispy ponytail. "I know you've been around the mill since you were a little thing, and who's better than you to help your dad out in his poor health?" Vera shifted the box before it slipped from her grip. "We heard you were gonna take over, and we just said, 'Thank ye, Jesus. She's comin'. Our Hailey's comin' back.'"

Hailey pressed her lips together and blinked to stem the sudden tears that sprang to her eyes. *Our Hailey. Lord, let me be worthy of their confidence.* She couldn't let them down. She just couldn't. She returned a tight smile to Vera and quickly looked away.

Hailey set her final box on top of the others in her new living room. Standing with her hands on her hips, she surveyed the all-too-familiar surroundings. Boxes and her small quantity of furniture sat mounded into a landscape of cubes in every room of the condo. One new addition was a flat box filled with sketches she'd done over the last few months in Colorado. It would take several more days to arrange everything. Again. Hailey sighed, bracing for a new round of settling in. As long as the bed was in the right place, she'd be able to function in the short term.

Her next priority was to see her father. When the last helper ambled toward the parking lot, she grabbed her keys and followed. Before slipping into the driver's seat, her eyes panned the quiet buildings. No sign of Alex. She hoped he hadn't moved away in the last five months.

Hailey drove across town toward her father's house, a large, two-story colonial she'd grown up in. Spindly bare branches along the wintery streets reached upward, waiting for their new leaves. As she passed the neighborhoods, strip malls, and wooded areas, it seemed as though she'd never left . . . or had just awakened from a long dream. A surreal haze filtered everything she saw. Could she have been gone for five months? Not much had changed in so short a time, yet she had changed, returning with fewer illusions, as bent as the branches on the trees.

The gravel crackled as she drove up the circular drive and parked in front of the red brick house. Disjointed memories tumbled from a distance, as through a long tunnel. The absence of childlike joy in those memories hovered on the shelf of her mind, leaving a chill behind.

Maybe in the coming year those feelings would lighten. Hailey stared at the house a moment longer before she turned off the car. She shouldn't build her hopes to unrealistic proportions. Her father hadn't changed personalities. He'd just become physically weak and perhaps as a result, more self-reflective.

As she stepped out of the car, she scanned the front yard. Normally clipped at perfect angles, the landscaping showed signs of neglect, with tendrils hanging out of lines and undergrowth near the roots of the hedges. Considering gardening was the only thing in her father's life that she could call his hobby, he must be truly weak.

Hailey slipped down from the car and let herself into the house with her copy of her father's key. Everything on the first floor was still and quiet, arranged exactly the same as she remembered. She almost called out to her father but stopped herself. Maybe he was napping or receiving a nurse's care.

Slowly Hailey mounted the stairs. When she reached her father's room the door was ajar and light spilled into the hallway. "Dad? It's me." Her voice was low.

A soft, scratchy tone emerge from inside the room. "Hailey, come in."

She gently pushed the door. Paul Anderson sat in bed, propped against several pillows and covered with a navy-blue afghan he'd had for years. She suppressed a cry of surprise when she saw his grayish face, tired eyes, and more wrinkles than she'd remembered. He'd lost weight and seemed to float in the billowing bedclothes. She approached the bed.

He held her gaze, a modest smile on his thin lips. "So glad you're here," he murmured as she bent forward to kiss his forehead.

She stepped back and pulled a chair toward his bed, not yet sure whether she too was glad to be there.

"Did you get moved in?"

Hailey nodded. "Thanks for sending the troops. They made the work go quickly. Now I just have to organize it all." She couldn't help but add, "Feels like I did this not too long ago."

Her father chuckled. "Should go quickly, then. You're a pro now."

"What's the status of your operation? Did they schedule the day?"

"Yes." His voice thinned. "Next Thursday."

"Do you feel ready, Dad?"

He shrugged. "Doesn't matter if I'm ready or not. I'll be glad when it's done."

"Me too." Hailey wouldn't let herself think of the possibility he wouldn't make it. Most people came through bypass surgery just fine. "You'll feel so much better after you heal up and get your strength back. Bet it will feel like you've gotten years younger."

"Yes, that's what the doctors tell me. That is, if I pull through."

"Of course, you will. Is there any doubt?" She held her breath.

Again, a shrug. "My condition is bad. But if it's my time, it's my time."

Hailey had stopped trying to talk to her father about anything spiritual years before. Though he attended church on occasion, it seemed more a social obligation than anything else. Yet, she couldn't judge his heart. "Just make sure you're good with God, Dad. That's the important thing. It'll give you comfort too."

Hailey was surprised when he didn't retort. Instead, he settled a tired gaze on her. "Yes, I suppose that's true, on both counts. Thanks for reminding me."

She started to ask him a question that might deepen the discussion, but he said, "I need to warn you about the mill."

"What about the mill?"

"Just the general atmosphere in the mill, the town, everywhere. Rumors, fear. People are nervous about their jobs." His voice rasped. He took a deep breath.

She reached out and put her hand on his arm. "You don't have to tell me now. Save your strength. We'll have time to talk."

"Some people have quit and gone somewhere else because they're sure it'll happen to them. Caulfield's let go of a lot of people. They didn't close, but they've got a much smaller staff now." He winced. A few moments later, he continued. "And of course, Pristine closed while you were still here. It's being turned into a shopping center. Tension's high everywhere. You'll see when you get there. Just wanted to warn you."

"In other words, I'll wonder what I've gotten myself into." She gave him a wry smile.

He half-smiled, then his voice became solemn. "Hope you won't. You're strong, though. And everyone there likes you. You can pull it together."

"Think so?"

He gave her a rare, close-lipped grin, but it was replaced by a grimace. He sank back against his pillow as if the effort took his last ounce of strength. His brows tangled together and his eyes fluttered closed.

"Are you alright?" When he didn't respond she said, "You're tired, Dad. I wasn't planning to stay long, but I wanted to see you. I'll go now." She watched his face for a sign he'd heard her, and for a relaxing of his pained scowl, but she saw neither. "Call me if you need anything." Again, no response.

She stood and watched him, unsure of whether to leave or call for help. "Are you okay?" When he didn't respond, she watched his chest to make sure he was breathing. As it rose and fell, she relaxed with relief. She slowly moved toward the door.

"Thank you, Hailey." The words emerged in a broken whisper, then trailed off.

Hailey fought tears as she hurried down the wide staircase and returned to her car. Clouds had formed in large dollops overhead, their gray tone almost matching her father's complexion. Weak and frail, he seemed to be grasping the hem of life itself, not sure of his ability to hold on. At the mill, she'd do what she could, garnering all of her energy, her best ideas, and her enthusiasm.

For her father, though, she could only pray and wait for the outcome.

Chapter Eight

Monday awoke gasping for air through a dense layer of fog. The beams of Hailey's headlights cut a yellow swath through the mist, but were quickly swallowed up. She could barely make out the imposing outline of Anderson Mill's main building beyond the rows of spindly winter trees separating her from the property. She drove past the empty guard house, where no one had stood duty in a decade. Despite its forlorn entrance, the parking lot was full and a faint whir of machine noises came from inside the imposing brick building.

The walk from the car to the front door was too brief. Hailey stopped and stared at the door, blinking in the smoky fog that clung to her. Here she was again. The last time she'd seen this structure, she'd been on her way out. Good riddance, and onward to a new life. The Rocky Mountains had called her and she'd answered.

So much for *that* decision. Yet here she was, in this place of possible redemption, for the mill and for herself.

Or maybe she was there just in time to go down with the ship.

A hand of panic gripped her throat momentarily. *Running back home, you couldn't make it out west, Daddy's patsy, pathetic puppet . . .* the cruel phrases ricocheted in her skull and kept her feet riveted to the ground. Who was she to think she could turn this mill around? Was she even capable of going into the building?

Hailey swallowed and hitched her purse up on her newly-squared shoulder. She could do this. Even her father thought so. She would show him, show herself, and show Hope that she could. She had to try, since she'd burned her bridges. God would help her. He *had* to. Hadn't He gotten her into this? She threw a pleading glance toward the sky

She entered the building, which looked and smelled the same as a year ago, the highly polished tiles reflecting milky light from the front door. She'd wanted to arrive a few minutes before the employees, just to get her bearings and let reality sink in at a gentle pace.

The reception desk was empty. Slowly Hailey mounted the wide, carpeted staircase toward the second-floor where the administrative offices were clustered. Just below, the factory, with its hangar-sized departments, processed cotton and other fibers through each step up to finished fabric.

"Hailey, I heard you were coming back to us." She heard a voice behind her, steeped in a genteel southern accent. Turning, she saw Emma Wright, the receptionist, whom she'd known since she was fifteen. The women exchanged hugs and both seemed surprised that their eyes were moist. They laughed together, and Emma added, "Back where you belong, Hailey. We've missed you."

Hailey didn't trust herself to speak, so she grinned and nodded. The surge of doubt that had assailed her as she'd entered the building was lifting by slivers.

"Have you seen your daddy? We're real worried about him."

"Yes, I stopped by the other day when I arrived in town. He's waiting for the operation in just a few days."

Emma's large brown eyes filled with unshed tears. "He's in our prayers every day. We hope for his full recovery. I'm sure you are taking a weight off his shoulders."

"I hope so. I'll do my best."

Several greetings later Hailey arrived at her father's office door. She glanced up at his name plate and was surprised to read, "Hailey Anderson, President." Her father wouldn't have thought to change the name plate on his office, would he? It had probably been a woman's thoughtfulness. Maybe Lenore, who had been elated at the news of Hailey's return.

Hailey unlocked her father's office door and turned the light switch. He hadn't been there in at least two weeks. The air smelled stale and dust had begun to accumulate in a fine bluish layer. She'd wipe it down later, but for now, she circled the massive hickory desk and sat in the worn black leather chair. Her desk, her place. She shook her head, still trying to believe.

The whirring and clunking of looms and the myriad machines below met her ears in steady but muffled waves, giving background sound to the silence of the big office. The third shift had been cancelled years earlier. The first shift would just be priming for the day.

She leaned back as her eyes canvassed the room, taking it all in. On every surface of the office were fabric samples, large books— she'd find out later what they contained—and stacks of papers. The walls, a sun-faded ochre color, were mostly bare, since her father never indulged in the frivolity of décor. A few puffs of raw cotton lay in the corners of the office, probably having fallen off of her father's suit after one of his rounds to the carding department, where the bales were first opened.

It was all hers now. Her challenges and, she fervently hoped, her triumphs over the textile mill's seemingly inevitable journey toward oblivion. She'd fight for it. That's why she'd come back. She only hoped she would know how.

"One day at a time, Hailey," she murmured to herself. For a moment she felt paralyzed at her desk. Where should she start? Daniel, her father's second-in-command, could show her the ropes, but she'd almost rather learn by herself. She'd seek out other tutors, if she had questions she couldn't figure out on her own. Perhaps the best first step would be to simply go from department to department, greet everyone, while making an appearance as the new president. She'd get the overview of the mill workings from a new perspective.

As she left the office she nearly ran into Daniel. He stepped backward and eyed her, his pasty face and pinch corners of his mouth showing no delight at her presence. "I heard you were due back today. Going to fill his shoes, are you?"

Hailey stared at him, at a loss for words, then recovered herself. "Well, thank you for the warm welcome, Daniel," then brushed past him.

"I'll need to go over a few things with you later," he called after her, "to bring you up to speed."

She turned and responded coolly. "I'll let you know when I have time. I know where to find you." She wouldn't give him the satisfaction of knowing how much she *needed* to come up to speed. Her current speed was just above park.

The encounter left a snag of irritation in her stomach as Hailey made her way downstairs. Daniel Carlton had always been a solitary player, rationing human warmth only to her father, like an over-eager son. She knew he wasn't well-liked at the mill, but no one said anything directly to or about him, since he was second in command. She hoped the other employees didn't share his lack of enthusiasm at her return.

She pushed on the heavy door of the warehouse and entered the vast hangar. On towering shelves all around her sat bales of unprocessed cotton. Hailey wasn't sure what she was looking for, but examined the rows and stacks before her as if she did. Truthfully, most of the time she'd spent in the warehouse had been as a child, as she chatted with the employees or watched the bales coming in from the trucks. She wished she had asked more questions back then.

"Well, if it isn't Hailey! Welcome back, my girl." Hank Winslow, supervisor of the warehouse, had been with the mill for the last twenty-two years. Hailey reached up for a hug from the older man, one of her many grandfathers.

Hailey grinned, softening from his warmth. "Yeah, who would have guessed?"

"I would have. You're an Anderson and you've always loved this place," he said. His voice was solemn, but his blue eyes twinkled in contrast to the white layer of grizzle on his jaws.

"You're right. It wasn't my plan to come back so soon, but I'm hoping to help out my Dad and the mill both." Suddenly she felt ridiculously close to tears, swimming in nostalgia, self-doubt, and hope that she'd somehow meet their expectations. She turned away, blinking rapidly.

"I know you will, Hailey." Hank turned to two other men who were moving in their direction. "Hey, look who's here," he called.

She greeted each of the other men, who grinned warmly and welcomed her back. "My son's working over in the dyeing department," one of the men said.

Hank added, "And mine has been in the mailroom for about a year."

They exchanged family news, then general information about the warehouse and its activities. Hailey took notes, not caring if it made her look like an amateur. That's exactly what she was, and among most of the mill employees, she knew she'd never be judged.

She left the warehouse and made her way to the carding department. Daily, bales of raw cotton were opened and separated on large machines known as cards, in order to shake out seeds and dirt. After the cleaning process it would be combed into parallel strands. As a child Hailey had always been fascinated by the transformation of each bale of cotton from a dirty wad of unruly fluff to a sleek, colorful bolt of fabric. She used to imagine some of the destinations of those bolts . . . elegant dresses, prim tablecloths, sturdy uniforms.

Hailey fished in her pocket for her earplugs. The roar increased as she approached the weaving department, and it wouldn't get any quieter until she returned to her desk. Each visit she completed in the carding, spinning, weaving, dyeing, and finishing departments progressed as in the warehouse, with joyful greetings followed by informative mill-talk. By lunchtime, she felt she'd gotten a decent overview of the mill workings and departments, though there were hundreds of details that she'd have to fill in over the next several weeks.

That afternoon she finally braced herself and picked up the phone to call Daniel. She didn't want to see him, but needed the bad news about the finances. They'd had a controller, but he had been offered another job in South Carolina. Being certain it was a matter of time before Anderson Mill closed down, he'd taken his opportunity. This left the books, and too much power, in Daniel's hands.

Daniel sat across the massive wooden desk from Hailey in the president's office. He shifted in his chair, seeming as relaxed as someone who'd just been fired. Hailey would collaborate with him only as much as was necessary. Along the way, maybe she could discern his attitude about her return, whether he thought *he* should be sitting in the black leather chair.

Hailey scrutinized the balances. Even as a non-mathematically inclined artist, she understood that the mill was in trouble. Maybe something could have been done long ago, but everyone had turned a blind eye. Or they'd made efforts too late, like drowning men treading water, to no effect. Hailey had little satisfaction knowing she'd been right in her predictions.

"The way I see it, the only way out of this is to go through an initial series of layoffs."

Hailey flinched at his words. Daniel's tone bore no grief over the news, as if he'd told her of a change in a vendor, or a new fabric design.

"Are you sure? There might be something else we can do before we resort to layoffs," Hailey insisted. "Maybe cut some expenses. I haven't even looked in detail at the expense figures, so maybe we can try some other things first."

"You mean things we haven't thought of yet? You've been gone, Hailey. Even before that, you were in design, and didn't know all the things we tried to cut expenses."

Hailey eyed him, bristling. "That may be the case." Her voice was frosty. "But I still need to have my own first-hand look at all of the expenses and figures. I'm sure that you and my father have done your best, but I can't neglect seeing *everything* and trying to come up with solutions. That's one reason I'm here." Intuition told her that it wasn't the last time she would need to remind him.

Daniel was already shaking his head, his expression closed like a steel door. "I don't see any way out of these layoffs. We've been talking about them for months. I have the list of positions."

Hailey reached out for his proffered list, even as her heart was sinking. As she scanned the names she couldn't muffle a small cry. "Bill Gatling? He's been with the mill nearly thirty years. He's worked in every department. How can we let him go?"

Daniel shrugged. "He's old school. He's in finishing and inspection now, but the number of workers there is too high."

"Let someone else go, someone younger. Not Bill."

"Hailey, this is business. You can't be partial to the people you like. We have to do what's best for the mill. Bill's close to retirement. Don't you think a younger worker will have more stamina, and in a couple years won't have health problems like we know Bill will? I *thought* you might be too close to everyone to be able to do the job."

"I can and *will* do the job," Hailey insisted, and felt she'd lost a shard of dignity by pleading her case to Daniel, of all people. "Just because I have human emotion for people I've known all my life doesn't mean I won't do my job, and I resent your implication."

Daniel shook his head and held up one hand. "You just have to be a lot colder about it. That's my advice."

Hailey grimaced and looked back down at the list. She hadn't asked his advice. But maybe he was right. "Oh no, Wilma Johnson? Becky Rowe?" The mounting sadness gripped her throat. She swallowed it down and took on a cool expression. "I'll keep this list and the budgets to study this evening."

Once Daniel had left her office she collapsed back into the hollow of her father's chair. Layoffs. Her grandmothers and grandfathers. She didn't come all the way back to Larkspur to strip people of their livelihood, the put them into the streets. She came to *save* their jobs. Was this the first thing she'd have to do? They'd surely blame her, just when they thought she'd be their rescuer.

She had to grudgingly give Daniel credit for one thing, the reminder to keep cool. To stay businesslike. It would be hard to do both, especially when she looked at people and saw the hope in their eyes, their confidence in her. She might have very well taken on too big a morsel, believing too much in her own zeal to save the mill.

At the day's end, Hailey drove to her father's house. She turned off the ignition and simply sat for a moment in the driveway. Her shoulders slumped with weary weight and she closed her eyes. Her first day was over. But it was not going to be her hardest day, not by far.

With great effort, she slung her legs out of her car, as if each one weighed over a hundred pounds. Maybe her father would have some encouragement for her. Her mouth quirked. Fat chance. *That* hadn't happened in at least thirty years. One could always hope, though. She knew he wouldn't invite her to stay for dinner, and for once felt relief. She needed to be alone to process her day, her re-entry into the world of Anderson Mill.

Sitting in the living room of the brick colonial house, Paul Anderson stirred his frosty glass of lemonade and slowly took a sip. "So, you got your feet wet today, eh?" His complexion hadn't improved, but his movements seemed less pained than a few days earlier. "Sure you don't want some?"

Hailey shook her head. "No, we're barely out of winter. I've been a bit chilled, so I'll go home and make a pot of soup. I need to think about everything I learned today."

Her father gave her a wry smile. "Yes, there's quite a bit to know. Like I said once or twice before, it will take time. But it won't be hard. You've been around this your whole life. Just need to get the overview. And don't try to be God, just do what you can."

Hailey gave him a crooked smile. He was right. She shouldn't picture herself as the Savior of Anderson Mill. She could get knocked down a peg very quickly, and already had, plenty of times that day alone. But maybe her father was right about another thing, that an overview and a little time was mainly what she needed. She hoped it was true. That, she could handle.

"Daniel told me today about the need for layoffs," she told him, watching his reaction. "I—I was surprised by how many there were, and some people who've been there for twenty years or more."

Her father frowned. "Yes. Daniel told me you two had talked today about the layoffs and that you'd taken it badly."

Hailey's eyebrows raised. "He did? He called to tell you that I *took it badly*?" She shook her head, scowling. "I was saddened, of course. These are people we've known for ages. You and I both know people like Bill Gatling won't find work easily. Daniel considers that strange. I just call it compassion."

"No need to be upset, Hailey. He was just telling it as he saw it."

"I could have discussed this with you myself, without him telling you in advance." The nerve of Daniel Carlton talking about her response to her father. Irritation bubbled hot in her stomach.

Suddenly she couldn't bear to talk about the mill anymore. Her father wasn't going to comfort her. She wasn't there for comfort, anyway. She'd come back to run a business. She needed to toughen up, and her father would expect that of her. She needed to expect it of herself.

"Everything ready for the surgery, Dad?" Her voice sounded abrupt to her ears. "Have you had all your tests and everything?"

She thought she saw him wince. He nodded. "We did all that the last few weeks. All I'm doing now is waiting until Thursday. They say this type of operation has good results, but I'm sicker than most. I'll be glad when all this is over." His voice was gruff as he glanced out the window. His hand tightened around the carved wooden arm of the chair.

The doorbell chime cut the silence. "That must be the visiting nurse. She checks on me and warms up my dinner at the same time. Nice lady. Name's Sharla.

"I'll let her in and be on my way. I'll call you tomorrow, Dad."

Her father nodded absently, then suddenly his gaze became sharp. "Hailey?" She waited. He moistened his lips and swallowed. "I'm glad you're here."

She smiled and squeezed his hand, then turned away before he could see the tears in her eyes.

As Hailey drove into the condo complex a foggy, dreamlike feeling assailed her, despite the familiarity of the buildings. It was almost too much effort to go to the block of mailboxes on the corner near her building, but it would only take a minute. She wanted to make sure the postal service had processed her change of address correctly. She sat in her driver's seat a moment while she leafed through the letters and ads. Everything looked in order, tidy address changes stamped on the bottom of the envelopes and a welcome packet from the post office.

As she stacked her mail and slid it into her purse, she noticed in her peripheral vision the bulk of a car in the opposite direction, pulling to a stop. She ought to free up the space in front of the mailboxes. Before she had the chance to change gears, a face appeared in her side window. She jumped back with a squeal of surprise.

Alex. His dark eyes connected to hers with an intensity she thought she'd never see again. And that same feeling like frantic bird wings banged against her chest. She quickly rolled down her window. His fingers curled over the edge of the window as he leaned toward her and peered into the car at her, only inches away. He looked the same as she remembered, as she'd imagined, so many times during her first month or two in Colorado.

For a second she lost her air supply.

"I thought it looked like you, then I thought I must be dreaming," he said with a tone of incredulity, though a smile twitched at his lips.

Hailey recovered, and gave him a warm grin. "Hello, Alex. It's nice to see you again." Yes, she'd start on the right foot this time, with plenty of warmth and friendliness, just as soon as she could breathe again. "I just got back to town a few days ago. Uh, my dad's real sick and he asked me to move back and run the mill."

Alex's expression sobered. "Oh, sorry to hear about your dad. So, you just got out there and had to come all the way back?"

"Uh, well, I could have said no. I had another job there, but the mill is important to our family, so I decided to come help out, and help my dad too."

He finally grinned, a rare flash of white teeth against swarthy maleness. "So, now you have the run of the mill," he quipped, then laughed. Hailey was so surprised she almost forgot to laugh with him. He'd always seemed so serious before, but maybe this was a new side of him. Or a side she hadn't seen.

And maybe he was glad to see her.

He stepped away from her car, crossing his arms over his chest. "You went back to your old place?"

Hailey shook her head. "No, my tenant's lease isn't up until late summer. But my dad heard about a unit available for rent here. So,

I'm almost back home, though not quite." She shrugged, afraid she was starting to ramble.

"Still neighbors." His eyes stayed fixed on hers until she felt warmth flood up her neck and into her cheeks.

"Yes, still neighbors. I'll try to be a nice one." They both laughed and he waved as he returned to his car. Two other cars waited behind him as he returned to his Jeep. He waved an apology to them.

Well. That was a surprise, a welcome one. How could she interpret his behavior except that he was glad to see her?

She couldn't make anything certain of that short encounter, but as she parked her car, gathered her things, and unlocked her condo door, she realized she was still smiling.

Chapter Nine

Hailey hugged her arms against an imaginary chill and glanced at her watch. Her father had been in surgery for three hours. He'd seemed fearful and bewildered that morning before a team of nurses bustled into his hospital room, smiling and full of assurances that probably meant nothing to him, as they surrounded his bed and prepped him for the final procedures prior to anesthesia.

Now the waiting room surrounded her in drowsy shades of pale green, vinyl blue seats arranged in a square, hushed whispers. White-clad nurses huddled around a counter, then came and went at intervals. A floral scent of cleaner accented the still air. There would be no news until after the operation, but Hailey wouldn't have been able to concentrate on anything at the mill, so she stayed at the hospital. She needed all of her attention on *this* moment.

Her phone let out a muffled sound inside her purse. She glanced down. It was Hope. They hadn't talked since her arrival a week earlier. Hailey hoped her sister would be less angry and hurt, given the gravity of the current circumstances. Maybe she'd finally understand what was at stake. "Hi, Hailey. Just checking on Dad. Do you know anything yet?"

Hope's voice sounded clipped and distant, as if it were a routine question, as if they'd never been best friends. Maybe it was too soon for understanding and forgiveness. "Hi, Hope. He's still in surgery. He might be finished within the next hour. He was in bad shape. I hope this will take care of him." Once again, saying too much.

Maybe Hope would pick up on her hints that the operation was more serious than she'd previously let on.

An extended silence made her wonder if Hope was still on the line. Finally, "I guess that would have to be the case if he's having heart surgery."

Hope was either stating the obvious to make conversation, or being sarcastic, and Hailey was too tired to try to discern which.

"These procedures, these plasty-whatever they're called, have a good rate of success," Hope continued, "if the person takes care of himself after. That's what I've heard, anyway."

"Yeah, I've heard that too." Hailey's voice trailed off. "How's Devon?"

"Fine. She's got a basketball game later on. All the athletic genes went straight to her, I guess."

Hailey nodded, wishing she could break the superficial stalemate in their relationship. It couldn't be forced, especially not now. It wasn't the time and she didn't have the energy. "I'll give you a call when he's in recovery. They'll know then if it all went well. You can talk to him later or tomorrow."

"Okay. Thanks, Hailey."

"Bye, Hope."

Hailey pushed the end button on her phone, a sharp sting in her eyes. Would things ever be like they used to be with her sister? Maybe their lifelong complicity was broken, dried up forever. Or would take months, years, to recover. She might save the mill, but feared she'd lose the closest relationship she'd ever had.

She grabbed a women's magazine and stared unseeing at its glossy pages and inane content. *God, I made the best decision I could. And I still don't know if it's the right one. Still don't know.*

The thought leaped into her mind. *That's why it's called a walk of faith. You walk it, day by day, trusting My voice, and trusting your own heart.*

She nodded and squeezed her eyes shut. Yes, that's the only way she'd know anything, day by day. A faint sense of comfort filled her inside.

The last hour passed quickly. When she heard, "Hailey Anderson?" her head jerked up. Dr. Cho, her father's surgeon, stood nearby in green scrubs and a white mask that hung around his neck.

She pulled herself up and scurried to his side, eagerly searching his weathered face behind black-rimmed glasses. "Your father came through the operation well, but he'll need to be closely monitored and have a long convalescence. He'll have to follow strict lifestyle changes, and he should be fine."

Hailey released a breath she didn't realize she'd been holding. Lifestyle changes. That confirmed the wisdom of her return to Larkspur. The lifestyle change her father had needed most was getting away from the stress of a failing textile mill. "These heart problems can come back again, can't they, Doctor?"

Dr. Cho nodded gravely. "The same conditions that led to the first operation can aggravate the heart all over again, if they're not changed. It is imperative that he lower his stress and follow a strict diet. Then there is no reason he can't eventually live a normal life."

"How long?"

"It will be several months before he'll feel normal. A month more and it should be safe for him to return to normal activities.

Some people bounce back more quickly, but given the previous attacks and your father's age, I wouldn't expect it."

"Thanks, Doctor. When can I see him?"

"Not for a couple of hours, at least. He'll be in ICU for a day or more, then moved to a regular room. If you don't live far, you could leave, but call before coming back, to see if he is ready to receive visitors. Otherwise, tomorrow."

Hailey drove back home as the late afternoon sun caressed the treetops, where feathery pale buds had begun to sprout. The early March temperature had risen since the morning, so she lowered the window and let the breeze bring soothing comfort.

Her father's surgery had taken her mind off the mill for most of the day. She'd taken two days off, and with the weekend she'd have four days to regroup, to rest her brain, and to focus on her father's needs.

She knew layoffs would be needed and dreaded the thought. The numbers clearly showed that if there were fewer salaries paid out, then there would be some relief for Anderson Mill. She'd seen for herself that some positions were superfluous and needed to be cut. And it still wouldn't be enough. They'd need to make major operational changes, if more layoffs in the future were to be avoided. She'd try hard to think like a businesswoman.

It was the only way, but she wouldn't think of it until Monday.

The following day she stood by her father's bedside and looked into his pale, pinched face. Three tubes emerged from his chest. An IV tube clung to his arm, as well as a catheter, and several other cables sprouted from his body and led to the heart monitor. A lump formed in her throat, but she smiled and murmured, "They have you plugged in like a Christmas tree, Dad."

The corner of his mouth twitched and she saw two fingers move. Hailey continued in soft tones. "Hope called yesterday. Twice. She thinks you had a minor procedure, but she's still worried. Everyone's glad you're doing so well, though. Might have a few visitors from the mill tomorrow. You've gotten a lot of prayers, too."

Hailey felt a presence beside her. She looked up and Daniel had come into the room, a concerned scowl on his face. Why couldn't he just say hello, like other people, instead of slinking in like a phantom? Hailey was annoyed but chided herself. Not a time for irritation.

"How is he?" His voice was low and his eyes darted around the room.

"He's done well. He's awake, you can talk to him."

Daniel leaned forward toward the bed. "Hi, Mr. Anderson. It's Daniel. Can you hear me?"

"He hears, but might not respond. He's very tired," Hailey told him quietly.

Daniel cleared his throat. "Mr. Anderson, everyone at the mill sends their best wishes. We all hope for your speedy recovery." Paul Anderson's eyelids twitched and Hailey thought she saw the corner of his mouth move again.

"He hears you. He tried to smile, did you see that?"

"Yes, I think I did. Well, I'm glad he's going to be fine. That's a big relief to all of us. I'll see you Monday, Hailey." Before she could respond, he'd turned and disappeared. Quickest hospital visit in history. But in his absence Hailey found herself relaxing her shoulders, which she hadn't realized were drawn up like a sling.

"Dad, that was Daniel. I don't know if you heard him. Yesterday you were in Intensive Care, but now you're in a regular room. You'll be able to have more visitors in a couple of days."

Her father moved a finger to show her he understood, then closed his eyes and slackened his torso, as if releasing all the effort the small gesture required of him. Hailey pulled a chair closer to his bed. Looking into his gray, pinched face, now softened by sleep, she tried to conjure memories from her past, mental snapshots of a happy family, but they eluded her. When she did see him in her mental archives, he was sitting stiffly in an armchair, as if listening to the news, but his expression showed his thoughts were far away. On what, she didn't know. On mill concerns, regrets, memories of his own, or just boredom. In any case, he was rarely present in the moment.

And here she was years later, alone by his hospital bed. In a way, she wasn't surprised that it was she who was here, not her mother or Hope. Though she wasn't close to her father, the link they'd always had was the mill, with the same loyalty, like a mission and a family all in one. Only her father would be in the position to understand. *You know the mill better than anyone, and more importantly, you love the mill. You have a heart for it.* He had understood, all along. So why had he never listened to her, affirmed her ideas or brought her into his inner circle? She had no answer except that he didn't have an inner circle. Even Daniel had not been able to fully scratch his way in. Her father didn't have to be a loner, he'd simply chosen it. She'd never known why.

Hailey released a long sigh and pulled a magazine from the bedside table. She'd been asking these questions for years. Her father was an enigma she might never understand. One thing she now knew, he trusted her with the mill, perhaps by necessity. It didn't make up for all the barren years of yearning for his attention and approval. But if it was all she could have, she'd take it.

℘   ℘   ℘

"I'll have another piece of that blueberry pie, Alice." Walt Baker gestured his gnarled hand toward the Pyrex plate on the dining room table. "I don't get this very often, so I make the most of it when I can."

Hailey laughed lightly and said to Alice, "It's really good. Did you make it yourself?"

Alice just smiled and slid the plate toward her husband. "He knows he's not supposed to eat too many sweets, doctor said, but I let him indulge once in a while. Mostly I don't do homemade. This time I wanted to, even though blueberries aren't in season yet. It's a treat to have you over, Hailey. It's been a long time."

"Yes, it has." Hailey gazed around the comfortable, simply decorated dining room of the Bakers, whom she'd known nearly all her life. Alice had already cleared away the plates from the roast beef and potato dinner.

"The coffee must be ready." Alice slid back her chair from the table and vanished into the kitchen, reappearing with a glass carafe. "Anyone for a refill? It's fresh."

"I'm still working on mine, thanks." Hailey smiled over the rim of her coffee cup at the kind face of Alice, whose wispy white tendrils clung to her forehead. Hailey had grown up with Walt and Alice's daughter, Beverly, but she was closer to Alice herself, who'd been almost a surrogate mother to her. Her screen door had always swung open easily. Whatever Hailey's hurt or disappointment, Alice had always been there with a warm tone and compassion pouring from her eyes, with homemade cookies and ample time, even when Hailey's own mother would crisply tell her to "be strong and move

85

on". Alice's husband Walt had worked at the mill for thirty years, and Alice herself had been there the last twelve.

"How's your dad doing? He's home from the hospital?" Walt reached for the carafe.

"He's been home for a week. A nurse visits regularly. He's still frail, but you know him. He's still ordering everyone around."

That brought a chuckle from Alice and Walt. "Some things never change," Walt said with a smile. "I haven't seen your dad in a while. In the last few months before he left sick, he'd stay in his office with the door closed. 'Course, I been working down in dyeing, so I didn't see him much anyway. I think he wasn't feeling too good there at the end. I was worried he'd just drop over one day, like his dad did."

Hailey's gaze darted up. "No one ever talks about my grandfather. He died just before I was born, so I didn't know him. He died at the mill?"

Walt nodded gravely. "Just fell over one day in his office. Heart attack. Your dad was already working there and he took right over. Though we were sad about it, the transition was real smooth."

Alice looked at Walt. "I heard the grandson of that guy has been working at the mill since last year sometime."

Hailey looked from Alice to Walt, and observed Walt's brows furrow, as if in warning. "Who?" She asked, not sure if she should.

Alice waved her hand in the air. "Oh, nobody. There was a man your grandfather had a conflict with years ago. Well, his grandson works at the mill. I'm kinda surprised he's still there. I hear he had a drinking problem and other things. Name's Sweeny, I think."

"Well, Alice, if he came last year and he's still there, maybe he's straightened himself out by now." Walt nodded toward her, eyebrows raised.

"I hope so." Alice's head lifted abruptly and she added cheerily, "Getting back to your dad, maybe he just thought he could get over it if he calmed himself down some. And that's why he didn't call you to help out sooner."

That would be the only explanation for her father allowing her to move away and settle across the country, only to ask her to come back six months later. He thought he could handle it himself, though he'd been having intermittent chest pains for months. "I guess it's hard for people to admit they need help. He's always been so capable at running things." She shuddered to think he could have ended up like her grandfather, lying dead in his own office.

"But sometimes your body just says 'no more, I'm worn out.'" Walt gave her a sad smile. "I kinda feel that way myself most days."

"You're no spring chicken, Walt," Alice told him with a smile. She looked back at Hailey. "We're just hoping his health will hold out and the mill will stay open until he retires in a couple years. Of course, we don't wish anything bad after that, but mills are closing all over the place. We hope we're not put out just before getting full retirement."

Walt glared at his wife.

"What?" she asked defensively. "Hailey knows all this. I'm not tellin' her something she doesn't know. I hope she'll prevent all that from happening, but I'm just being honest." She looked at Hailey. "I guess you know people are scared. We're scared. It's tense around there. We just pray every day and thank God we have another day's work."

87

Hailey scrambled through her mind for something useful, comforting to say to this dear older couple who were almost like family to her. Should she assure them they weren't on Daniel's list? She didn't think they were, but couldn't be certain. Did they wish to influence her? Immediately her mind was flooded with shame. Of course not, not the Bakers. A year earlier she'd never have had such a thought. Now that she was acting president of the mill, her relationships weren't as neutral, especially when layoffs hung over them all like a loosely-bolted guillotine. She wondered if her contacts at the mill would now be tainted with suspicion and fear. So far, no one but she and Daniel knew. But it had to have crossed their minds daily.

"I'm not surprised that the staff is nervous," she said. "Many mills are closing. They need to be creative, because they can't do things like they always did." How many times had she said the same things to her father?

"Why now? Textile mills have been around for over a hundred years in North Carolina. Don't people still need fabric and fibers?" Walt thrust his fingers through thin, graying hair.

"Markets change over time. And I'm sure you know that foreign imports are having an impact." Hailey sipped her tepid coffee. "There was an agreement made a while back to limit imports for several years, but that period ended a few years ago. Lots of mills didn't make any changes, even though they knew that agreement was ending and those limits would be lifted. It's hard to compete with the wages of some countries like China and Pakistan."

"What about the whole 'made in America' campaign?" asked Alice. "Thought that was supposed to help out."

"Oh, it did. But just not enough. When the price is much higher because of labor costs, people usually don't care where something is made."

Walt snorted. "Sad but true. Guess that won't be changing anytime soon."

Alice turned weathered blue eyes to Hailey. "I hope it's not too late for us. I hope you can turn things around, Hailey."

Hailey smiled sadly, yet felt the familiar thud inside, seeing the hope in Alice's eyes. She hoped she was up to the task, she who had never run a textile mill. "I'll certainly do my best." Seemed she was saying that phrase to someone at least once every day. "I'll do everything I can to keep the mill open as long as possible."

"You're only human, but I know you'll do whatever you can." Walt touched her forearm gently, and the compassion in his eyes brought a lump to Hailey's throat. He added, "And if it doesn't work out, it's not your fault. Some things are just meant to be."

"I don't think it's meant to be," said Hailey quietly. "I just hope it's not too late."

Chapter Ten

As soon as Hailey entered the building Monday morning she sensed it. Emma shot a glance up from behind the reception desk and mumbled a greeting. Should she ask her if everything was alright? Normally she was cheerful and gentle-natured. Hailey shouldn't pry.

When she saw Lenore's pinched, ashen face, she had to ask. What had happened? Maybe an employee had died over the weekend and she'd been too preoccupied with her father to know about it.

"Lenore, is something wrong?"

Lenore's head jerked up. "Uh, hello, Hailey. Why do you ask?"

"Everyone looks as though someone died. I hope no one has. Is it my imagination?"

"It's about the layoffs. We heard we're gonna have layoffs. I'm sure you know, since you're the boss now. Isn't that right? Some people are gonna get laid off?" Her round blue eyes searched Hailey's face and her pointed chin trembled.

Hailey swallowed. How had this news gotten around? Supposedly only she and Daniel knew about it. Surely, he wouldn't have said anything. Still, it would have been an easy rumor to spread, since it wasn't a rumor at all. "Where did you hear this?"

"I'm not sure who told me. It's kind of been running through the mill for a week or so."

Hailey scowled. "It is possible—" she began, measuring her words carefully, "that in the next couple of months a small-scale layoff will be necessary, but more than that, I can't tell you just now. It might be avoidable. Of course, I'll do everything possible to keep it from happening." She finished with a sheepish smile and a shrug, realizing she'd contradicted herself. "I'm sorry, I know that's vague. But I'll keep communication open so employees know what's happening."

Lenore sighed. "I guess that's all you can do. I know you're doing your best, and geez, you just got here a couple weeks ago."

"I've hardly had time to catch my breath, with my father's health, and all."

Lenore gasped and splayed both hands against her mouth. "Oh, Hailey, I totally forgot to ask about your dad. He had open-heart surgery last week, didn't he? I was too caught up in my worries to think about his surgery."

"It's understandable. He came through very well, but he's still weak. I go see him every day after work, and a visiting nurse goes frequently to check on him."

Now that her father's surgery was finished, she really needed to focus her attention on the mill, like a bulldog attacking a bone. Even before she'd returned to Larkspur, the mill was hanging on a thin limb. All she needed now before she could even get established were rumors and panic rippling among the employees.

She turned back to Lenore. "Are many people talking about this?"

Lenore nodded. "It's sort of building up day by day. I think the more nothing is said, the more people worry."

"Do you think it would be helpful to address it openly and set things straight, even if it's bad news?"

Lenore gulped and nodded again. "Everyone's afraid, but at least we'll know what it is we're afraid of."

"I may do that. Let me think about it." As she returned to her office, Hailey's mind churned. How could this have started? It only took one statement for rumors to start sparking small fires of panic all over the mill. The previous week she hadn't noticed anything unusual in the employees' demeanor. Or maybe she'd been too preoccupied to see it.

The previous week she'd spent large chunks of time in each department, being tutored by each supervisor in the processes that went on there each day. From carding to spinning to weaving to finishing. She'd wanted to discern what changes could increase productivity without necessarily laying off employees. Were the processes efficient? Were the operators well-trained? Were there too many in one department but not enough in another? As she circulated through the noisy compartments of the mill she made abundant notes to herself, filling up a small notebook by the end of that week.

When she realized she couldn't avoid it, she called Daniel in for a meeting. He sat across from her, a dispassionate frown on his pale face. "I think the mill is doing too many things," she told him without preamble. "There are few mills nowadays that do all that we are doing. We spin, weave, and finish, while other mills buy the prepared yarn, weave it, then send it elsewhere for finishing. There are many ways we can do this, but it will involve reorganizing the staff. And that will require retraining some of them."

Daniel pursed his lips and listened without comment. She wondered if he had suddenly become supportive, but then he said, "You're kidding yourself if you think you can avoid layoffs, Hailey. You saw the list we went over together."

She glared at him. "I *know* layoffs may be needed, but I will examine every possibility first. I am trying to get a baseline on the mill's efficiency before making decisions that will affect the futures of so many people. Layoffs can't be done rashly, as I'm sure you agree."

He swung back in his chair and swiveled slightly, a mocking expression on his face. "It's not like people don't expect it. Haven't you sensed the tension in the air?"

"Yes, I have. It seems to be increasing, and I wonder what or who is responsible for that. No new mill closings in the area have been announced, have they? Why the upsurge in panic?"

"Just the times we live in."

"I'm thinking of calling a meeting and addressing the question head-on."

"Why on earth would you do that? That will just throw everyone into hysteria."

Hailey leaned forward on her desk. "Because if it isn't addressed, the fear will increase. Imagine you think you have cancer but you aren't sure. Whether you get either a confirmation or a clean bill of health, you're better off knowing than not knowing. If the news is bad, you'll know what you need to do next."

"Maybe you should wait until you know what you're going to do."

"I agree that a layoff can't be avoided. I want to prepare them for the possibility, at least." Hailey looked at Daniel just in time to see him roll his eyes then quickly try to look concerned. She frowned. She regretted that she couldn't count on Daniel for support or good advice, amidst her pressures and uncertainty. At times the burden, even after just two weeks, sagged heavily on her shoulders as she considered the employees and the future of the mill.

Her tendency might be to put the needs of the employees over the company's needs. She wanted to save jobs, but not at the expense of Anderson Mill. If the mill went down, everyone would be laid off. Getting the mill back on its feet and healthy enough to employ even more people was her objective. But at the moment, she had a long way to go and bore this burden alone.

Of course, Daniel wanted to keep his job. But he'd never sat at the knees of spinners and weavers and dyers as a child, listening to their tales of growing up in a mill village, in the days when the works were powered by a waterwheel, and how sometimes entire families and towns were sustained by a textile mill. Hailey used to sit for hours, enthralled by the stories of mill towns, self-contained cities surrounding the life of the mill, with their own schools, sports fields, stores, and even governments.

Now there was just the mill by itself, but its roots still went deep and spread wide in the life of each worker and the identity of Larkspur. For Daniel, this was a job and perhaps an ambition. How much ambition, she still wasn't sure.

After dismissing Daniel, Hailey sat alone in her office and stared out the window from her leather chair. What would Dad have done? She tried to put herself in his place, tried to imagine all of his forty years of experience at the mill. She could always ask him, couldn't she? He'd be a support with the decision. He may be physically frail, but his mind would be available to help her think of aspects she didn't yet understand. Why hadn't she thought of it sooner? She still had a long-term brooding reluctance to come near her father with personal matters.

But this wasn't personal. After the work day she alerted him to her arrival then drove directly to his house. When she entered the living room of the big colonial house he was sitting in his recliner facing an unlit brick fireplace. The television was muted and several lamps cast a warm glow throughout the dusk-darkened room. He greeted her with his usual reserve, but his color had returned.

Hailey lightly touched his shoulder and sat down in the upholstered wing chair near him. "How are you feeling today, Dad?"

He shrugged. "Same as yesterday. Same every day. The doctor said it would be long, so I'm trying to get used to it. I'm about to die of boredom."

Hailey grinned. "I guess all the pressure is lacking in your life. It might be a good idea to find some hobbies, since you'll have some months yet to go. Are there any books I can get you? Puzzles?"

He snorted and shook his head just as a woman appeared in the kitchen doorway, the same one she'd seen before. The woman was attractive, about sixty, with curly salt-and-pepper colored hair and a warm, broad smile. "I've got your dinner warming in the oven, Paul, so I'll let myself out." When she saw Hailey she said brightly, "Oh, hello. Are you Paul's daughter?"

"Oh, yes, Sharla, this is my daughter, Hailey. Hailey, my nurse, Sharla."

Hailey smiled and said, "Hello, Sharla. Thanks for taking such good care of my dad."

Sharla blushed. "Oh, it's a pleasure. He's no trouble at all." And to her father, "I'll be by again tomorrow to check on you."

When Sharla had gone, Hailey said, "She seems nice. She comes every day?" She watched her father closely, curious about Sharla's blush.

"Not every day, but often enough. She came some before the surgery, to help with medicines and take vitals and whatnot. So, she kept coming, knowing I'd need some help afterwards. She's becoming a friend, I'd say."

His last words nearly confirmed Hailey's suspicion. "I was wondering if she was a friend too, not just your nurse. I'm glad you have a new friend." Hailey grinned at her father, who blustered and looked away.

"She's a nice lady and she comes by often, so that's all. She's good company."

"Well, if she *were* more than just a friend, or one day became one, I think that would be just great."

"Now, don't go getting ahead of yourself, Hailey." Her father looked uncomfortable.

Hailey knew when to drop the subject, but liked the idea, which had never occurred to her before, that her father could be attracted to someone. He'd been alone for more than ten years. Maybe a new relationship would keep him from driving himself into another heart attack.

"Dad, I have some things I want to run by you, if you don't mind."

"I was wondering when you'd come and ask for help or advice. I didn't send you over there to figure it all out by yourself. I know we haven't always agreed, but you can ask me whatever you want and I'll do my best to help you from my experience."

Hailey felt strangely touched, even though her common sense told her that was normal. It wasn't something she took for granted, not when he first asked her to return to Larkspur, and not any time since. "Thank you, Dad. It means a lot to me to know that you feel that way."

"Well, of course. Now, what is it?"

She summarized her findings about production, personnel needs, and what she'd gleaned talking with each department supervisors. Then hesitantly she added, "I'm thinking of cutting out one or more of the stages of production, like carding and spinning. We can order yarn from another manufacturer and weave it, then take it to finishing. That would cut out some workers from those departments and they can be retrained or some can, um, be laid off, as much as I don't want to do that." She stopped and watched his face. They'd had a similar discussion over a year earlier and he'd nearly shouted her out of his office.

For a moment he didn't speak. She almost held her breath. Finally, he said, "I have thought of that before, but everything was always so urgent all the time and I knew it would take a massive reorganization, so I never did it. Also, I felt it would be a shame to cut out some of our functions, like all the other mills around us. It's been in our family so long and always stood for something. But now, if you think that's what we need, I would do it."

"Really?" Was he agreeing with her? Trusting her conclusions? "The mill will always stand for something, Dad. Changing the production process won't ever change that. Customers won't even know. And what if there are layoffs? That would be a shame too, don't you think?"

He shrugged. "I've held them off for over a year and we just bled, so it's time. It's never easy, but it may save the mill. Daniel told me you two had spoken about it."

Hailey's brief sense of camaraderie with her father was abruptly shattered. "Daniel called you? Why is Daniel always calling you to tell you what we've talked about?" She realized her tone had risen. "It's like he's some kind of spy who has to report everything before I can come tell you myself. I can't stand him getting in the middle like that."

Her father chuckled. "Now, Hailey, he's just trying to keep me in the loop. He's not a spy, he's been in the mill many years and wants me to stay informed."

"But it's not his place to report to you whatever he and I talk about, discuss my reactions, my decisions. It's not his *place*."

"Tell him yourself. Don't get into a dither, Hailey. Keep your calm."

Hailey fell silent, flooded with shame. Some president of a company she was, letting impatience and anger, and perhaps jealousy too, carry her away. She thought she had changed. Was she still the impulsive, short-tempered brat who left town almost a year ago? Hadn't she changed at all? Maybe she *should* tell Daniel about her feelings. But how to do it without sounding petty and jealous?

Was it so bad that Daniel wanted to keep her father up to speed on matters at the mill? Maybe not. It depended on his reasons for doing so, which she still didn't trust. As she looked at surveyed her father, she couldn't help but sense his interest in the mill seeping away. He hadn't been there in over a month and rarely spoke of it to her, unless she talked about it first. Maybe Daniel's reports were beneficial to her father.

He stared at her. "Does that help?"

"Yes, it does. I was thinking that was what we ought to do, so I'm glad to hear you'd thought of it before. That means we'll certainly have layoffs, since fewer departments will require fewer operators. It won't be easy, but I guess it has to happen."

The conversation drifted to healing and medication then dwindled to silence. Hailey had been nagged by curiosity about something since her dinner with Alice and Walt and decided to find out. She broke the silence. "Dad, I didn't know until just the other day that your father died at the mill. How tragic that must have been."

Her father looked startled as she evoked the topic he had always avoided. He grimaced and didn't speak for a moment. "Yes, it was a difficult time. I was the one who found him. But we all had to go on, there was nothing else to do."

"Yes, I'm sure. Seems he had some kind of conflict with someone before that."

"How are you hearing this, Hailey?" Annoyance laced her father's voice. "I don't think it's that important, what happened so long ago."

She shrugged. "Just curious. Once in a while I hear a vague reference to my grandfather from someone at the mill who might have known him. They know more about him than I do."

"Not sure it's that important, since he's gone. We all have conflicts with people, no sense in talking about it to the subsequent generations." He turned his head in a way that said the discussion was finished.

Hailey smiled weakly. "Yeah, I guess you're right. We probably have enough troubles of our own."

The following day Hailey nervously paced her office, glancing at the clock for the sixth time in twenty minutes. She'd scheduled an emergency meeting for all the employees just before the end of the first shift. It was a rare event, but perhaps they were expecting it. Tension layered up throughout the day as they likely wondered what she would say. Daniel thought the employees should learn about layoffs when they occurred, but Hailey preferred to follow Lenore's suggestion, bringing the possibilities out front so that the employees knew what they were facing. They were adults who deserved to know.

She made her way to the large auditorium on the first floor, heart hammering in her rib cage. Maybe this was the only time she would have to address them all together.

As she stood before the sea of expectant faces she felt almost faint. *You're the president, Hailey. This is one of the things presidents have to do.* She took courage from that lonely truth and uttered a silent prayer.

She swallowed what felt like raw cotton and glanced down at her notes. "Thank you for stopping your work day to come to this short meeting," she called out. Her amplified voice rang through the vast room and a hollow echo shadowed back. She was eager to be finished, with the truth on the table. "I will be brief and straightforward with you all. First, I am aware there is a lot of talk and worry about the possibility of a layoff. You know this has happened to other mills in our area, and some have even shut down. I want to address your concerns. I wish I could say that this is pure rumor and it won't happen, but I cannot guarantee it at this time."

A loud murmur rippled through the crowd. Hailey could see eyes and mouths across the room go round with fright. "Of course, we are doing everything possible to avoid this, but in all probability, there will be a small-scale layoff within the next several months. This will be necessary to preserve the mill and the remaining jobs.

For those who will be affected by this, you will have over one month's notice. The community college is offering free courses for those who wish to retrain in another profession. And lastly, I will do *everything* possible to bring back, as soon as possible, those who will be affected. I can't make specific promises, but that is my hope and my intention. That's all I can tell you at this point, but I thought it was fair to prepare you. I sincerely regret this bad news. I hope it will allow you to prepare, in case you are affected."

She glanced at the clock on the far wall. It was twenty-five minutes before the end of the work day. She leaned back toward the microphone. "You are all free to go home now. We will keep you posted." As she stepped away from the podium a lump lay heavily in her stomach. She didn't know if she'd done the right thing. Was it better to let them find out when it happened, as Daniel suggested, or to warn them in advance? Some would find other jobs, and others would mentally and emotionally prepare themselves with a transition plan. At least she hoped so.

She started back toward her office and heard behind her, "Bravo, Hailey." Daniel stood smirking, arms crossed in front of him. "Now you've started a full-scale panic attack. It was under control before that."

Hailey whirled to face him, a geyser of rage beginning its ascent through her torso. "Daniel, I've had enough of you talking to me like I'm equal to you. I am the president of this mill now—"

"Temporary president."

She fumed. "I make decisions according to what I think is best and you need to remember your position. I don't appreciate your snide remarks and I don't appreciate your reporting to my father every conversation, every meeting we have. If you need to be reminded what the associate does, I'll be happy to do that. The associate director *helps* the president accomplish her job. That

101

doesn't mean you call my decisions into question or undermine my attempts to run this mill. Are we clear?" For all her firmness, her insides felt like jelly. He was either buying it, or reading her fear and self-doubt.

He gave a small bow and said, "My apologies, Hailey." Yet the derision remained stamped on his face.

"Are. We. Clear." She stood rooted in place, staring at him.

He avoided her glare and nodded, turning abruptly and disappearing around the corner. She returned to her office and shut the door, trembling from head to foot. She stood still for several moments. Confrontation was not her favorite, and she avoided it whenever possible. Yet this time her frustration had propelled her like a rocket. She'd have been unable to stop herself.

Hailey trudged to the window and looked down at the crowded parking lot. All was still except for a man hurrying toward his car. She shut the blinds to the parking lot below and fell into her chair. She closed her eyes and murmured, "Lord, have I taken on too much? Am I now in the lion's den? Are you going to rescue me, like you did Daniel in the Bible?"

Peace did not come immediately. She repeated "I am not alone, I am not alone," several times, picturing herself nestled in God's strong arms. She felt calmer, stronger. She had to pass through these waters before being able to straighten out the mess at the mill. At least the employees had been warned. That was the first hard step. The next one would be the layoff itself, but she'd have another month to prepare for it.

That thought comforted her temporarily. Her comfort evaporated, however, as she approached her car to leave for the day, and splattered across the windshield were several shattered eggs and a crudely written paper stuck underneath one windshield wiper. It read, "Go West Again!"

Chapter Eleven

Hailey pulled into her numbered parking spot in front of her condo and sat, glued to her seat. She forced out steady breaths. In the left corner of the windshield a smear of egg yolk still clung.

She couldn't believe that one of her grandmothers or grandfathers at the mill, or one of their children, could have done this. They didn't even know yet if they would be laid off. The mill was in a dark season, likely to get even darker. Like it or not, they'd all have to brace themselves to walk through it. Her included.

No point sitting in the car. Hailey got out and reached to pull a canvas tote from the back seat. She locked the door and saw Alex walking in her direction. She couldn't help but notice the way he filled out his T-shirt and faded jeans as he strode toward her with manly nonchalance. She thought he was returning from the mailboxes or dumpsters, but he angled purposefully toward her, stopping a few yards from where she stood still near her car.

For a moment she wondered if he was going to say anything. Finally, a subdued smile. "Hey, Hailey. How is it going since you've been back in town? Everything going okay over at the mill?"

Had he heard something? Maybe he was just being kind and solicitous. In that case, she was touched, and the fact that he asked, cared—that *someone* cared—was a cool balm over her stretched-out nerves. She let her shoulders sag and looked at him ruefully. "Not really. I guess I knew I wasn't coming back to a healthy, happy mill."

His dark brows gathered. "What happened?"

She circled the front bumper and stood in front of him. "Today I announced that we'll have a small layoff sometime soon and—" she gestured toward the windshield and remaining smear of egg yolk, "—this is what happened."

He leaned forward on the front bumper. "Someone egged your car? I guess people don't like the idea of being laid off and think you're responsible."

"It wasn't *my* idea of bringing great news, layoffs soon after taking over at the mill." She shook her head. With an unexpected jolt of boldness, she added, "We could sit on the porch for a few minutes, if you have time." Besides that, she didn't have the energy to stand any longer.

Alex's face warmed just slightly. He followed her to the porch where a painted wooden bench sat covered by a quilted throw blanket. "I'll get us some cold water if you'd like." At his nod, she disappeared into the house and threw her bag and purse onto the couch. She quickly filled glasses with ice and bottled water, though her heart pounded wildly with anticipation, and she fought an adolescent urge to scream with glee.

Hailey calmed herself and returned to the porch. She handed Alex a cool glass.

"Thanks." He took a long gulp then wiped his mouth on one wrist. "You're sure that layoffs can't be avoided?"

Settling beside him, she was aware of his nearness on the small bench. She couldn't believe that Alex Moreno was sitting only inches away, acting like a concerned friend instead of an annoyed neighbor. He really *had* been glad she'd returned. At least that was her favorite theory. He smelled good, as if freshly scrubbed with soap after a long day. A trace of stubble shadowed his jaws, giving him a rakish look.

"Unfortunately, yes. Since coming back I've been going through every department and all the accounts. We need some big changes." Hailey sipped her water, the coolness sluicing down her dry throat.

Alex listened with interest and took another sip. A mild breeze flowed through the porch in a smooth caress. The wind chime swinging above the railing trembled a musical sigh.

"I won't bore you with too much mill talk," Hailey said, "but I'm planning to cut some of our operations and outsource them instead. That will eliminate some employees, unfortunately, but it's the only way we can stay afloat."

"Better than closing."

His deep brown eyes latched onto hers. For an instant she couldn't pull her eyes away, as a prickle of warmth crept up her neck. "Yes," she murmured, then caught herself before she was mesmerized. "Of course, the . . . the current state of the mill is the result of years of keeping the status quo." At least she uttered a coherent sentence. Did his look mean anything, or was he simply a good listener?

Hailey hoped she wasn't being disloyal to her father, but she'd said the truth. "Drastic measures should have been taken a long time ago, so they're happening now." She shrugged and threw him a wry smile. "I'm just the one who gets to do it."

He grinned and leaned back. "Lucky you."

Her tension slowly dripped away. "I'm glad I don't have a fancy new car. Maybe worse things will happen to it before this is all over."

Alex frowned. "Do you think anyone would try to hurt you?"

"Oh, no, I don't think so. A little egg is just an outlet from someone who feels helpless and frustrated. Many of our employees have known me my whole life."

"But not all of them."

"No, not all."

"And it's possible that some of them have no affection for you because they don't know you. To them, you just appeared, took over, and started turning things upside down."

Hailey paused. "Yes. That does makes me feel better about the egg, since it's likely not someone I know, but worse about the prospect of other things happening. If someone doesn't know me, he won't necessarily be patient or understanding."

Alex leaned forward and fished a wallet out of his back pocket. "Here," he said, pulling a small card from the wallet. "Here's my number, if you ever need help with anything." He slid a pen from his breast pocket. "I'll put my cell on it too."

She watched as he scribbled his number on the back of the card and gave it to her. "Don't hesitate to call if you're afraid or if someone is bothering you. I just live a few doors away."

"Thanks." She took the card and fingered it in her hand. Maybe he was just worried, and nothing more. But it was a start. Still, she felt a stab of disappointment.

As if reading her thoughts, he added in a low tone, "And don't forget, you promised to stop by one of these days."

She smiled. "Yes, I owe you an overdue visit." To distract the mad fluttering inside she glanced down at his card. "Oh, you're a—

oenologist? Did I pronounce that right? Some kind of botanist? I didn't know that. How interesting."

"Yes, close enough. A botanist and a chemist both, I guess. An oenologist is a winemaker. A vintner cultivates the vines. I like to dabble in both. I work at a local vineyard developing new formulas and testing the ones we have. We experiment with different types of grapes, though certain ones are standards of the North Carolina crop, like scuppernongs. But we also have European vines, like cabernet franc and chardonnay. They're more fragile, since they come from a different type of climate."

"I had no idea. Are there many vineyards in North Carolina?"

"There are dozens of wineries, and seem to be growing in numbers every year, and at least a couple hundred vineyards."

Hailey's eyes widened. "Almost the Napa of the east. Sorry for my ignorance, but what is the difference between a vineyard and a winery?"

"The vineyard grows the grapes and the winery makes the wine. A winery may order grapes from a vineyard, just like any company orders a raw material from a vendor in order to make its product. Lots of establishments do both. I like to be involved in the whole process, from vine to bottle." He smiled and shrugged. "It's kind of an art form."

Over the past two years of her mild crush on him, she'd never known exactly what he did. She would watch him drive in or out of the complex, or carry trash and recycling to the bins or get the mail. She might have seen him at church, but she wasn't sure. Hard to know anything about someone that way. She'd guessed he was some kind of engineer. "That sounds fascinating. You must spend a lot of time outside."

"Not as much as you'd think. In the lab, in front of the computer, as well as out in the fields. It's interesting and varied. A lot of the old tobacco farms have been turned into vineyards, and it's been a few years now . . ." he chuckled, "a few years of really lousy wine, but now some of it's quite good. Some varietals haves even won prizes. Pretty soon they'll be able to compete with more established growing regions. Some vineyards already have."

"How long have you been interested in developing wines?" Hailey noticed Alex had shifted slightly toward her and his left arm crooked on the back of the bench. A spring breeze gently tousled his slightly wavy black hair.

"My grandparents had a vineyard in Mexico. My dad decided to go into medicine instead of follow the family vineyard, but I was always interested in it, so I guess the family passion skipped a generation and fell to me." His face was animated when he spoke. Hailey could almost picture him as a small boy, trailing his grandfather through the rows of gnarled vines, asking dozens of questions, listening to the older man explaining how certain kinds of weather affected the sweetness of the grapes.

"Did you grow up in Mexico?"

"No, we came here when I was small. My dad did his medical school in Durham, but I spent lots of summers back there."

"Why did you stay here instead of working on your family's vineyard there? You could have taken over the family business from your grandfather."

He frowned. "My grandfather and my father had a falling out a couple of years after we moved to the States. I never knew all the details. Besides that, I'd been here since I was young. I felt more American than Mexican, even though I went back often." He took a sip of water. "My grandfather sold the vineyard, and later died. I think it broke his heart to sell, because he wanted to pass it on to either his son or to me, but we were all up here."

"Oh, how sad. But it wasn't anyone's fault. You just lived where your parents brought you and decided to stay. I'm sure he understood that at some level."

"Yeah, we talked about it just before he died." Alex's gaze had shifted beyond her as if he were remembering. His jaws tightened. "We made our peace. He did leave me some uncultivated land down there and a big house. I'm not sure what I'll do with it, so it's being used by some cousins for the moment. I guess you could say it's my vacation house." He grinned at her and she was startled, as always, by the brilliant whiteness of his smile against his tanned skin.

"A vacation house. That's more than I've got." She laughed, seeing his face open again as if shucking the negative memory far away.

"But you have a textile mill. Troubled, yes, but it's yours, more or less. You followed the family passion and now you're running with it."

Hailey pursed her lips thoughtfully. Her heart for Anderson Mill hadn't exactly been cultivated at her father's knee. Given her father's aloofness and the pain it caused, it was amazing she still had such an attachment to Anderson Mill.

"I'm running with it, but it's crushing me already." She leaned back against the bench and let out a short laugh, shirking off the newly-accumulated tension that had gathered between her shoulder blades. "Sometimes I wonder if I thought I was superwoman, coming back to save the day."

"You told me your dad was sick. That was a factor too, wasn't it?" His voice became softer, his face relaxed. Hailey felt drawn by the deep music, the gentle strength, in his voice. And compassion that nudged a deep place inside her.

"Yes, a big one. I'm not sure which was the bigger draw, the need to help him or the chance to help save the mill. I'd tried in the past to suggest things and he would never listen to me." She tightened her lips and shrugged. "That's why I moved to Colorado, out of frustration. Then one day he just dropped the whole thing into my lap. I didn't feel that I had a choice, given his need for months of recovery. Aside from that . . ." she released a deep sigh, "it was a challenge I'd waited for. I couldn't refuse."

Alex grinned at her and slowly rose to his feet. "Sounds like it was meant to be. Unfortunately, I need to go now. It was nice talking to you, Hailey. I guess that's the first real conversation we've ever had."

Hailey also stood. "Yes, I believe it was. Very neighborly of you to stop by." She grinned. Standing next to him, she guessed he was about five inches taller than her five foot six. A perfect complement. "Do it anytime. And thanks for listening. I—I feel calmer." It was true. For the first time since her return, she felt like she had a friend, besides Nina, who was tied up with wedding planning.

"Good, I'm glad. Now call me if you need to, okay?" He was already walking toward the sidewalk, glancing back at her. She nodded and waved. She'd prefer he called her, but maybe it was too soon. She should have given him her number too, but wasn't sure if it was her place or his. Still, a puddle of warmth spread inside, almost enough to erase whatever unpleasantness went before.

CR CR CR

April crept in with gentle breezes, bringing people outside of closed doors to sit in their yards or on porches, prepare for spring planting, and take walks. The Bradford pear trees exploded with white blossoms like overgrown fluffy snowflakes. When they began to fade, small purple flowers reached out from the native redbud trees. Fuchsia and salmon-colored buds burst from azalea bushes, along with the antique white and pink blush of dogwood flowers. The city was ablaze with a celebration of color.

Hailey breathed in deeply, marveling at the beauty all around her. Several times over the weekend she stopped to snap pictures of the ephemeral spring rebirth. She'd forgotten how North Carolina could enchant at that time of year. She'd enjoyed the dry climate and near-constant sunshine of Colorado, but had never felt bathed in green like she did here. She ought to paint a still life of the pastel blooms, if only she had time.

Thursday morning, her buoyancy was tempered by the event of the coming day: layoffs would be announced.

All month long she'd agonized about which positions to cut and who to move to other departments. In the end she was guided by the changes she made in the operations. The carding and spinning departments would be removed and all the equipment sold. In return, more looms would be brought in to increase weaving capacity. She'd been thrilled to find a mill that was doing a similar change in the other direction, and was able to strike a deal for an exchange of equipment. It had cost a fraction of what new looms would have cost. Hailey spent long hours during work and late into the evening researching and negotiating the changes, and praying the risk wouldn't turn the wrong way.

She sensed a certainty that her decisions were sound and that she'd sacrificed as few employees as possible. This didn't stop her from losing sleep and silently mourning each day prior to the announcement.

In the final numbers, fifty-five positions would be lost, out of a total staff of three hundred twenty, a small layoff by comparison with layoffs of other mills. Small comfort, however, for those targeted.

Not surprisingly, Daniel thought it should be a much higher number and opposed the idea of retraining some of the older employees. "As long as there's a layoff, why not cut some dead wood?" he proposed during a heated debate with her.

Hailey cringed at his choice of words. "Why not save the jobs of loyal employees who know the mill better than you or I ever will? Doesn't that experience count for something?" She leaned back in her chair and crossed her arms. "Would you rather get a twenty-year-old who has to be trained with the basics, and who will probably be gone as soon as something more elegant comes along?"

"We'll have fewer internal problems with as many new staff as possible. That's what I would do if I were president."

"Well, thank goodness you are not. These people have given their careers to the mill, and you'd put them out without a second thought, bringing in people we don't even know." She shook her head. This kind of conversation was becoming commonplace as well as tedious. "Doesn't make a bit of sense, Daniel. The idea is to have as *small* a layoff as possible, not use it as an opportunity to clean house." She sighed. Wasn't this hard enough already?

In the three weeks that passed since she'd spoken on the porch with Alex, she'd only seen him once, a shared wave as they passed in their cars one afternoon. Not much to build on, Hailey thought glumly. No further incidents of vandalism had occurred so she didn't call him, but she did send a text message to thank him for his offer of help. She was sincere, but also wanted him to have her number too. She thought that was pretty clever, and hoped he'd pick up on it. So far, he hadn't.

It was payday. Pink-slip day as well. Tension flowed like a strong electrical current through each department of the mill as employees awaited the verdict. When the news finally went out, Hailey locked herself in her office. She didn't want to hear any comments, wails, or shouts. It was already agonizing to be the responsible party.

Maybe she wasn't cut out for running a mill after all.

As she arrived home that day feeling wrung out emotionally. At least it was over. Glancing down the street she saw that Alex's jeep wasn't in his space. Many times, since that day on her porch, she spooled their conversation back in her mind, remembering his caring focus on her as she spoke. She wondered if it had meant something, if somehow, he might be interested in her. But there had been no follow-up, no phone call to check in, no suggestion to get coffee or take a walk. She must have imagined his interest.

How she longed to talk to him just then, tell him how torn she felt, how hard her month was, what a wrenching decision it had been. She'd begun to think of him as a friend, the only person who knew the stress of her current predicament. Though she'd been able to catch up with Nina, her friend was less accessible than before, with a fall wedding date and so much to do. Hailey hesitated to seek her out, and ended up feeling alone much of the time, especially in matters of the mill. She hadn't yet reconnected with all of her church friends, either. She could always talk to her father, but doubted that he'd provide reassurance or a sensitive ear.

Hailey dialed Alex's number. It rang several times and his voicemail picked up. She hung up quickly. Her face flushed with embarrassment. Maybe it was for the best that he hadn't answered. What would she say, that she just wanted someone to talk to?

The following day Hailey again holed up in her office, claiming to be tied up by emergencies and phone calls. She did need to call some sales reps to outline the changes at the mill. But in truth, she didn't want to see the faces of those who were serving their final weeks of employment at Anderson Mill. The majority of employees were likely weeping with relief, but it was the others who broke Hailey's heart. Her despondency was slightly lifted by a fierce determination to bring them back, whatever it took.

At the end of the day she pulled into her parking spot at her condo. Looking up from her car, she spied something dark on her front door. She approached the door and the stench enveloped her. She cried out in horror when she saw the ugly brown stain that stretched from one side of the carved molding to the other. Someone, maybe the author of the egging, had smeared horse or some other kind of manure on her front door. Though the evening was cool, beads of perspiration broke out all over her neck and forehead. She fervently regretted not living in a gated community. She shot a glance in every direction, but saw no one.

Hailey covered her nose as she dashed through the front door. She changed quickly into a pair of jeans and torn tee shirt then returned outside. With a garden hose, she squirted down the front door and walkway with a vengeance, gagging as she held a bandana over her nose. She glanced several times in the direction of Alex's condo, but his car was still not there.

After a thorough shower and a good cry, she drew the blinds closed and collapsed in a heap on the couch. *Oh, Alex. Where are you when I need you?*

For the first time since her return from Colorado, Hailey was afraid.

Chapter Twelve

She'd give laid-off employees an extra month's salary, that's what she'd do. A minuscule severance, to be sure, but it still put a deep hole in Anderson Mill's bottom line for the month. Hailey would never admit that fact to Daniel, who had thrown his head back in exasperation, but said nothing except, "It's your mill."

What was one more month? It would help the workers make ends meet during a transition none of them had asked for. The mill would benefit later on from fewer salaries. For now, however, she'd chosen to be generous.

"Guilt money," she overheard one woman say as she cast a smoldering glance in Hailey's direction. It was partially true, but Hailey knew the woman spoke from sadness and anger. Hailey's good intentions wouldn't be understood by everyone. She had only God and her own conscience to answer to. Hopefully that would be enough.

At least that's what she told herself, against the leaden despondency that mounted like layers of ash after a fire. As she'd moved through each department in the weeks leading up to the layoff, workers watched her furtively, with pinched, hollow faces that reflected back anger, despair, and hopelessness. Conversations hushed as she walked by, and sometimes blatant hate and contempt burned from their eyes.

Other times, the response was very different. "Hailey, don't you go blaming yourself, now. We knew this was possible a good bit before now." Bill Gatling's kind eyes were shadowed with sadness. "Probably shoulda happened a long time ago. Your dad was just as soft-hearted as you are, and he didn't want to let people go either."

"Oh, Bill." Tears squeezed through Hailey's eyes and left a hot trail down her cheeks. She couldn't stop herself from reaching her arms around his burly shoulders and squeezing him tightly. "You don't deserve this, Bill. You've worked everywhere in this mill, and I'm going to do everything I can to bring you back as soon as possible. I need your experience here." She'd tried to find a place for him in another department and had finally given up.

He smiled gently down at her, like the grandfather he'd always been, his gray-black whiskers blanketing his long jaws. "That would be real nice if it happened. But don't worry about us. The good Lord will take care of us, He always has." He cocked his head, an expression on his face that she couldn't interpret, then added, "This company might have belonged to *another* family, after all that happened before. It stayed in Anderson hands, so I reckon there's got to be a reason for that. Keeping this ship afloat is your main job, Hailey, and your Daddy would want that first of all."

Fred Murphy from the carding department told her, "You're picking up the pieces of a tough situation, Hailey. We know you're doing your best with it."

Gratitude flooded her heart as she spoke to these people, and it gave her a partial balm against the hostile attitudes of others, those who blamed her and pined for her father's return. He'd have done the same thing sooner or later.

She wondered later about Bill's words. What did he mean when he said the mill might have belonged to another family? What family, and under what circumstances? And his phrase, 'all that

116

happened before.' Maybe he was referring to the struggle of the textile industry over the previous decade and a half, and how easily they could have gone under during those years. They weren't out of danger yet, however, even after layoffs.

Hailey sighed. If only she had a faster reflex to lean on God, especially now. The mill's problems gave her ample opportunities to trust and develop that relationship, if only she would take them. That serenity always escaped her, probably due to her own dogged need to prove something to herself. That, and her fear that He didn't want to be involved. Having felt invisible to her parents led to a similar expectation with God.

The day finally arrived, some employees dubbed Black Thursday. The work day ended early for all laid-off employees, so they could gather their belongings, turning the lock on careers, short and long, that only a month earlier, they'd thought were secure. From an inconspicuous spot Hailey watched as employees hugged each other over choked-up goodbyes, their hopeless faces streaked with grief and tears as they carried small boxes full of personal belongings out of the building.

The following day Hailey entered the front door, imagining it quieter than before. Emma smiled at her from the reception desk. She'd recovered her cheerful demeanor once she learned that her job was safe. "Here's some mail for you, Hailey, including yesterday's." She extended a small stack to Hailey, who tucked it under one arm and headed upstairs to her office.

She cradled a cup of hot coffee and settled back at her desk. It was over, the specter she'd dreaded. "I survived my first test, didn't I? I didn't back down." Her voice sounded thin and uncertain as she spoke aloud to the empty walls, not at all sure if it finally gave her legitimacy, to face the ugly challenge of a layoff without falling apart. Why did she still feel like an impostor, walking in shoes that didn't fit?

She glanced across her desk, which still seemed like her father's, though she'd been acting president for over two months. She rose and walked slowly around the office. She hadn't touched it since her arrival. Since she'd be here a while longer, maybe it was time to make it her own.

Hailey gathered dusty fabric swatches into a pile and shoved them into an empty space in a file drawer then straightened and dusted all of the other surfaces. She eyed the far wall, a blank stretch of marred paint. The framed sketch of Anderson Mill should go there. Plants would add a nice touch, and perhaps drapes. Her thirst for beauty and color had been neglected for far too long.

In her files at home were a few late nineteenth-century photos of the mill when it was purchased by her great-great grandfather Isaiah Anderson. One photo, faded with age, depicted the mill's original buildings, including the water wheel that powered it. Its owners stood in front, stiff and unsmiling. She'd have it framed and place it alongside a photo of the current mill that hung in the lobby. Anderson Mill would have a rebirth, breathe a fresh draught of air.

Hailey returned to her desk, and her gaze fell to another photo of the mill, this one on the front page of the newspaper. She eagerly spread it out on her desk as the headline leaped at her. It read simply, "New Layoffs at Anderson Mill".

She frowned. That was misleading, since Anderson hadn't had layoffs in years. Eagerly she skimmed the text, wondering if this article did as so many others had, shouting out the misfortunes of ailing or dying companies. Was that really what people wanted to read?

"'Fifty-five jobs were lost this week at Anderson Mill in Larkspur, a company of over three hundred employees,'" she read aloud. "'This makes the third layoff in Forsyth County this year, rivaling mill layoffs at the same time last year. Acting president, Hailey Anderson, took over in late February. New leadership was unable to turn the ship around and avoid the loss of jobs. In other parts of North and South Carolina, the same trend emerges, as mill leaders struggle to keep the looms running.'"

They hadn't asked her for an interview, but still wrote about her actions, her *failure* to stem layoffs, for the whole city to read about at the same time she was reading about it.

Frustration welled up inside her. She rummaged in several of the drawers of the massive desk and found some blank paper. Maybe it would only be therapeutic.

"Letter to the editors," she scrawled at the top of the paper, then sat for several minutes sifting through phrases that leaped into her mind. "I've just read your thought-provoking article about another mill closing. It seems you could re-use the same article many times and save yourselves the trouble of writing. As president of Anderson Mill, I'd like to share my version of the story, since no one on your staff has asked me for my comments—"

She stopped and laid down her pen. No, this wasn't at all the tone she wanted to convey. The letter she'd begun was simply a bubbling frustration over an ignorant, shallow article. She had vented on paper. Now, she wanted to rise above venting, to make the citizens of Larkspur proud of Anderson Mill and of her father. *Lord, please help me do that.*

She closed her eyes briefly. Then, picking up her pen, she started again. "I have just read your thought-provoking article about mill closings in Forsyth County. I agree that it is a sad trend in our beloved institution, once the strongest in North Carolina. In the same way as many other industries, textile mills must re-evaluate their practices and be sensitive to changing economic climates. Foreign imports have forced many mills to change their way of doing business. But that's not always a bad thing. Sometimes jobs are lost along the way. Indeed, some mills have shut their doors."

She paused. How to turn a negative newspaper article around, to give rather than take away hope? She took her pen again. "The goal is to make the industry stronger in order to not only avoid further layoffs, but hire more people. Our layoff at Anderson Mill was very small, only a sixth of our total workforce. That doesn't imply a lack of sympathy for those people who lost their jobs. As a company that has been a part of Larkspur's landscape for over a century, we ask for your compassionate help instead of passionless commentary about yet another mill layoff. Instead we should strive to build ourselves up as a community, and encourage the Larkspur workforce. We ask businesses in Larkspur to hire those laid off from textile mills. We ask residents of Larkspur to buy American-made textile products, as your participation in this country's economy. If we band together we can revive our homegrown industries and be strong leaders again. We can do it with your help."

There, that was better. Should she send it? Who was *she* to send it? Shaking her head, she fought the stab of self-doubt and signed the letter.

A small smile emerged on her lips. Hailey Anderson, President, Anderson Mill. She put the letter in a drawer of her desk. Tomorrow she'd reread it and perhaps send it.

Hailey dialed her father's number at home. "Hey, Dad. I guess you heard the news about the layoff."

"Yes, Daniel—I mean you already told me about it yourself the other day. I assumed it had already happened."

"Yesterday. The notifications went out a month ago, and yesterday was the last day for fifty-five of the operators. It's sad. I guess within a few weeks we'll feel more normal."

"That's the hard reality. It will help the finances, of course. I'm sorry you had to be the one to do that." He cleared his throat.

Hailey smiled. Slowly the older man was changing. Some emotions were leaking through his crusty exterior. "I survived my first big test as acting president."

"Probably won't be the last one. You did well, Hailey."

A lump formed in her throat and ached with pleasure. It was almost worth it all to hear his words. "Thanks, Dad."

She hung up the phone and a smile lingered on her lips, tentative, like a nervous butterfly, but emerging from a deep place within her. Daniel had been proven wrong, she *did* have what it took to take the often-hard measures that went along with leadership. She still felt like an impostor, but slowly that taunting voice was fading.

Gradually her thoughts drifted to Alex. No word from him. She'd been encouraged too quickly by their conversation on her sun-swept porch, when she felt like she was opening up to a friend, and he to her. It meant nothing to him and he'd forgotten about it already. She didn't dare call him again.

She rewound his words in her mind, since they were likely all she would get of her Alex Moreno fantasy. Suddenly her cell phone rang, a smothered sound deep inside her purse. She pulled it out and saw Alex's name. A smile tugged at her lips. How had he known?

"Hi, Alex."

"Hey, Hailey, I haven't talked to you for a while, but wondered if everything was okay, you know, with the layoff. Has it happened yet?"

"Yesterday. Thanks for asking. The announcements went out shortly after you and I talked that day and, um, yesterday was their last day."

"Oh. Time goes fast, doesn't it?" She could hear road noises through the phone. He must be driving, or else near a parking lot. "I read something about it in the paper so I thought I'd see how you were holding up with everything."

Hailey frowned. His weren't the words of a man who was interested in her, but rather those of a concerned neighbor, a good Samaritan, a nice guy. He hadn't even remembered. He'd seen it in the newspaper.

"Okay, I guess," she said. "I'm glad it's over. I was really sad for the people laid off. I've known quite a few of them my whole life, so it's a bit like betraying family."

Alex was silent. Then, "I guess I never thought of it that way. That's rough."

"People tell me business is business. I'm not so sure I'm cut out for business, in that case." She gave a hollow chuckle.

"Sure, you are, Hailey. You're doing great. But like you said, you knew the mill was in tough shape when you came, so this is par for the course, hate to say."

Hailey tightened her lips and nodded. "Yes, I guess it is. I just have to keep that in perspective and move on. Hey, by the way, I'll be home this afternoon if you want to come grab a place on the porch. I made some iced tea yesterday."

Her heart pounded. Was she being too bold? Hadn't she also invited him the other day? And left her number for him to call? *Back off, Hailey!*

"I'd really love to, Hailey, but I have an appointment I'm headed to right now. I hope we can do it another time."

His voice was affable through the phone, but Hailey felt a thud inside, and her face burned. Of course, he had things to do. There was a reason she'd hardly seen his jeep in his driveway for nearly a month. He was busy and she wasn't on his radar. Except when he became worried for her safety, like a big brother.

"Sure, another time would be nice," she said lamely. "Thanks for calling, Alex. It's really nice of you."

He paused. "Um, yeah, well . . . I *do* want to get together soon. My schedule will calm down soon. I'd like that. Really."

"Bye, Alex."

Hailey leaned back and let her shoulders fall. So much was said and not said. Was he sensing her disappointment and being the ever-helpful compassionate guy, not wanting to let her down? Why had she done it again, made the first move? She'd never been a girl who pursued and wouldn't take hints. Alex had been kind and neighborly. Nothing more.

Why did she dream she'd stand out for him, stay in his mind? When he saw her in the neighborhood he was friendly, but he was probably the same with other neighbors. Out of sight, out of mind. Easy to leave and forget, just like she'd been for Joel so many years ago. It hadn't taken him long. Maybe if she were knock-down gorgeous, or a brain surgeon, or a best-selling author . . .

Seemed that returning to Larkspur to save the day didn't make her any less invisible. Doing her best at the mill wasn't enough. Even just being Hailey apparently wasn't enough.

Chapter Thirteen

The smooth ceramic surface of Hailey's second cup of coffee warmed her fingers. She glanced at the kitchen clock. She should leave for the office, but there were two birds perched on the fence alongside the tiny patch of grass behind her townhouse. Their colors drew her like nectar, their orange-red beaks topped by a black band. Soft taupe feathers covered their backs and breasts. She pulled out her phone and snapped a photo. Maybe she'd pull those colors together for an office makeover.

Two hours later, Hailey was in the warehouse, halfway through her daily rounds of each department. A sense of calm had returned among the employees following the layoff. That storm had passed. Now she sought to monitor with vigilance the changes she'd made, especially tracking the accounts, hoping the reorganization had made a difference. Slowly, it was staunching the hemorrhage.

Once in the design department, her former domain, she leafed through pencil sketches and sample swatches of the sole designer, Laurel. Reviewing designs in the department where she'd worked for six years felt awkward to Hailey, as if she was passing judgment. Maybe she was. Most of her visits left her dissatisfied. She was still a designer at heart, an artist. Fabric design was of utmost importance. Otherwise, what would distinguish them from anyone else?

"This one is nice," she told Laurel. "I like the colors." She groped for something positive to say, but most of Laurel's designs lacked imagination and vibrancy of color. Hailey's mind drifted to the birds she'd seen that morning. Now, *that* was vibrant color.

Hailey tightened her lips into a grimace. The creative department was anything but creative. Where would new ideas come from? One idea percolating in her mind for over a month was to have a brainstorming session with some of the staff. If the employees themselves contributed to the ideas of the mill, they might feel more ownership and have a higher morale.

"Hailey, this has never been done. A brainstorming session?" Daniel's voice cut like a rusty blade.

"Is that a reason not to do something, because it's never been done? How many things wouldn't exist today if people kept that attitude?"

"But they're factory workers. What kind of ideas could they have that could possibly help the mill become more cutting edge?"

Hailey shook her head as they walked side by side to the small conference room. She was expecting about a dozen employees who'd been given leave of their looms or dye vats to come to the meeting. "You just never know, Daniel. It's not so much the ideas I'm looking for, but the spirit. It will give them a feeling of participation. But I'm also expecting some of their ideas to be great. They've been here far longer than either of us have."

"But you'll look weak, if you ask for their ideas, as if you don't have any of your own."

She stared at him. "That's not the point, Daniel. I have plenty of ideas. But I'd like to hear *theirs*. What if they have tons of ideas, but no one has ever asked them before? What if they knew that their thoughts actually counted? That helps morale, and morale is something we need. And since you're mostly interested in the monetary side, when morale improves, production improves, or so the studies say." If the employees felt more involved, it would affect every department in a positive way. But there was no use trying to convince Daniel of that.

He said nothing, but his face had closed like a metal box.

"You don't have to come, Daniel. I mentioned the meeting, but never thought you'd be interested in attending."

"I wouldn't miss it."

Hailey overlooked his sarcasm and focused attention on the men and women already seated in the conference room. She smiled brightly and panned her gaze across the group. "Hello, everyone. I appreciate your participation in this brainstorming meeting." She'd just pretend Daniel wasn't there.

"As you all know, our efforts are now more focused on weaving. I appreciate all of you and your cooperation in this reorganization."

She scanned the attendees and attempted to make eye contact with as many as possible. Some employees looked perplexed, still not sure why they were there, and others seemed pleased to be included and eager to speak.

"Our desire is to become more competitive and offer the best quality and service to our customers. I'd like *you* to think of how we can do this even better. For example, in training, hours, process, working conditions, products . . . who has an idea to share?"

One middle-aged woman, Martha, timidly raised a hand. "All of them things are okay, I guess. But what would be nice is to be able to work overtime. That was a big help in the past, especially at Christmastime."

Hailey nodded. "Thank you for your suggestion, Martha. I guess the overtime will be a result of getting more orders and more customers. But how do you think we might be able to get more customers who will buy fabric?"

"We can do different colors at different seasons, you know, like the clothing stores do," said a younger man, Carl, about thirty-five. "I mean, maybe we already do that, but we can do it even better than everyone else."

"Excellent, Carl," said Hailey. "I was already thinking along the same lines." Carl looked pleased. She turned her attention to another woman who had timidly raised her hand just below her ear. "Helen? Do you have an idea for us?"

"Well, I know the internet is getting so big. We should think of ways to use it more to expose our fabrics to everyone. Maybe we could attract regular customers, like ladies who like to sew, or schools that need uniforms, things like that."

"And to follow up on Helen," said a pink-faced younger woman named Jennie, "We can have merchandise online that people can order. Now we just have fabric, but we can have that fabric made into things, like curtains or bedspreads, and then take orders online."

"Great ideas." Hailey nodded her encouragement to Jennie.

More hands raised and suggestions began coming like bullet-fire, as the noise and enthusiasm in the room increased. Hailey had asked Lenore to take notes. Lenore's hands kept moving and flipping pages of a yellow legal pad. Some of the ideas were clearly impractical, but Hailey could cull through them for inspiration.

Thirty minutes later, Hailey held up one hand and the room quieted. "Thank you for sharing your good ideas. I'll consider everything that was said and see which ideas we can try. Before you all go back to your departments, I want to let you know that we'll be doing a Fourth of July staff picnic, so mark your calendars. I know we haven't done that in a few years, but we'll start again this year."

A cheer went up as the noise increased again. The room emptied out and only Daniel remained, a pinched look on his pale face, arms crossed over his chest. She ignored this and said lightly, "That went well."

"You think so? And can we really afford a picnic? That'll cost a lot, Hailey. We're starting to save, following the layoffs, but you're going to give it all away, it seems."

Hailey sighed. "Yes, it seems that I will." She turned and left him standing with his mouth twisted like a scar.

She returned to her office and closed the door. Glancing at the clock, she settled into her high-back chair and drew toward her the list that Lenore had compiled from the suggestions. Some, she eliminated with a black felt-tip pen. Others caused her to pause. She circled them and made some notes in the margins. With new ideas swirling through her mind she embarked on a brain-storming session of her own for the next hour until she noticed it was past time to lock up and leave.

With a satisfied smile she gathered up the sheets, covered with spider-like diagrams and margin notes, arrows and parentheses. She rummaged through a drawer where she'd seen some folders and pulled one out. As she arranged the brainstorm sheets inside it, her eye caught a yellow folder wedged into the back of the drawer. She gingerly pulled it out, noting it bore the name "Spencer-Shapiro", scrawled on the front. Maybe it was a client.

Hailey opened the folder and was surprised to see a designer's sketches and margin notes. She didn't recognize the sketches from any of the designs she or staff designers had done the previous years, but she did recognize the fabric, because it had been one of their top-selling products. She spied a date, two years earlier. It had been done before she'd moved to Colorado. She'd probably been too pressured then to notice that one of Anderson Mill's new products had been designed by an outside artist.

Hailey bit her lip, perplexed. The vibrant colors on the design leaped off the page. The lines were fluid and regular, but the dye pattern gave the impression of a weathered fabric.

Leafing through the folder again, she noticed a business card that read "Judith Araujo, Textile Design". The firm was Spencer-Shapiro in New York. Had her father hired a designer in New York, even though she'd been his staff designer?

A flood of jumbled emotions coursed through her. Her work must have been unimpressive enough for her father to hire an outside firm. Why had there even been a design department, in that case? She knew that many mills outsourced all of their design, but she had believed for years that she was contributing her special talents in design to her family's company. Was it all a farce? Had her contribution been useless all those years?

Maybe her designs had looked as ordinary to him as Laurel's did to Hailey. Maybe that was why he'd never praised her, never validated her ideas. And when he was utterly desperate and had no other options, he'd called her and convinced her to come back to Larkspur. It was either a matter of abandoning the mill to its fate, or calling faithful doormat Hailey.

"Don't be ridiculous," she chided herself in a gravelly grumble. "If he wanted an outside designer from time to time, it doesn't prove anything, does it? My department was still doing the lion's share of design work."

But it was true that the New York designer's work sparkled with an indefinable quality that elicited a second look, one that remained in the mind's eye and memory. Better than Laurel's and even Hailey's own work. She squirmed with the realization.

During years of her father's indifference, she'd comforted herself with the thought that she was infusing the mill's designs with *her* creativity, and that effort somehow compensated for the constant feeling of being slighted, or invisible. Now she wasn't so sure that had been the case. Why had her father hired her and kept her on?

And in bringing her back to Larkspur, was it really for the reasons he had said, because he knew she had a heart for it, because she understood it? Or had he realized he had no other choice? Of course, he'd known she would come running back.

Then as now, the pathetic puppet.

Chapter Fourteen

Tears blurred Hailey's vision as she drove the familiar route from the mill to her condo complex. She didn't see landscape, renovated buildings, time-worn landmarks or the signs of early summer in full bloom. Instead, her mind churned as she turned past the decorative sign at the entrance of her wooded neighborhood and swung her car into her numbered space.

For once she didn't glance down the street, scanning for Alex's jeep. And for once she wondered if she'd done the right thing in returning to Larkspur to save the day. She must be so predictable for her father to have known that she'd come running back.

Hailey was swabbing her swollen face with a moist washcloth when she heard the doorbell ring. Nina. In her distress she'd forgotten that Nina was coming over to share news and pizza together, like old times. A flood of gratitude washed over Hailey. Nina would have comfort and wisdom to share.

"Hey, Hailey." Nina's soft voice and slight southern lilt greeted Hailey when she opened the front door. Nina's rounded blue eyes were framed by dark brows and lashes, giving her a surprised and alert look. Several wisps of wiry dark hair escaped from her thick braid.

She stepped into the living room, accompanied by a cloud of pizza aroma from the large flat box she carried. Her brows furrowed. "Hey, it looks like you've been crying. Are you alright?" She set the box on the kitchen counter.

"It's stupid, really." Hailey gave her an embarrassed chuckle. "My self-esteem has taken a hit today."

Nina gathered her into a tight hug. "Tell me what happened."

Hailey reached for a tissue then grabbed a pitcher of iced tea from the counter. "Let's sit and I'll fill you in."

When they were seated at the dining table she said, "I learned that my father hired a designer from New York at least once while I was still there. I know I'm acting like some kind of betrayed wife or something. I just—when I saw it I felt so useless, like I'd been some kind of a place-holder while all the important designs went outside the company."

"Oh, Hailey." Nina leaned forward to squeeze Hailey's arm. "Don't you think companies do that once in a while, even when they have staff designers? That doesn't mean he didn't value *your* work."

Hailey nodded glumly. She pulled a wedge of pizza from the box and bit off the point. It steamed with the fragrance of Italian sausage and green peppers. "All along I knew I was overreacting, but I felt worthless. I guess it opened up old wounds."

"We all have days like that, when the smallest thing can make us feel like we're nothing. Like the other day, when Justin's mother questioned one of my decisions about the wedding. I spent the day thinking my future mother-in-law hated me." Nina took on a lopsided grin and they both laughed.

"We're so fragile sometimes. Of course, you want your mother-in-law to like you, but having a difference of opinion doesn't mean she doesn't. And my father getting an outside designer doesn't mean anything either. I mean, her design was excellent. I would have wanted to hire her too."

Hailey stopped, holding her glass of tea in mid-air.

Nina looked back at her. "What?"

Hailey turned an earnest stare to Nina. "Nina, maybe I should. I mean, hire her. I can outsource to her once in a while too. She's good, and she may be what we need. It'll be an additional cost, but once in a while a fresh design . . ."

"There's my old Hailey. You're springing toward a new idea already. God has recycled this catastrophe."

Hailey laughed. "Well-said. In fact, I think I'll go to New York and meet with her myself. I need to go see some clients and reps there anyway. It would be good for me, as the new president, to meet her and talk about the new vision."

"Which brings out an important point. As the president, you don't have time to do your own designs. You'll need people like this designer even more than your dad did."

A summer breeze puffed the sheer curtains at the kitchen window and wafted toward the table. Hailey felt a lifting of the weight she'd carried before Nina's arrival. "You're such a good friend, Nina."

Nina gave Hailey her understated but kind smile. "What I'm telling you is true. And here's another thought. Maybe your dad simply liked having you around so he found something that was needed and you were good at, even though he could have outsourced it. He spent money he couldn't really afford having a creative department. He kept you there, not only because you had a gift, but because he *wanted* you there."

Hailey's brows furrowed and she was silent for a moment. Her eyes searched Nina's. "You think so?"

"Is it so hard to believe that he would want you there? He loves you, Hailey. A lot of men from his generation don't know how to express their feelings very well, to their kids or anyone else. That doesn't mean he doesn't have fatherly love toward you."

"It's so hard to believe, when I grew up longing to hear that he was proud of me. So many things hurt me, and of course, I was over-sensitive too. When I was in high school I worked on the set of the school play. I was really proud of it, but my dad didn't come to the play because I wasn't acting in it. The main skill I had didn't have value for him. At least that's the way I felt then."

"Well, he was wrong and I'm sure he's regretted it since then. You have lots of talents, but design is a valuable one you've contributed to the mill. Tell me, where would textile mills be without design? Everything would be gray and brown, solids and stripes. What boring clothes we'd all have. We'd hate putting them on, they'd be so ugly, and we'd want to stay in our pajamas." Nina expressed herself with an exaggerated voice and hand motions.

Hailey laughed and added, "We'd all look like inmates in a prison somewhere, if we didn't have designers."

"It would be like wearing uniforms every day." Nina paused. "Everyone thirsts for beauty, Hailey. Now it's your time to give it to them."

CR CR CR

The shrieking horns and loud city rumble of New York City hushed as the glass door of the immense office building slid closed behind Hailey. She looked around at the glistening marble floors and walls and the rich dark wood trim, feeling like she was in another world.

As she waited for the brushed metal elevator doors to open, several people attired in suits and dresses gathered around her. She heard a bing and the doors opened. The silent crowd filed in like obedient soldiers. She glanced surreptitiously around, observing the mask-like faces, inhaling the varied scents of cologne and shampoo.

What would it be like to do this every day, instead of going to Anderson Mill, where she was always greeted like family? She knew that many people aspired to these jobs in vibrant, exciting Manhattan, but she never had. A wave of gratitude engulfed her. She didn't have to come daily to this sleek, elegant office building. Not only did she have a secure job in Larkspur, but she was in a position to make decisions that would influence the future of the company. And that particular day, that was what she hoped to do

Outside the elevator a plush carpeted hall led her through imposing double glass doors etched with the words, "Spencer-Shapiro Design". She approached the mahogany reception desk.

"Good morning. I have a nine-thirty appointment with Judith Araujo," Hailey told the middle-aged receptionist, who looked up at her through narrow rectangular glasses. "I'm Hailey Anderson from Anderson Mill." Felt good to say those words.

"I'll let her know you're here."

When Hailey entered Judith Araujo's office, she faced the woman's profile as she spoke on the phone. Her dark, shoulder-length hair curled, thick and unruly, around her pale face. When she turned to Hailey she smiled and gestured toward a chair near her desk.

Hailey settled into the comfortable leather chair and let her eyes roam around the office, which was anything but sterile and corporate. Though there were no windows, the impression of natural light glowed outward from several oil paintings depicting a sun-soaked meadow. Fresh flowers billowed out of several vases, filling the air with a faint floral scent, while other brass and pottery containers held ferns and ivy.

A kindred spirit. Hailey smiled. She'd come to the right place.

Judith hung up the phone and leaned forward. "I apologize for that. It rang probably just as you were coming down the hall. It's nice to finally meet you, Hailey."

She extended her hand and Hailey shook it across the desk. "I've known your father for years but haven't had the pleasure of meeting you. Or I should say, I met him once or twice and we've had periodic phone contact over the years."

"Have you worked with Anderson Mill longer than six years? That's how long I was there as a designer."

"Oh, yes, much longer than that. But my projects with Anderson were sporadic. Sometimes a year or so would go by with no contact."

Hailey leaned back and relaxed her shoulders. "It's nice to finally meet you too, Judith."

Judith's intelligent dark eyes danced impishly, enlivening and softening her pointed, birdlike features. Her warmth immediately put Hailey at ease.

"How is your father these days? I haven't spoken with him in over a year."

"He's had some health issues, but he's doing better. He's asked me to take his place for a while in leading the mill."

Hailey instantly regretted her words. She sounded temporary again, like a fill-in president, a place-holder. "I'm the acting president now. I have wanted to meet you. I really like the work you've done for us in the past." That was better. She made an effort at direct eye contact.

"Thank you. I hope that relationship will continue."

"That's why I came. As you might know I was in the design department for several years, but now as president, I can't do design, but still have ideas. We've had to let go of some of our designers. You may have the creative touch we need right now."

"I will certainly help in any way I can. Do you have any initial concepts in mind?"

"Yes, I do. For a while I have felt that our designs are ordinary. They don't leap out at the eye, or say anything special. The exception is the ones you have done for us. And as I look around at your lovely office, I feel so much at home. I know we'd work well together. People need beauty, and I want to bring it to them in the fabrics they buy from us." Hailey smiled, aware that she had quoted Nina nearly word for word. But her heart had so fully agreed that she'd adopted the sentiment as her own.

Judith nodded vigorously. "We do have a similar perspective, Hailey. I also feel that most designs I see are lacking heart and imagination."

"Of course, we'll continue with some of the standards people are used to, but I'd like to experiment with new colors and patterns. My current ideas have been inspired by the colors of spring in North Carolina, where I live. I brought a few sketches with me, but first would like to show you these photos." Hailey turned on her phone and pulled flipped to the photos she had taken. "These first photos of flowering trees . . . dogwoods, Bradford pears, and here are some redbuds."

"Hmm. This is lovely. Something could be done with this shade of purple here, a sort of plum-pink."

"And this bird. That reddish orange against black struck me, and here next to taupe—I knew we had to do something with it, pulling the colors and ideas straight from nature. Here's a cardinal. Look at that red on him," Hailey marveled.

Judith nodded. "The only time I get to see this color is from the traffic jam right in front of me as I'm late for work."

Hailey grinned. "I think most people are inspired by color. Bold colors included. Now here's something softer." Hailey advanced the photo and the screen was filled with pastels. "This is a photo I took of a bank of azaleas, more of a pastel theme. We can eventually do a sea theme as well. I could call it 'tones of nature', or something like that."

For the next thirty minutes the two women wove new ideas, brain-storming themes, products and patterns. When Hailey finally stood up to leave she had a folder of scribbled designs, notes, and new vision for Anderson Mill.

Hailey stuck out her hand and Judith grasped it warmly. "I think we'll work very well together." She also felt like she'd made a new friend.

She left the building and was again enveloped in the energy of the city, honking horns, people scurrying, and a layer of noisy tension around her. She glanced at her watch. Three more hours until her flight back to Winston-Salem.

Judith hadn't been able to see her until the final day of her trip. The previous days were well-spent, however, as Hailey met with sales reps, long-term clients, and potential new ones. She'd also made time to visit the Museum of Modern Art, stroll through Central Park, and see a play on Broadway.

The urban pace was an exciting change from Larkspur, but Hailey drew comfort in the fact that she'd soon return home. Home to a slower rhythm, friendly smiles, and fluffy green trees as far as the eye could see. She'd enjoyed the rugged landscape of Colorado, but it hadn't been her place. North Carolina was her place.

Time for one last stroll through the shopping district on the way back to her hotel. Hailey slowed her steps, not so much drawn to shop windows as to people. Thronging the sidewalks were families apparently on vacation, business people, and couples holding hands, talking and laughing together.

A pang pierced through her contentment. She was alone, alone on the streets of New York City. Central Park, Broadway, Times Square, all of these should have been shared with a special person. She'd enjoyed herself, but only now at the end, she thought of how much nicer it would have been with a companion. Would she one day be part of a couple, like the ones she saw, a life partner at her side sharing the experiences of a new city?

Was running Anderson Mill enough for her? Would it be in the future? Even if it became a leader in the industry, she wondered if it would still satisfy her, if she returned home every evening to a solitary meal, to sketch or read into the night.

She was accustomed to that routine, often craving the quietness of her condo after a day full of pressures and decisions. Other times the quiet was too loud. She longed to share her reflections of the day, the good and the not-so-good, or ask for feedback about an issue. She'd love to cook a meal alongside someone special, planning it together, dividing the tasks, and have something completely different to think and talk about than the mill.

Alex came into her mind and disappointment sliced a cold path through her. She'd been filled with hope after their chat together on her porch, but he seems to have evaporated like smoke on a windy day. She hadn't even seen his car in over a month, let alone crossed his path at the dumpster. There had been no sense in stopping by his condo in order to keep her promise to him. She'd taken too much initiative already, and he clearly wasn't home.

More clearly, he hadn't thought about her in the meantime.

"Oh, Hailey, don't waste your last hour in New York being gloomy." She chided herself under her breath. It had been a good visit and she should be encouraged. She decided she would be. And be thankful. For starters, she'd come full circle from a disappointing survey of the Anderson design department. And she was starting to notice a shift in her view of herself, as the mill's rightful owner.

Ownership. It felt different. These days her mind was more often on the mill's potential, not on impressing her aloof father. When had it happened? Nina's words had been a comfort, and her own decision to go to New York had made a statement, if only to herself, that she was in charge. God had given her the challenge. Finally, she would give herself permission to be the president of Anderson Mill, for as long as she was able.

At least her next mission was clear in her mind, to bring beauty to people through fabric. She was both an artist and mill-owner, and finally understood it was okay to be both.

Beyond that, she'd only know with time.

Chapter Fifteen

Hailey scanned the gently sloping hills of the park, dotted with multi-colored parasols and booths filled with local products and handmade crafts. She gestured with her hand. "Let's go over there near the food trucks and look at some of the art booths," she suggested to Nina. "Maybe I'll get inspired again."

She and Nina wove through clusters of people, who flowed like rivers in every direction. Sweet and tangy aromas from pizza, cotton candy, bratwurst and hamburgers saturated the air, along with waves of conversation and laughter.

"I'm glad we came to the festival early today." Nina cupped one hand over her eyes. "Looks like the crowds have doubled since we arrived."

"And *I'm* glad we put a pause on our crazy lives to come today. I'm on the verge of becoming a workaholic. We needed an activity that's completely out of our ordinary routine." Hailey smiled back at her. "And I've missed seeing you."

Echoes of music from the nearby band shell floated toward them as if on a cloud. It was a nearly perfect, dry day under a velvet blue sky, ushered by a light breeze.

The women approached a white awning with paintings in various styles hanging on makeshift partitions. "Do you still make time to paint and draw, like you used to?" Nina cocked her head to look more closely at a canvas splashed with an abstract design.

Ruefully Hailey shook her head. "I miss the days when I used to grab my sketch pad and head downtown or into the woods. I did that more when I was in Colorado, but now I don't make time. There's always so much to do. I'd really like to start again. I *need* to."

"I like your sketches and paintings. You have a real talent. But I know it's hard to carve out space to do what nourishes us and gives us balance. I have trouble with that too, with endless wedding preparations and the little details that keep popping up."

Hailey peered upwards at a landscape painted in warm colors. "That's lovely, isn't it?"

Nina made an approving sound and wandered to the next painting.

"This is nice too," murmured Hailey. "On the flight from New York I promised myself I'd start drawing and painting again. I was so inspired by the designer I met, that I realized how much it's part of me. I miss it."

They continued to wander to the next booth, displaying pottery. "Oh, I love this," Nina murmured, holding a vase carefully in both hands. "We haven't had a chance to talk about your trip. Was it a success, then?"

"Definitely was. I know I want more than just a company that runs smoothly and in the black. I want the fabric to be exceptional in some way, and of course after quality, the first thing that comes to mind is design. The beauty of the fabric is what should stand out. You encouraged me in that thinking, remember? Hiring an exceptional designer is a service I am willing to pay for, because I think it will give back in the long run."

"Does that mean you hired her? Freelance, I mean."

"Yes, she'll be our main designer. The one we still had on staff will now be a contract position. I'll give her the more standard jobs, the ones that require less pizzazz. When she understood that she could stay home with her son and still have a job, she was glad."

"Sounds like you did her a favor and saved money at the same time." Nina grinned. "I love it when that happens."

"We'll save money on her salary and benefits, which will help pay for Judith. When I got back to Larkspur there were some bad attitudes at the mill, and I'm not sure of the cause. It's as though someone keeps stirring up trouble, but I can't identify the culprit."

Nina's brow furrowed. "I wonder if someone wants to challenge your position, since it happened while you were gone."

"That's a good point. Before I left, the employees seemed optimistic and encouraged. But when I came back there was this shadow of suspicion again, as if they were expecting another layoff."

Hailey decided she wouldn't allow it to mar her day. She needed a mental break from the mill, and the previous year she'd missed the annual festival. These days it was rare that she took a day for herself just to enjoy time with a friend. Soon, Nina would be a newlywed and less available for girl time.

Hailey caught her breath as she spied a familiar face in a nearby booth. "Oh, look over there at the wine booth," she whispered to Nina as she slid behind a family of four. "Remember my neighbor who I have a crush on? That's him there, working at the stand."

Nina peered around her. "The tall guy, dark hair? Hey, he's handsome. I think I've seen him at church a couple of times. He looks familiar."

"Maybe he goes to a different service. I haven't seen him even in my neighborhood in over a month."

"I remember you telling me he works at a winery. There are a lot of wineries at the festival today. Aren't you going to go talk to him?"

Hailey frowned. He'd been avoiding her for a month. Should she just sally up to his booth and greet him, probably looking desperate? Or would it just be taken as a friendly, neighborly—

"I see you hesitating. Go talk to him."

"What if he thinks I'm pursuing him? I'd be mortified."

Nina rolled her eyes. "Hailey, really. You're his neighbor and a casual friend. He won't think anything. And you said yourself you haven't seen him in a while, so that gives you another legitimate reason. Go."

"I guess you're right. He might not think anything of it."

"We'll say hi then I'll disappear so you can talk to him."

Hailey made a sound in her throat. "Nina, he's busy working. We'll just say hi and *both* disappear, okay?"

Nina's eyes narrowed. "Hmm, I can tell him I have things to do at home for work tomorrow, or the wedding . . . that might work. I've had enough sun anyway."

"You don't have to leave, really." Hailey blew a wisp of hair from her forehead. "I feel like I'm thirteen again. I'm really out of practice."

Nina laughed and gently nudged Hailey at the same moment that her hiding place, the family of four, moved on. Hailey sighed and approached the booth where Alex was pouring a small quantity

145

of wine through a tiny metal spout into a proffered plastic cup. When he saw Hailey, his eyebrows lifted and a wide grin spread across his face.

"He looks glad to see you," Nina whispered behind her as she pretended to study a brochure she'd picked up.

They stood for a moment in front of a pyramid of wine bottles at the booth until Alex finished with his customer. He turned to Hailey and Nina, wiping his hands on a white half-apron around his waist. "Hi, Hailey. It's a nice surprise to see you here."

Hailey smiled. "It's a nice surprise to see you at all—I mean, I haven't seen you around." She felt a flush of embarrassment creep up her neck. *Way to put the foot in, Hailey.*

If Alex noticed her discomfort, he didn't show it. "It must have seemed like I vanished into thin air. I was out in California for the last month, doing some training at one of the wineries in the Napa Valley."

"Oh." Hailey nodded. "I know that Napa's a famous area for wine. Alex, this is my best friend, Nina. Nina, Alex Moreno."

"Nice to meet you, Alex." Nina shook his hand over the makeshift counter.

"I need to wait on these people, but don't go away." Alex held up a finger. He turned to serve a small group clustered around the counter. Hailey was relieved to have a moment to regain her composure.

"So, apparently he *did* have a reason not to call you. He wasn't in town." Nina's dark eyebrows lifted. "And all this time you thought—"

"That doesn't prove that I was wrong. It just makes it look—" Hailey pressed her lips together, "less bad, I guess. I was thinking the worst."

"You? Thinking the worst? Never, Hailey."

Hailey laughed. "Now, stop."

Alex turned back to them. "I'm actually getting off in just a couple minutes, if you can wait. We can go listen to the music together if you want."

"Great, sure. I'll probably need to go, though . . ." Nina began, but Alex had turned back to a new customer, plastic cup in hand.

"Stay with us, Nina."

"Not on your life. I'll slip away discreetly and you can get to know Alex better." By the time she finished her phrase, Alex had circled the booth and stood beside them.

"Ready?" He looked each of them.

"Um, I'm afraid I can't stay." Nina looked at her watch. "You guys go on, I have to work early tomorrow. Have fun."

After she left, Alex turned to Hailey and shrugged. "Hope it wasn't anything I said."

Hailey laughed and shook her head. "No, she really did need to leave." In a way it was true. Fortunately, Nina had come in her own car.

"I brought a blanket to sit on for the concert." Alex shifted a canvas tote bag higher over one shoulder. As they approached the band shell the music grew louder and the crowds thickened. People sprawled on colorful blankets, in folding chairs and on the grass, surrounded by coolers, wine bottles, and paper plates.

147

"Do you mind if we stay on the edges of the crowd?" he asked. "That way we can talk. Otherwise it'll be too loud for us to hear each other."

"Sure, that's a good idea." It would have been disappointing to be drowned out by music, after all of the time she'd waited to see him again.

Alex chose a plot of thick grass near a tree and spread out the blanket. He gestured for Hailey to sit down and sat beside her, smoothing the blanket around them. His tan had deepened in the last month and his hair hung below his collar, giving him the look of a dashing pirate. Yet his face showed relaxed interest and kindness.

"So, tell me about California." Hailey was glad she had an easy conversation-starter.

"I had the opportunity to do some training at a leading vineyard in Napa, called Roberson Vineyard. I learned some techniques I hope to implement here." He gave her a crooked grin then said more softly, "I should have let you know I was going to be gone. I told you to call me if you had any problems, but then I disappeared. Not very nice, huh?"

Hailey shook her head gravely. "No, not at all. I'm kidding. You don't have to tell me whenever you go out of town." She kept her voice casual, but was glad it had crossed his mind. "It sounds like a wonderful experience. What did you do out there?"

"The owners of vineyard where I work know the owners of Roberson so they worked out a training opportunity for me. I was able to go there for a month and see their whole process, from vine to bottle. Some things are the same in every vineyard, like clarification and aging, but there are also special techniques, different kinds of barrels or additives, and so on, which affect the taste."

Hailey couldn't help but notice the sparkle in his eyes as he spoke of his experiences. This didn't keep him from holding her gaze, though she wouldn't read too much into that.

"Of course, the major success of a wine is in the grapes, and they are finicky things. Depends on growing seasons, soils, topography, weather, pests. And it can all change with the land it sits on. For example, in Italy there's a river in the d'Abruzzo region where the same type of grape has a different taste on either side of the river. Same thing happens in the Bordeaux region of France. Soils and growing conditions are different."

Alex leaned back on his elbows and crossed his ankles, looking more relaxed than he had the other day on the porch. "It was great to see the whole process of a big vineyard. I got up early every day and followed people around, did what they told me to do. By the end, I was like an employee, with my own responsibilities."

"Sounds exciting. And of course, it's a beautiful part of the country."

"Yes, it was beautiful, like a dream." He leaned on one elbow, a sudden intensity in his eyes. "Hey, I'm doing all the talking. Tell me what happened while I was gone. Was there any more vandalism?"

"No, that settled down, thank goodness." Hailey pulled some rogue curls away from her face. "I think someone was simply afraid of being laid off. Once the layoff was over, nothing else happened."

"Good, I'm relieved." He glanced up. "Look, they're switching bands. Any idea who's up next?"

"None at all. When I'm outside and the music is live, I'm not as picky. I just enjoy almost any type of music, since it's more about atmosphere." She'd listen to about anyone if it meant she could stay there with him on that faded blanket under a balmy summer sky.

"I like being here on a summer night, with all these people. Some of them have drunk too much wine, but most are just relaxing with their friends and family. It's one of God's gifts, times like these."

Hailey was touched by the gentleness in his voice and by his observations. "You're right. God gives us so many good things to enjoy, but so often we focus instead on what's going wrong." Speaking for herself. Clearly.

"So true. You told me you were planning to do some changes at the mill. Have you started that yet?"

She nodded. "You have a good memory. A lot has changed since I last saw you. I got rid of a couple departments, so I hope that will help us be more efficient. I just got back from New York a few days ago. While I was there I met with a designer whose work I like, someone my father had used for design a few times."

"New York City and only work?" He lifted his brows.

"I hadn't been there in a long time, so yes, I tried to enjoy it too. I went to the modern art museum, took in the local atmosphere, Central Park, uh, what else? Broadway, Times Square. I tried to squeeze in a little bit every day after my appointments. It was a good trip, productive but fun too."

"I'm not a big-city guy, but I'd enjoy going there for a long weekend. I would think you'd fly to New York every month or so, schmoozing all the clothing manufacturers and designers." He grinned. "I can see you doing that."

Hailey laughed. "Really? I never thought of myself as a schmoozing kind of girl. In fact, when I first came here to take over managing the mill I had a huge case of self-doubt. I wasn't sure I could really do it, even though for years I thought I knew exactly what needed to happen."

Alex pulled up to a sitting position. His tanned forearms brightened the turquoise of his T-shirt that bore the logo of his company. "Don't we all do that sometimes, even when in our heads we know we're qualified?"

"But that's just it, I wasn't sure I *was* qualified. And so much was riding on my efforts. I—I risked a lot to come back here," she said quietly.

"I can imagine that the stakes are high, when you're talking about a company. But from the start I never doubted you." He spoke with certainty, not flattery.

Hailey's chest ached at his words. "I'm touched that you think so, but you don't know me that well. How could you be sure I'd succeed?"

He leveled his gaze at hers until she felt his dark eyes piercing her soul. He said, "I see more than you think. Call it intuition." His mouth quirked. "Women aren't the only ones who have that."

Hailey's scalp prickled and she felt warmed. She swallowed, blinking into his direct gaze. When her voice came out it sounded tinny, childlike. "Really? I'm afraid to ask, but what do you see?"

Alex was silent for a moment. He circled his parted knees with loosely linked arms, and stared at her intently, as if peeling back the outer skin of the self she projected each day. "I see . . . a woman who is smart and determined, yet deeply compassionate and passionate about things that really count for her. Am I right?"

Hailey's eyes burned. She blinked and nodded. Her throat ached. It was as though he saw things in her she almost didn't know herself. Somehow, without knowing her, he'd seen into her soul.

He grinned suddenly. "*And* you can be feisty." They both laughed then. "You've changed, Hailey. You seem gentler now. Less

151

out to prove something, but still slow to give up." He cocked his head. "I like that."

Hailey shook her head. "I—I don't know what to say. I'm glad you think I've changed. I really wanted to. I fought that Scottish temper for a long time."

Alex chuckled. "I thought it was the Irish who were known for their tempers."

"They are, whether it's justified or not. But somehow it got mixed in with my Scottish family. Not so much temper, but frustration when things aren't right, and when people don't do the things that seem *obvious*." She laughed again. "I guess that's arrogant, isn't it? But to me, it's so clear."

He nodded with an amused smile teasing his lips. "That's why you're the perfect person for the job. You know what needs to be done. And now, is it going smoothly with all the changes you made?"

"I guess time will tell. We bought more looms so we've increased weaving. It's been about a month, but things are slowly starting to turn around. I'm going to try new designs and test them in the market. I'm tired of boring fabrics."

"Yeah, me too." He pulled on the front of his brightly colored T-shirt. "This is from one of the biggest French designers, Fruit de la Loom."

They both laughed. Hailey made a face and looked pointedly at his T-shirt. "It's pretty, but not exactly what I meant."

"I assure you, it's very trendy."

Hailey grinned at him, enjoying the light-hearted banter and the prickling of attraction that tingled everywhere inside her. For nearly two years she'd been drawn to Alex from afar, but had no idea if there was any like-minded substance, anything deeper than physical attraction. There was a *lot* of that. She'd also appreciated the clear-headed, balanced way he expressed himself in owners' meetings. So, he could be playful too, and seemed completely secure in himself, unlike her.

"Yes, okay, if you say so." She patted his arm as if he were a small child and they grinned at each other. He held her gaze with curved lips until warmth pool inside her chest and fan up through her neck.

"What about your dad?" he asked quietly, breaking the magic covering that swirled around her. "Isn't he the one who convinced you to come back? Does he help you out, you know, give you guidance?"

Hailey sighed and looked down at her clasped hands. "I ask him things once in a while. Sometimes I really need to hear his perspective, out of respect for his years as president, and of course, as my dad. We haven't always had the same philosophy, but on certain things he's very helpful." She shrugged. "Part of me wants to do it alone, though. I'm not sure just yet if I'm trying to prove something to him or to myself."

"Maybe both, though he was already convinced, since he called you back. And now you're becoming convinced. Aren't you, Hailey?"

She paused at the tenderness in his voice, as if he were again peering into the deep parts of her. Was she convinced she had something to offer, a voice worth hearing? Yes, slowly it was happening. "Little by little. With God's help."

He grinned and nodded. "Atta girl."

Later they were quiet as Alex walked Hailey back to her car. "This has been fun," she told him as she reached her door. "I'm glad I ran into you."

He stood beside her, the picnic blanket gathered loosely in his arms. The evening breeze ruffled his dark hair and a subdued smile hovered around his mouth. "Me too. I should have called you when I got back in town. Once I got back to work, it was as if the ceiling crashed down on me, there was so much to do. But I think I'm getting caught up and I shouldn't have any trouble making that call, if you don't mind."

"I'll look forward to it." Her voice was soft. She hoped it conveyed openness, invitation. With a final smile, Hailey slid into her car. She backed up and with a last wave, drove toward the exit. Through her rear-view mirror, she surveyed him. He stood still, watching as she drove away.

Chapter Sixteen

Hailey leaned back against fluffy pastel pillows and scanned the sketch pinned to the wall, of two birds playing in a birdbath. She'd made an effort to sketch at least twice a week in a bid to recapture her artistic identity, endangered by the demands of textile manufacturing. She'd even begun sketching ideas for jewelry design and stashing them in a folder. She might one day still have a chance to do freelance design in her free time.

Her eye wandered to a framed photo of Hope and Devon propped on the wooden table near the clock. She hadn't spoken to Hope in weeks. What a far cry from their previous warm complicity, the weekly phone calls she'd taken for granted in the past. Back then it didn't seem like they lived so many miles apart. Now, they were worlds apart.

Hailey braced herself and reached for the phone. "Hi, Hope," she said brightly. "I was just thinking of you guys. What's going on out there?"

Hailey noticed the lilting "Hello" when Hope answered the phone change to a dull, "Oh, hi, Hailey. Not much. Just working a lot lately. Devon's the one who needs a social secretary. We're into the teen thing now."

"What is she up to?" Hailey's eyes burned. Would they ever recover the warm, bantering tone they'd had all their lives?

155

"Sports, primarily. She loves soccer and she's pretty good at it. But she squeezes in a tennis match once in a while. She has a new group of sports friends, it seems." Then silence. What should Hailey say next?

"Any interest in boys yet?"

A small, dry chuckle. "Now that you mention it, there's this guy, Scott, who works at the tennis club. He's a junior. She's enamored with older guys."

Hope continued talking about Devon and her schedule, her friends, her mood changes, but didn't ask Hailey anything. No point interjecting comments about happenings at the mill. Hope had written the mill out of her life fifteen years earlier.

During the phone call, despite a tiny trickle of tears, Hailey managed to keep her voice even. When she hung up, the fragile dam burst and hot tears coursed down her cheeks. Hope, Hope. She'd lost her only sister. She'd crammed down the urge to say three, four times during the call, "I miss you," but could predict her sister's retort.

If only she could hear Hope say with her typical affection, "I understand, Hailey. You did what you thought was the best." But Hailey had little hope of that. *I miss you.* Four months had passed since Hailey had driven away from Colorado. How long would it take for Hope's heart to heal, for the forgiveness and understanding to spring out of dry ground?

Whenever Hailey called, she'd muster her energy as if it were an unwanted chore. Each time, she'd hear Hope's dull tone on the line. But if she persisted, maybe one day she would be able to shatter Hope's walls. Those walls had shut her out when she most wanted to share an experience of her week or a secret pleasure.

One such pleasure was Alex, who was no longer a filmy figure glimpsed two blocks away on a routine trip to the dumpster. The memory of his words at the festival surged frequently through her mind, flooding her with warm, fluttery joy. Something had changed between them that evening. She'd seen it in his eyes. She longed to share this news with Hope, but didn't dare.

Her thoughts went to her father. She called less often lately, since the operation was over and he was recovering well. She'd gotten caught up in her new life, forgetting her father, the catalyst of it all.

Hailey picked up the phone again. "Hi, Dad. Sorry I haven't called in a few days. How are you feeling?"

"Oh, things are coming along, I guess." Her father's voice was subdued, somehow softer than in the past. "I'm about ready to start moving around more. I was able to play golf this week."

"I didn't know you played golf."

"I didn't. Not much, anyway. But I figured that I'd die of boredom if I didn't get out of this chair and do something. Thought I'd give it a try."

"It's not too soon?"

"Nah, I took it easy. Just hit a few balls. Unbelievable how bad at it I am." His throaty chuckle warmed Hailey.

"You'll have a chance to improve," she assured him. "Everyone starts at the same place."

"You mean, really bad?"

"The basics, then with some practice—"

157

"Yeah, I know. What's happening with you? You don't call to fill me in anymore."

Hailey winced at the gentle rebuke, which sounded sad to her. "I'm sorry, Dad. You know how busy things get over there. I think I told you about letting Laurel go and hiring Judith up in New York. Things are just starting to turn around. I expect it to continue."

"So, you're satisfied with what's happening? That's good. You're doing good work, Hailey."

"Thanks, Dad. Means a lot to hear that from you." A wave of gratitude surged through her. She expected him to ask more questions about the mill, but he didn't. "Anything else happening over there?"

"Not sure what to say, really. I found a new show I enjoy watching. Comes on Thursday nights at eight. Sharla comes by once in a while to see me. No one else. I guess I never had lots of friends before, worked too hard."

"It's never too late to start. Are there any clubs or activities you can get involved in? Things in the community?"

"You mean like bridge or horseshoes?" Her father snorted. "Not that desperate yet. I'll get back into gardening soon. I'll see what I can find over there at the community center. They might have a Retired Codgers Program, or something."

Hailey laughed. "I wouldn't call you a codger yet, Dad. Although I did see a park bench you'd probably like. Just go there with your breadcrumbs and the pigeons will join you."

Her father laughed. First time in Hailey Anderson history that their laughter mingled together. He had changed, become lighter.

Hailey's humor was tempered by the sobering realization that her father had grown detached from the mill, almost like Hope. It was as though the powerful engine that had fueled most of his adult life had sputtered to a halt, replaced by a Thursday night television program. She wondered if she should try to keep him involved, to give him a renewed sense of passion. When he was healthy enough to return to the mill . . .

The thought was unsettling and triggered thoughts that lingered after she hung up. She'd been there for four months. The doctor said her father would have to stop working for about six months. Maybe she only had two months more to work as interim president of Anderson. And then what? When she agreed to return, she hadn't asked that question in enough detail, though it had weighed heavily in her mind. How could she step down, now that her heart and plans were fully invested in the mill's present and future? Her father hadn't said what he had in mind for his return to Anderson Mill.

And she didn't have the courage to ask.

∽ ∽ ∽

"I want to commend you on your article, Ms. Anderson." Bridget Fleming, a journalist for the *Larkspur Sentinel*, sat opposite Hailey at her desk. The woman smoothed her suit jacket and adjusted her dark-frame glasses. "It was positive, yet not sugar-coated. I intended to write a follow-up article before now. I apologize that it took me so long to get back with you."

A knock came on the door and Lenore entered carrying two cups of coffee, then discreetly disappeared. Bridget scanned the article Hailey had written two months earlier and sipped her coffee. "Here's the phrase I liked, 'We ask businesses in Larkspur to hire those laid off from textile mills. We ask residents of Larkspur to buy

American-made textile products, as your participation in this country's economy.'"

She looked up at Hailey with a glimmer in her eyes. "This gives a call to action, instead of just a complaint, like so many editorials do. And here's the best part, 'If we band together—' I love that, 'band together'. It's so rousing. 'We can revive our homegrown industries and be strong leaders again. We can do it with your help.' That's great. It restores pride in our town. People really responded to that."

Hailey leaned back. "Really? Was there any kind of response?"

"Oh, yes, didn't you see? We had dozens of letters in response to your editorial. We've been publishing them ever since that date, there were so many. It's kept a buzz going about Anderson Mill."

"I—I guess I didn't keep up with it afterwards." Hailey felt a flush of pleasure rise up within her. Maybe she should have read the paper in the following weeks. People were talking about Anderson Mill? "I said my piece and went on with my work." She gave Bridget a wan smile. "Do you have any of those editorials with you?"

Bridget nodded and rummaged through the file on her lap. "Oh, here's one you'll like. It says, 'I want to respond to the recent exchange of articles about Anderson Mill. I think we need a business like this as an example in our community. We fall on hard times, but we rally together. We need to stand behind them, not just moan about it and then ignore them. Let's all do our part, as the president said we should.'"

The woman thumbed through more papers in the folder. "Here's another one. It just says, 'Here, here. We shouldn't throw in the towel on textile mills. It's part of our heritage.' Then here's one: 'We should rejoice that only a few people lost their jobs at Anderson Mill. One can see that every effort is being made to save jobs, not let people go. Maybe we should all buy American made even if it costs more. It will save our jobs in the long run.' That's just a few of them, Ms. Anderson."

Hailey swallowed the lump that had formed in her throat. "I had no idea," she murmured finally. "I didn't know that people felt that way about a textile mill. It's actually part of their identity as residents of the town, isn't it?" Why hadn't that thought occurred to her? It had always been part of *her* identity, as an Anderson. Yet the mill provided jobs for many residents of Larkspur, present and past.

Bridget nodded and grinned. "This company has had its ups and downs, for your grandfather and your father alike. Yet it's always survived. And it's nice to see a company passed along, kept in the same local family, instead of owned by some big conglomerate. I'd like to do a follow-up on where your company will go in the future, what are the plans and so forth. Can you make some comments on that?"

Hailey hesitated. "Um . . .we're still in the process of a major reorganization. It's difficult to say exactly where we will be headed, but our desire is to focus our energies on weaving, with innovative designs. That may sound obvious, but we've streamlined our processes. I would love to be able to hire back people we had to let go, but have to wait and see." She held up her hand. "Don't print that so that it sounds like a promise. It's my hope, but not at all a guarantee. I would do that first before hiring new people, but I certainly want to do both."

"Yes, of course I understand." The woman scribbled in her notebook.

After several more volleys of questions, Hailey asked, "Ms. Fleming, I have a question about the first article you wrote. I was surprised the day I read it because I hadn't given an interview, yet there was information about the layoff. Did you speak with anyone else on my staff about the layoff before writing the article?"

"I spoke with a young man in your employment, though I'm not at liberty to say his name."

Hailey nodded. "I have an idea of who it might have been. Can you at least tell me if he was thirtyish with straight brown hair? That would fit our associate director, who would have had the information you needed for your article."

Bridget just smiled, but nodded almost imperceptibly. "He just gave me facts about the layoff, nothing deeper than that."

"But he did it in a way that wasn't favorable to the mill, it seems to me. Ms. Fleming, for any future articles concerning this company, I'll be glad to speak with you myself."

After a cordial goodbye, Hailey sat back in her chair, with a mélange of emotions swimming inside her. She was pleased and touched by the community response to her article, yet she still fumed. Fortunately, her editorial had smoothed the damage of the first article. The last thing Anderson Mill needed was negative public relations.

Daniel Carlton should know that.

Chapter Seventeen

Hailey pressed her foot gently on the brake as she eased toward the stoplight. A long stretch of boiling, humid weather had broken and a gentle breeze floated through her open car window.

Over her left shoulder she scanned the row of shops that had done business on that sidewalk for as long as she could remember. A woman was waving at her. Connie Parker, a longtime neighbor of her parents. Hailey waved. So much had changed in Larkspur, yet was still bound together by a comforting framework of relationships and businesses that were part of its history.

A small light on Hailey's phone indicated a message. Maybe it was from her father. At the next stop light she listened to it, and the warmth of Alex's voice filled her ears. She smiled. He'd finally called.

"I'm sorry, I didn't call as soon as I'd hoped. I thought of you a several times, but only had about forty seconds, and I wanted to talk to you for more than forty seconds, so ended up putting it off."

Hailey laughed. He was rambling. Kind of cute. Either he was nervous, or it was a quirk she hadn't seen before.

"I'm sorry it's short notice, but would you like to get some barbeque tonight? You probably missed that Carolina tradition while you were in Colorado. I can pick you up at six if you're available. Just let me know." Normally Hailey was a big-time ahead-planner, but she could learn to let go and seize the moment. Especially with Alex.

She called back and got his voice mail. "Hi, Alex. I'd love to go for barbeque. I'll wait for you at six." Hailey pulled into her parking spot and glanced down at her watch. She didn't have much time. She dashed into the house and straight up the stairs.

Thirty minutes later, a heap of clothes that she'd tried and discarded lay on the bed. In the full-length mirror she surveyed herself. She'd pulled her thick hair into a high pony tail and added gold dangle earrings. A colorful sleeveless blouse complemented slightly faded crop jeans and sandals. She was striving for casual but cute. She should do some shopping soon. Another neglected personal task.

When she heard the doorbell ring she added some coral lipstick and hurried down the stairs. Usually when she saw him he was dressed for vineyard work, well below casual, with faded jeans, sometimes holey at the knees, and a T-shirt. That night he wore a crisp plaid button-down shirt and dark blue jeans. A fragrance of fresh soap and cologne drifting toward her. As always, the first sight of him caused a flutter inside.

"Hi, Alex." She suddenly felt timid. It was like a first date. It *was* a first date with him. "It's better to see you at my door than at the garbage bins."

He chuckled. "Much better. You look nice. Ready to go?"

She locked the door behind her and walked beside him toward the parked cars. When they reached his jeep, she caught a glimpse of the two of them side by side in the jeep windows. They looked good together, like they fit. *Stop rushing things, Hailey.*

Alex drove with one hand loosely on the top of the steering wheel, occasionally glancing over at her as he drove. "Apparently

North Carolina has been doing barbeque for over three hundred years," he said. "They used to cook a whole hog for hours over live coals, just painting the sauce on the whole time."

The nervous flutter in Hailey's stomach had begun to dissipate as a quiet comfort took over. "Must've been delicious. I guess there's a good reason why the tradition has stuck around for so long."

"Sure thing, and we're about to find out. Barbeque in eastern North Carolina is different from that in the west, but you probably know that. I've heard there are several regional varieties. I plan to find out one day when I take an eating tour." He turned his head and grinned at her. "I think you'll like this place tonight. They have great sandwiches or platters, whichever you want. They say it's pit barbeque. Maybe that means it's cooked in a pit."

He seemed relaxed, comfortable in her presence, and more talkative than she expected. She'd take that as a good sign. "I've had barbeque a few times as a child," she said, "but when my mother went through her health kick, it was out for a while. She thought the meat was too fatty. But you're right, I did miss that in Colorado, among many other things."

"Ah, I knew it." Alex's long jaw dimpled. "I know Colorado is beautiful. I've seen pictures, but it's not the same as here." He shook his head decisively. "Not as green, for one. Or as humid."

"You're right about that. The mountains there are beautiful, though. And the aspen trees have white bark, like birch. I loved the dry climate, I admit. My hair does too, gets less frizzy there. Oh, here's the restaurant. That wasn't too far. Looks cozy."

The jeep pulled up into a crowded gravel parking lot, tires scraping underneath. The stained wood siding of the restaurant reached up and met a sloping red metal roof. A checkered valance topped large front windows. Through them Hailey could see clusters of people eating around wood tables.

After ordering sandwiches and drinks, the gentle temperatures coaxed Hailey and Alex outside to picnic tables around the back of the restaurant. She held the steaming barbeque sandwich with both hands, as morsels of sauce-laden pork spilled out of the other side onto her plate.

"What else did you miss when you were in Colorado?" Alex nibbled a stringy morsel of pork hanging out of the bun. The air was warm but comfortable, and overhead a colorful string of lights framed the picnic area with a festive glow.

Hailey pondered his question as she savored the tangy sauce and chewy strips of meat. She liked a guy who asked questions, putting her at ease and drawing her out. Alex had that ability, yet was willing to talk about himself too without being self-absorbed.

"When I first got to Colorado I felt relieved." Hailey wiped her fingers on the checked paper napkin and leaned back, mentally reviewing the last few months. "For so many years I'd tried to make some kind of a difference at the mill. At first, I just wanted to contribute to the family business once I was out of college. Then when the textile industry started falling apart, I felt more pressure to help turn it around. But—" she shrugged, "I finally gave up. Once I was in Colorado, I felt like I was starting all over with a clean slate. I loved being near my sister and my mom, for the first time in years."

She sipped from her icy mug of lemonade and searched her memories, trying to recall when her attitude had changed. "But it was also hard being new everywhere and trying to find my way around. The newness can be exciting too, that is, until it gets old. Until you start missing old, dear friends and familiar places, until you long to be comfortable somewhere. I hadn't realized how much a part of me this place is." She shrugged. "That's not the reason I came back, of course, but lately I've become more aware of those roots."

"Now you're back home with your roots and your old friends, but you don't have your mom and sister nearby." His voice had a solemn ring.

Hailey winced at the sudden stab inside her, and her shoulders slumped. Her voice became quiet. "That's truer than you know." She looked up at him and said glumly, "My sister and I were really close all our lives before I went to Colorado. She never understood why I would leave so soon after getting there. And she still hasn't accepted it."

"Didn't she know about your dad's surgery?"

"She knew he was having a procedure, but she didn't realize how serious it was. He asked me not to tell her or my mom. I guess he didn't want them to worry."

Alex's brows gathered. "If she thinks you moved back because you simply changed your mind, maybe that's why she's peeved."

Hailey shook her head slowly, her lips tight. "I honestly don't know what she thinks. I told her that Dad wanted me to take his place at the mill, that the mill was struggling and he wanted my help. But she thought I was running back just to please him. We've always had this disagreement where my father is concerned, because I try too hard to get his approval, while Hope—that's my sister—she couldn't care less. She's the maverick. And the two of them have never gotten along well."

"I would expect things will improve between you and your dad, since you saved the mill."

Hailey let out a muted laugh. "I don't know if I've saved anything yet. I took over for him, which he greatly appreciated. And we've gotten a little closer recently."

"Things might also heal up with your sister over time. Bottom line, though, it's your life and you did what you thought was best. She'll just have to get over it."

"It's been four months and no sign of thawing on her part." Hailey shrugged and leaned her elbows on the grainy wooden picnic table. "I was really sad years ago when she moved to Colorado, but it never occurred to me to be angry at her. If she was happy, I was glad for her."

"Maybe you think everyone else has the right to be angry, but you don't." He cocked his head to one side as he gazed at her.

Hailey narrowed her eyes at him. "Are you playing psychologist with me?" They both laughed. "Really, I don't see any reason to be angry, then or now. It hurts that she's angry, but I understand it's mostly disappointment and sadness. She's wanted me to move out there for years, and when I finally did, it was over too quickly. Poof, like it never happened."

"That must have been annoying for you, moving all the way back when you'd just gotten settled out there."

"Yes, you could definitely say that. But I saw no other choice." Hailey chuckled. "I was also embarrassed to come back home after making such a dramatic exit."

Alex's laughter rang out. "I've never had these dilemmas, just never moved once I got here. Don't plan to, either."

"The thing about plans, Alex," she said quietly, "is that you just never know what will happen."

A comfortable silence fell between them for a moment then Hailey said, "Where is your family now?"

"My dad's been gone ten years, I have one brother who lives in Charlotte, and my mom is in Clemmons, not too far from here. I have a little sister up in New York. She's a singer, trying to break into the big time."

"Have you been in Larkspur all your life, ever since you moved from Mexico?"

Alex shook his head. "We've lived in Durham and a couple of smaller towns, then finally settled in Winston-Salem until I got into high school. I liked the bigger towns better because it's easier to be a foreigner in a bigger place. People are less likely to treat you like you don't belong there."

"Really? I didn't know people were still prejudiced like that."

Alex snorted. "Believe it. They still are today, though less than in the past. If you're Hispanic, people assume you're going to run a restaurant or work in one. I tend to be a workaholic, but I'm trying hard to break that. Maybe I'm overly sensitive, but I always felt like I had to work harder to prove myself."

"That shows you're strong and determined. You might have wanted to prove something in the beginning, but I can tell you want it even more for yourself. Your eyes light up when you talk about vineyards and grapes."

A half-smile curved his lips. "That's a good point. What I wanted was even more important to *me* than trying to please everyone else. After a while I didn't care. God helped me to understand my value, regardless of what others think."

That was a lesson she too needed to learn. Before she could respond to him, he startled her by leaning toward her, both elbows on the table. His eyes latched onto hers and he softly said, "I enjoy talking to you, Hailey."

She blinked. A thump echoed inside her chest and her voice came out in a whisper. "Me too."

"I didn't plan to lose contact, uh, repeatedly." He chuckled, but lowered his eyes away from hers, as if suddenly shy.

Now was the moment to say something to let him know how she felt. She could always tell him she knew he was busy and that it was okay. How lame. He'd given her an opening and she should take it.

She swallowed. "I *was* kind of disappointed when I didn't hear from you, because we'd just started getting to know each other."

When he looked up and locked her eyes again, a hint of a smile playing the corners of his mouth, the tight springs inside her loosened. Then she added, "Okay, I was *really* disappointed. Didn't cry myself to sleep, but I wanted to egg *your* car."

The air filled again with his laughter. She'd gotten her point across, she hoped. As they laughed together warm fingers of contentment closed around her heart.

"Don't want that to happen," he said. "And I don't plan to be scarce anymore. I'd like to see you more, Hailey."

"I think you know where I stand on that idea," she said softly.

He made a small bow with his head. "Duly noted." He leaned down to the side of the bench and when he'd straightened he was holding a purple aster. He held it toward her and held it out to her. "I like your eyes, they're a beautiful green."

A wave of heat returned, lapping outward through her whole body. She noticed he'd inched closer and his elbow touched hers.

He grinned and added, "I first noticed them while you were yelling at me during the owners' meeting a year or so ago."

Hailey laughed. "I wasn't yelling at you. I was just passionate about making my point, whatever it was back then. Anyway, I thought Latins loved to argue. That's not true?"

He was shaking his head, still smiling. "A stereotype. But if you really want to know the truth about that, you should hang around me more often."

"Oh, you mean, so we can argue? I had other things in mind." Hailey clapped a hand over her mouth then pulled it away. "I mean—like picnics and, uh, barbeque sandwiches, for instance."

Oh, she'd done it again, humiliated herself, and all so innocently. How to pry that foot out of her mouth? Her face burned again, but for less romantic reasons. She simply shook her head, but Alex was laughing.

"You're cute, you know." He pulled his long legs one at a time from under the picnic table and stood up. "Shall we walk? There's a path over there near the lake."

She nodded, grateful for the smooth transition. Alex gathered the paper left over from their supper and shoved it into a nearby trashcan. She grasped his outstretched hand as he helped her up from the picnic bench. They stepped gingerly around roots and stones as they walked along the path encircling the lake. The sun had sunk even lower, spilling fuchsia streaks across the sky.

Hailey slowed her pace and fell into step beside him. "Do you see your mother often? Are you close?"

"I try to see her or talk to her every week. It's been hard lately, since I've had so much work, but I try to fill in with a phone call. My mom's wise and very smart. She's had a hard life, but has always had this quiet dignity about her, like a queen. She's a good advisor and sounding board when I need one, but she doesn't meddle. She knows I need my space. My dad was a workaholic and at times an alcoholic. He died of a heart attack when I was twenty-two."

"That's a shame." Hailey paused then asked, "How old are you now?"

"Thirty-one."

"I'll be thirty-one, too, in a couple of months."

Alongside the dirt path the lake stretched out, glassy, a melted pool of pink from the setting sun. Fireflies dotted the falling darkness with tiny points of light. Alex and Hailey passed a few couples and families on the path, though fewer and fewer, until they reached a worn wooden bench near the edge of the lake. Alex gestured toward the bench and she sat down.

He leaned back and linked his fingers across his stomach, lifting his face to stare at the fraying canvas of blurry pinks, purples, and blues overhead. "Have you ever come close to getting married in the past?" he asked her, still staring skyward.

Hailey shook her head. "My last serious relationship was about three years ago. At the time I thought we could be headed toward marriage. Then my boyfriend, Joel, got a job in Boston. We planned to keep in touch and see how it went, and I was ready to move up there. But it just fizzled."

As she spoke, Hailey felt like she was speaking of another person, another life, not her own. "What about you?"

"I dated some in my twenties. But I was always too focused on my work to give serious priority to relationships. Remember how I disappeared for weeks at a time? I used to do the same thing when I was in a relationship, so that didn't go over too well. I kind of woke up one day and realized it was important to me, like it hadn't been before. I knew I needed to be more present, physically and mentally, if I was going to develop anything with a woman."

Was he revealing his intention toward her? Or was it some kind of warning? "Yeah, it helps to be around," Hailey teased.

His voice softened. "My need to prove myself was mostly subconscious until recently. I thought I was just excited about my work, which I am, but realized I was more driven than I should be. So, I'm making a conscious effort."

Hailey nodded. "I'm glad. I think being aware of something unhealthy is the first step to changing it."

A look of what seemed like relief passed across his face. "True."

"I have areas like that too. At some point I realized I was trying to matter to my dad, to the world, in my efforts at the mill. That was another factor that made it hard to come back. I didn't want to fall into that again."

"I hope you don't. You matter, without the mill, without your dad."

Their eyes locked. Hailey smiled then looked away. A comfortable silence ensued. Fireflies lit the air with specks of light as the sun began its descent and the air cooled.

"So, we're the same age, go the same church, I discovered. Saw you last week." He nodded at her, a smile quirking one side of his mouth. "We live on the same street. What else do we have in common? Do you have hobbies?"

Hailey leaned back on the wooden bench. She fingered its rough texture as she looked across the tranquil lake. "I like anything artistic. I draw and paint, and take pictures. I'm trying to spend more time doing art, because I stopped for a long time. I had to give myself permission, since it wasn't validated in my family. What about you?"

"It's hard for me to find time for hobbies these days. I throw Frisbee with my dog in the park, garden a bit. I played the saxophone when I was a teenager, so I'm starting to pick that up again, when I have time."

"I remember at the festival you said that you like jazz. I do too."

"And I like to cook. Got that from my mother. Used to hang around in the kitchen when I was real young. I grow plants in a big window greenhouse I built, and also in the little yard out back. I'd like to have a big garden and greenhouse one day, once I have the time to work in it."

A man who cooks, plays music, and grows plants? Hailey was more intrigued every moment by his many facets and surprises.

"Next time, you can come over and I'll make you dinner," he promised. "My work is going to lighten in the next week, thank goodness."

At the thought of this idyllic moment repeating, not in three months, but possibly the following week, Hailey shivered with pleasure. "I'd love that."

"Before you left for Colorado you seemed a bit feisty for me. When you came back, we had a chance to start from zero."

She was glad he'd thought about her before. And 'start from zero'? That had definite potential. "I'll never hear the end of that, will I?" she grumbled, but grinned.

"I like feisty, as long as it's not directed at me."

"Cook me a good meal and all will be forgiven."

"You got it. Like I said," his voice was husky now, his gaze direct. "I'd like to see you more. If food will do the trick, I'm willing to try."

She met his bold stare and held it a moment. Slowly with deliberation, she said, "I'm in."

Chapter Eighteen

Hailey stared at the figures on the computer screen, rereading the same columns, striving to focus. It was a losing battle. Her mind wouldn't stay put, but kept drifting back to Alex, to snippets of conversation by the lake, a joke, a look in his eyes that said he was drawn to her.

For months she'd had little in her head but the mill and what she could do to help it thrive. Now, it was difficult to keep her thoughts from wandering. She hadn't felt this way about anyone in so many years. Joel had cured her of that,

Or so she thought.

A lazy smile pulled at her lips. She'd come down to earth eventually.

After leaving the barbeque restaurant a few days earlier, she and Alex had talked for over an hour in his jeep. He'd pulled up in front of her condo and she'd invited him in to continue talking over coffee, not wanting their evening to end. Although he insisted he needed to get home, it seemed he couldn't leave, as they embarked on a new conversation. Since that day, he called once just to see how her week was going and texted once. Things were definitely moving in the right direction.

Hailey allowed the springs of her leather chair to rock her gently backwards. Her eyes swept across the room that she'd recently had redone. Fresh paint in light ochre covered the walls. Stained wooden crown molding hugged the ceilings.

The framed sketch of Anderson Mill dominated a central place on the wall, but softer artistic efforts graced each corner. A large ceramic pot of fresh flowers sat on a credenza near the large window, which now held a floral print swag that coordinated with the walls. The two threadbare chairs in muddy brown that had always sat on the other side of her father's desk had been replaced with contemporary chairs in soft plum. Of course, she'd been inspired by Judith Araujo's décor in New York. Finally, Hailey's office was modern-looking and functional without sacrificing an unapologetic explosion of color. On the wall just next to her door was a framed painting of a lily pond that she had done several years ago, which had been one of her favorites.

The phone startled Hailey out of her reverie. "Hailey Anderson," she answered.

"Hi, Hailey." It was her father's voice, with a surprising lilt. He hadn't called her at the office in a month or two. Immediately a sheet of alarm fell down over her.

"Hey, Dad. Is everything okay?"

"Yes, everything's fine. I was thinking I'd like to come to the mill today. I haven't been in so long, and I'm feeling up to it. I wanted to let you know ahead of time, if it's a good day for you." His tone lacked the former authoritarian coolness of the past.

"Sure, Dad. Today would be fine. I don't have any appointments."

"How about eleven?"

"Great." She added, "You know where to find me."

"Sure do. See you then."

Hailey hung up the phone, her mind suddenly churning. Maybe it was just a visit to drop by and see everyone. Or maybe he was preparing his return to Anderson Mill as its president. He hadn't said so, but it could be a first step. He'd come back to visit then realize he missed the place. Or else this was part of his schedule, as soon as he'd fully recovered and his energy had returned. Perhaps it was time.

Where would that leave her? She had toyed with the question, then pushed it away several times over the last five months. Somewhere along the line she'd stopped seeing herself as a fill-in employee on a temporary assignment and had stepped into the role of a visionary leader with a heart for the company and a stake in its success. Would she be forced to step down and find something else to do?

Going back to the design department was out of the question. With Alex in the picture, returning to Colorado wasn't an option either, not until she saw how their relationship would develop. Or not.

Nothing was guaranteed, not Alex, not her position at the mill. Even her home was a rented condo on a twelve-month lease. One phone call had thrown her world, seeming secure ten minutes ago, into a whirlwind of uncertainty. One phone call had done the same thing five months earlier.

Another question, weighty and dark, almost obscured the first one. What would be the fate of the mill, if Paul Anderson were to return? Would he undo the changes she'd made? Maybe he'd reverse the mill's progress with his previous practice of closing his mind to innovation and risk.

Would it all end up being for nothing?

By the time Emma buzzed her office to announce her father's arrival, Hailey's nerves were gathered into knots. She murmured a prayer and attempted to shove her worries into God's hands and smoothed her outward expression to erase signs of anxiety. Her father probably wouldn't have noticed anyway.

He finally appeared in her doorway looking years younger than he had when she'd stormed out of his office and fled to Colorado a year earlier. His face looked less lined, his countenance less stern, somehow softer. And he had more than a hint of a suntan.

"You're looking great, Dad." She stood up and waited as he surveyed her office.

"Looks real nice, Hailey. You've got the artist's eye. I guess it wouldn't be hard spending much of your day in here, not like the practical tin can office I had."

Hailey felt her face flush. He had begun surprising her on a regular basis. Against the pleasure of his words, her heart struggled with what he must think of her redecoration, as if she'd never intended for him to return. In truth, she hadn't.

"Thanks. Have a seat. New chairs, you'll like them."

He reached out to rub the fabric on the back of the chair facing Hailey's desk. Then he lowered himself slowly onto it and settled back. "It's nice, comfortable."

"Have you seen anyone downstairs yet?" She slid back into her own chair.

"Just the receptionist. Can't recall her name. I'll make some rounds later, just to say hello. Then if you want to and if you're free, I'd like to take you to lunch. There's a new place that just opened up in the Bloomfield Mill Mall, you know, the one that used to be Bloomfield Mill before it closed."

Hailey smiled and blinked quickly to keep tears from leaping into her eyes. In nearly thirty-one years she'd never had lunch alone with her father.

"Yes, I know the one. They've done nice things with the mill's demise, haven't they? Just glad it didn't happen to us. We don't need that kind of reincarnation."

He chuckled. "Very clever. Reincarnation, is it? Anyway, are you up for lunch?"

"Absolutely. I've been wanting to try one of the new places over there. Do you want to do your tour around the mill first, then we can meet back?"

"Yes, we'll do that."

"I think I told you about the Fourth of July picnic we had for the staff. It was really a fun time. I wish you could have been there."

"That sounds nice. It sure was a scorcher that day. But it's good you did that. I'm sure the employees appreciated it, since we hadn't done it in a few years."

He didn't move but looked at Hailey expectantly. "Hailey, I want to tell you something before I go visit the departments."

She tensed. At least he wouldn't hold her in suspense for long. She'd rather know sooner than later what his intentions were, so that she could adjust toward plan B.

He cleared his throat, as if he felt awkward. "I've made a decision. It wasn't a very hard decision for me, with you handling everything so well over here. I've decided to retire. I won't be coming back to Anderson Mill as the president. I want you to take over as permanent president from now on, if you want to."

Hailey's mouth fell open. "Really? Are you sure?" She felt a weight of pressure roll from her back and dissolve into dust. Another lighter weight, like a mantle of trust being passed on, slipped into its place.

He nodded gravely. "Yes, I'm sure. The stress of this place just about killed me. Now, I do not hope that for you, of course. But I think you're more able than I would be in my present condition to handle the pressures and decisions here. I've given my best years, and now you can do the same. You belong here, using your ideas and energy for the future."

Hailey smiled at him. "Thanks, Dad, for your confidence in me. As long as you're at peace with the decision, so am I."

He smiled back, and it was so rare, it seemed to electrify his face. "Why would I want to come back here, Hailey? Golf is fun, and I'm making some new friends out there at the club. I started gardening again last week, and even though it was hotter than blazes, it felt good to get out there again. I wouldn't have time to come back and work at the mill."

Hailey laughed aloud. "Sounds that way to me. And then there's a certain lady named Sharla. I assume she's still part of your life?"

His face pinkened, but he smiled again. "She has become a good friend, someone I greatly appreciate. That's all I'll say for now. Well, I can tell you that I've started inviting her places, just once in a while. Feels good to go out with a lady again. It's been a long time."

"That's perfect. I'm happy for you, Dad. Isn't it nice not to have to worry about things here anymore?"

"Very nice. I actually sleep through the night these days. Now, why don't you accompany me on my tour? I would like to be escorted by the president herself."

"Gladly." Hailey stood and circled the desk, then proffered her arm to her father.

Before they went through door he glanced up and saw the painting of the lily pond. "That's pretty. Don't think I've seen that before."

"I did that a couple of years ago."

Surprise registered on his face. "You did? Well, Hailey, you have quite a few talents I don't think I realized. You were always artistic as a child. You're quite good."

"Thanks, Dad. That's nice to hear." Hailey's throat filled with emotion. She swallowed and then smiled at him. "Ready?"

Later, they sat at a table washed by the afternoon sun that poured through the mullioned windows of the restaurant. Just like a father and daughter. Now they were like the families she'd envied during her youth, when she'd see a father and daughter talking and laughing together. It had seemed so natural for them and so foreign to her, even unimaginable.

Until now. Somehow, the relationship had flowed easily into a new phase, not close, but a good bit warmer than in the past. No reason to think that couldn't continue. Hailey sighed in contentment and took a long gulp of iced tea.

"Now that everything is settling down in your life and in mine, can I tell Hope about your operation? I'd like her to know how serious it was and that you're doing much better. I think she has the right to know. I'd also like her to understand why it was necessary for me to come back. She's still miffed at me."

Her father's brows furrowed. "Oh, that's too bad, Hailey. You girls were so close growing up. She must have been happy when you moved there. I didn't think about how it would affect her when you came home. I just knew the mill and I both needed you here." He shrugged apologetically. "Maybe your explanation to her will help smooth things over. And be sure to tell her I've made you the president."

CR CR CR

"Hey, Hope. How are you guys doing?" Hailey clutched the phone with a moist hand. She didn't want to waste any time before calling her sister.

"Oh, hi, Hailey. I just woke up from a nap. That's why I sound groggy."

"You take naps? But you're Miss Energy, aren't you?" Hailey teased, reminding her of a high school nick name.

"Not anymore. I'm thirty-five, remember? Mother to a teenager. And I had to work late last night on a big deadline so I got to bed around two. Today I left early and came home."

"Is the deadline finished?"

"Yeah, but what a pain. I told them I'm taking tomorrow off too."

"Good for you."

"So, what's new with you?" Hope's voice was softer, less defensive, it seemed. And she asked Hailey a question. A change of heart?

Hailey swallowed. Here goes. "Um, well the big news is that Dad is retiring from the mill, permanently. He hasn't worked there since his operation last March."

"Since March? I thought he'd had a simple procedure. I'm surprised he hasn't gone back to work."

183

"He made me promise not to tell you before now. I guess he didn't want you to worry, but he had a bypass operation." Hailey heard Hope gasp. "He was very sick. His doctor told him he wouldn't be able to work fulltime for four to six months. The stress at the mill would have done him in. That's the reason he asked me to move back."

"You all left me *completely* in the dark regarding my own father." Hope's voice rang out, laced with irritation.

"I'm sorry, Hope." A tightness squeezed her chest. Just when she thought she'd be smoothing things out with Hope by telling her the truth. "I felt caught, trying to respect his wishes."

"Well, you'll always do that, I guess." Her voice slid out like metal, then Hailey heard an audible sigh and her tone softened. "Is he okay now? What is his condition, since he can't work anymore?"

"He's much better. I don't know if he *can* work, but he chose to retire. He seems younger and happier now. He's started playing golf and working in the garden again. He couldn't do any of that for the first three or four months after the operation. He had a couple of minor heart attacks last year."

"Oh, my God," blurted Hope. "I wonder why he'd keep that information from his own daughter and ask you to do the same."

Hailey pressed her eyes shut and searched for words. "Maybe he wanted to keep you from worrying. It put me under a lot of strain knowing you were upset, but be unable to tell you the full reason I had to leave. I hope you understand better now."

"Yes, of course I understand, better than I did." Hope's voice came out muffled, as if she was fighting tears. She cleared her throat. "But he'd have found a solution without you going back there. What about that guy, the assistant lackey?"

Hailey almost laughed. "Daniel? For whatever reason, Dad trusted me more than Daniel. I don't trust Daniel either."

"Well of course he'd trust you more than someone else. You're an Anderson, and you worked there for years. You know the place. And you actually love that place, though for the life of me, I can't understand why. Dad knew that."

"I'm sorry for the pain it caused you. I was also very sad to have to leave."

"I know you were." Hope's voice was gentle. "And maybe you weren't really ready to leave Larkspur in the first place."

"It's possible. It's nice to be back, despite the summer heat. I guess in our own way we each have to build new roots or else go back to our old roots."

The warmth hadn't fully returned to Hope's voice, but now there seemed to be an open door. It was enough for now. Hailey would love to see that blossom and grow, just as it had with her father.

She fought the temptation to tell Hope about Alex, biting back her words. First, there was nothing to tell, not officially. She couldn't say, "I'm seeing someone," when all he'd done was buy her barbeque and call a time or two. And he told her she had beautiful eyes. In the past Hope was the first person she would have told, official or not, but their current state didn't yet welcome sharing the breathless account of the man who preoccupied her thoughts. Not yet.

ભ   ભ   ભ

The wooden screen door was still moist from the earlier rain when Hailey knocked firmly on it. The paint had mostly peeled away from years of neglect. She stood on the porch of the modest home, as rivulets of perspiration trickle down her back and between her breasts, though it was after six in the evening. Faint footsteps grew louder until the big wooden door behind the screen opened.

"Hailey, what a surprise," cried Bonnie Gatling as she clasped her hands together. "Come in out of that heat. I'll make you some tea."

"Hi, Bonnie, I was close by and wanted to see you both. I'm sorry for not calling first."

"Oh, my dear, no need to call first, especially you. Come in." She turned toward the living room. "Bill," she called. "Can you come? Hailey has dropped by."

Bill Gatling lumbered toward the living room from a hallway in the back. "Hello, Hailey, come in and sit down." They sat on the worn leather couch in the living room while Bonnie left the room to prepare iced tea. "What brings you out this way, Hailey? Hope everything is going well for you and the mill."

No bitterness showed on the older man's lined face, though he'd been out of work for over three months. Hailey felt a swell of affection for the couple. They'd always been gracious and even-tempered, regardless of what was happening. She looked up as Bonnie set a tray of tall glasses on the coffee table and began pouring tea.

"Thank you, Bonnie," she said. "How refreshing on a day like this."

When Bonnie had sat down, Hailey looked at both of them. "I just wanted to see how you two are doing, you know, since the layoff. Have you had any prospects for new employment? You know I'd love to give you a good reference."

Bill leaned forward and gave Hailey a kind but tired smile. "No one wants to hire a man my age. Less than ten years and I'll be ready to retire. I keep asking the Lord if He wants me to retire early, but I'm not sure how we'd live. Bonnie works but it isn't a great salary."

"I take in some ironing too on the side. Even with that it's a bit tight."

Hailey tightened her lips and nodded. "I'm so glad to see you both, but I wanted also to find out how things were going, because we have some funds available to help out. I'd like to offer that to you, if you'll accept."

She pulled her purse from the floor and placed it beside her on the chair. This dear couple didn't need to know that the funds were not some kind of Anderson Mill emergency fund, but had come from her own savings. She figured since she hadn't bought the house in Colorado she could afford to help out some of the families affected by the layoff.

"Oh, Hailey. Why, I don't know what to say." Bonnie pulled her folded hands from her lap to her chin. Tears glistened in her eyes. "It sure would help about now. My car is in the shop and I need it to get to work." She looked to her husband. "Bill?"

"I guess we can't say no, but I will try to pass along some help to someone else, once we get on our feet." His voice was gruff.

"That's a sweet gesture, Bill. Just accept this as a gift. I wish it could be more, but maybe it will help for now." Hailey was already writing the check, her heart filled with the joy of being able to offer a small help to them. She'd been able to do the same for several other families under financial stress. She looked up at both of them and extended the check. "You both deserve it, believe me."

The following day Hailey unlocked her office door and found a paper wedged underneath. She bent down to retrieve it and saw scrawled across the top, "Petition to request Hailey Anderson to step down as president." Her mouth went dry. She closed the door behind her and slid into her chair. Who could have done such a thing? And why?

With over three hundred employees, there were bound to be some who were disgruntled, but to start a petition?

She looked down at the signatures, but there were only three. What was the point in letting her see a petition with only three signatures? Anna Lockhard, Michael Sweeny, Mona Munson. She didn't even know them. Which meant they didn't know her either.

Hailey rose from her desk and left her office. She knew who to talk to. In the dyeing department she spied Vera King, who had been with the mill for many years and with whom she had a friendly relationship. She was astute and didn't talk much, but carried calm wisdom through her mostly menial activities.

She found the woman standing in front of a tall metal dyeing vat, surveying the progress through a small window. "Vera, do you have a minute to talk?"

A smile spread across the older woman's face. "Sure thing, Miss Hailey. This is finishing up anyway."

When they'd walked to the side of the room, Hailey showed Vera the petition. "I wonder if you've seen this petition or know anything about it?"

Vera studied the paper carefully, her brows gathered. She looked up at Hailey and alarm showed in her eyes. "I haven't seen it, so maybe it didn't get around to everyone. I wonder who would do that. Seems to me like you're doing a great job here, turning things around, even though we had that layoff a while back." She shook her head. "I wonder who would do that." she said again.

Hailey was relieved that the petition hadn't gone throughout all the departments in the mill, but regretted that talking to Vera hadn't provided clues to its origin. "Vera, would you do me a favor? Please let me know if you do learn anything about the petition. I'm not asking you to spy on anyone, just to let me know if you happen to hear something that would help me."

Vera nodded vigorously. "I sure will, Miss Hailey. Don't pay any mind to that paper there. It's just somebody who's ticked off about something. Let him deal with it himself. I think you're the best thing that's happened here at the mill. If you don't mind my saying, better than your dad, and a far sight better than your granddad. Your dad was just fine, but I think you understand us all better than he did. He was always kind of distant, you could say."

"And my granddad?" Hailey prompted. Seemed she was hearing references to him lately without learning anything about him.

"Well, he was before my time, but I heard people say that your dad was a better president than his father, and that his father was a drinking man. Beyond that I don't rightly know. Maybe your dad can tell you more."

Not much chance of that. Hailey had already tried. "Thank you, Vera. I'll let you get back to your work."

Why couldn't Hailey get any information about her grandfather, Benjamin Anderson? She'd never been curious about him before, since he had died before she was born, and he'd been as much a workaholic as her father. And apparently, an alcoholic. That was news. Maybe his drinking habit interfered with his work. Was that why no one was willing to talk about him? Maybe it was too long ago and didn't matter anyway.

At least, she hoped not.

189

Chapter Nineteen

August rolled into Larkspur, sluggish and humid, slowing nearly to a halt every living thing. Even the trees stood still, with not even a light breeze to break the impression of a painting. Inside the brick building, looms ran rhythmically, oblivious to the conditions outside.

Hailey surveyed the screen in front of her, and nodded her approval to Curt, a web designer. "This will give us a far more modern look." She leaned back in her chair. "Early next year I'd like to talk to you about setting up the site for online distribution of household textiles."

"Just give me a call when you're ready to move ahead on that. You can even send some rough ideas beforehand. It's a great step, expanding the reach of your products."

And hiring more people. Already, Hailey had rehired two employees. The best part of her job to date was hearing Jenny Sanders cry into the phone, "You did it, Hailey! You said you'd try to bring us back, but I didn't think it would happen."

Hailey smiled. She'd make one more call before the day's end. The phone rang four times, five times. A groggy voice responded.

"Hello, Jeremy. How have you been?"

"Oh, alright, I guess." The young man's voice sounded sleepy or depressed. "I haven't found another job so that part could be better.

But we're all healthy and Josie is working fulltime. But we just found out we're expecting. That's a mixed blessing, I guess, with the extra expense, but we're happy about it too."

"That's wonderful news." Hailey was eager to tell him the rest. "I have more good news for you. The reason I'm calling, Jeremy, is to tell you that the mill is doing better now and we have a position for you in the finishing department, if you'd like to come back."

"You serious, Miss Anderson?"

"Yes, I am. If you'd like to talk more about it, why don't you come by tomorrow between ten and eleven and I'll tell you what the position involves. I know that isn't exactly what you were doing before, but we can train you."

"Thank you, Miss Anderson. I'll be there for sure tomorrow."

Hailey still had a grin spread across her face and a warm simmer inside when her cell phone rang.

"Hailey, I'm finally inviting you over for dinner." Alex's voice was breathless and she heard shouts and clanging in the background.

She laughed. "Well, in that case, I'll be there. Are you still at work?"

"Yeah, we just got some new vines in from South America and there's a lot of physical work to get them situated. How about Saturday, six thirty?"

"Perfect. Can I bring anything? A salad or dessert?"

"Nope. I'll just pamper you."

Her brows lifted. "Well, then, how can I say no? Can't wait."

Her day had just gotten better.

႙   ႙   ႙

The flutter in Hailey's chest kicked up as she prepared for her long-awaited dinner with Alex. Like a teenager on her first date. Well, they'd already had their first date, so why the nerves? Maybe it was the realization, or hope, that their relationship had moved with unmistakable momentum since that first day on the porch.

Remembering that day, she'd been unsure if anything but neighborly friendship lay between them, but lately she'd noticed how he looked at her or leaned toward her. He himself had said he wanted to know her better.

Hailey tried different earrings, pulled her hair up, let it fall down, changed clothes again. She finally settled on lightweight green pants, casual but flattering, and a print blouse with a string of matching beads. When she finally looked at herself for final approval she had a silly grin affixed to her face.

It took only a few minutes to walk three blocks to Alex's condo. The summer breeze licked her bare arms with mellow warmth. The sun had begun sinking, painting purple and rose streaks behind it. As Hailey approached his building, she could see warm light spilling through the windows onto the hedges and front porch. She imagined him in the kitchen shifting from the oven to the fridge, distracted, perhaps wearing a manly apron.

When Alex came to the door he wasn't wearing an apron, but a wide-checked shirt open at the neck and tucked into jeans. He always dressed casually and she liked that he was never messy or baggy. His face lit with pleasure when he saw her. She didn't miss the fact that his eyes scanned her as she entered the foyer.

"You look nice, Hailey." Before she could respond he gestured her inside toward the living room. "Welcome to my place."

The living room drew her with earthy tones, dark wood, and colorful oil paintings. A wrought-iron coffee table topped with terracotta-colored ceramic tiles sat in front of a dark brown leather couch, surrounded by a thick textured area rug. Plants flourished in each corner and some hung from the ceiling.

In the adjoining dining area, a table had already been set for two. A dimly-lit chandelier bathed it in a subtle glow. Hailey felt invited by the rich, warm décor, and by the dark-eyed man beside her.

"It's really beautiful," she said. "Certainly not the stereotype bachelor pad. You've taken care in so many lovely details."

Alex seemed pleased. "I live here every day, so it's important to me how it looks and how I feel here."

"I think exactly the same way. So many people use their home as just a place to eat and sleep. That's fine for them, but I want something beautiful surrounding me when I come home."

"I'll show you around, though it's the same floor plan as yours."

After passing through a well-equipped kitchen filled with enticing aromas, he led her to the backyard, a small fenced-in square of grass and a patio slab that each condo included behind it. The first thing she saw was a tiered shelf filled with plants sitting against the fence. Nearby, a small brown and white dog looked up at her, his tail wagging.

"This is Spencer." Alex squatted down and scratched the dog's head with both hands. "Hey, Spence. That's my good boy."

He sat back and the dog rushed up to Hailey. She bent down and stroked his head. Spencer sniffed at her and continued to wag his tail.

"He seems well-trained. He didn't even jump on me. What kind of dog is he?"

"Mutt terrier, I guess. I don't like when dogs jump all over people, so I trained him to stay until I call him. A friend of mine moved out of the country a couple of years ago and gave him to me."

"He's really sweet." She pointed to his vertical garden. "That's creative."

He grinned and shoved his hands into his front jeans pockets. "Yeah, with such limited space I had to get innovative. Did a bunch of research on different structures, and that's what I came up with. It's worked well so far, and I like having home-grown vegetables and herbs. You're having some tonight, by the way."

"Can't wait."

Hailey stayed on the patio with him as he grilled steaks and talked about his week. Back in the kitchen, she offered to help, but he'd already done everything, saying, "No, this time you are my special guest."

Happily, she leaned against the counter watching him and talking as if they'd known each other for years. She noticed he'd adapted the standard condo kitchen to fit his love of cooking, with gleaming metal pans hanging from a lattice on the ceiling, and an array of knives and kitchen machines along the counters.

Finally, they sat down at the dining table. Spread before her was a colorful bowl filled with homemade steak fries, a spinach and tomato casserole, and the steaks with mushroom butter on the side. Two thick candles flickered in the center, casting a blush of warmth across the table.

If his objective had been to impress her, he'd succeeded beyond expectation. Her own cooking was acceptable, though nothing to rave about. His meal was nothing short of delicious and the comfortable ambiance was like a hug to her senses.

Their conversation flowed easily throughout the meal and for nearly an hour afterwards. For dessert Alex served peach mousse. Hailey's romantic jitters abated, replaced by simple enjoyment of his company.

She hadn't wanted to discuss work, but as often happened, it came up easily and often. "I never did find out who was responsible for the petition," she told him after he asked about it. "Just some disgruntled person, I guess."

"You've hired back people and the bottom line is stronger, from what you've told me." Alex pushed his empty dessert bowl away. "I guess there's always going to be someone who isn't happy with anything. He or she should just go somewhere else."

"Hiring people back has been such a thrill for me, not just because it's a sign that we're doing better, but I just enjoy giving good news and seeing people happy. But for the people who never lost their jobs in the first place, I'd think they would simply be glad to have a job, and encouraged that I'm making improvements little by little. I can't change everything overnight. I've never run a textile mill before." Hailey finished her dessert and licked her spoon. "That was amazing. I've never had peach mousse before."

"Peaches are in season now, as you know. Cheap and plentiful, so I made ice cream too."

Hailey marveled. "Is there anything you don't do? I keep discovering wonderful things that you do in your free time, but you seem to have so little of that."

Alex gave her a modest smile. "I enjoy it."

"Me too. Everything."

195

For just a moment their eyes locked and held. Hailey realized she'd held her breath as the tingle began. She let it out and smiled at him.

"So, the petition just died away?" he asked, and it broke the tension of the moment.

Hailey swallowed and cleared her thoughts. "Seems like it. I asked an employee if she knew anything of the petition's origin, and she didn't even know there was one. I was relieved that it hadn't gotten around the mill very far. She thought I was doing even better than my dad."

"You've turned it around."

"She said something strange, though. She said I was a better president than my dad, and a *lot* better than my grandfather. I don't know much about my grandfather, except that he died right in his office. He keeps coming up in conversations, but I haven't been able to learn anything about him."

Alex swirled his glass, watched the liquid cling to the sides, then took a sip. "Do you think it's important?"

"I don't know. Just makes me curious. I get the feeling he had a lot of weaknesses that might have gotten in the way of good leadership, and possibly good parenting, too." She thought of her father, who'd never spoken openly of his father. It had never seemed strange to her before. Now it did.

Alex leaned toward her, his forearms on the table and a lazy smile on his lips. "At least you're the permanent president and no one will take that from you. Not a petition and not your dad." He paused. "I'm very glad you have a permanent job and won't be going anywhere."

"I'm glad *you're* glad," she said lightly, observing his expression, which had shifted, deepened. "Being the real president makes me feel bolder in things I want to do. It allows me the freedom to build something." She knew her the words carried a double meaning and wondered if he picked it up.

He stared at her for a moment, a small twitch in the corner of his mouth. "Sky's the limit. Want to move over to the couch? It'll be more comfortable."

The soft leather couch was like smooth butter against her skin, cradling her as she settled into its back, again giving her the impression of being hugged. Sitting beside her, Alex talked about the new vines and production schedule, slipping away from the previous emotional undercurrent.

She listened attentively, picturing him testing the sugar content in a wine, clipping vines, working in a laboratory. One day maybe he'd take her there and explain the winemaking process to her. His work seemed such a fit with the man she was discovering, closeness to the earth, a natural lifestyle of simple pleasures like growing plants, making food, playing with the dog.

She loved everything she'd learned about him so far. Of course, he must have faults, but she hadn't seen them yet. Soaking in the moment was what mattered, there in the dim light with his low, rich voice caressing her, his closeness like an enticing cloud of incense swirling around her.

A comfortable silence fell between them as the soft notes of a jazz station drifted from the kitchen radio. Hailey gazed at the candle flame that danced on the coffee table and cast distorted shadows across the shiny wood surface.

Alex's subdued voice broke into the silence. "Last year before you moved away, did you know that I liked you a little bit?"

Hailey looked up at him. The mood had shifted again to a focused intensity, with his dark eyes on her. Slowly she shook her head. "You did? I thought I annoyed you."

He laughed softly. "I can see how you'd think that. Things were kind of problematic back then with us."

"I guess what worries me, though," she began, watching his face, feeling her own heart, almost hearing it pounding like a drum, "is that it sounds like you're speaking in the past tense."

Without breaking eye contact he leaned forward slightly, a faint smile on his lips. "Speaking in the past tense, I liked you a little bit. But in the present tense, I'd have to say I like you a *lot*. And it's growing."

He reached out and gently pushed a strand of hair away from her face. "I think about you a lot, Hailey, more than any other woman I've known. And in a different way. I like being with you. I look forward to seeing you. May not seem that way to you, since I'm busy a lot, but you're in my thoughts."

As he spoke, his voice soft and hypnotic, Hailey felt something leap inside her, joy, hope, a tangle of breathless emotions she couldn't quite identify. This was Alex, beside her, telling her these things. Alex. "Me too," was all she could think of to say. He was certainly in *her* thoughts as well.

It was as though he hadn't heard her because he continued speaking softly, but with directness, his dark eyes clinging to hers. "When you left I was angry with myself for being so distant with you. I don't know why I was. When you came back I knew I had a second chance. I'm ready to think of something besides work. There's more to life than work, there's the need to share it with someone." He paused. "I want to see where this will go."

"I do too," she murmured again, feeling stupid for repeating his words, but what else could she say, when he'd uttered the cry of her own heart? "I—I like you too, Alex. A lot." She felt almost adolescent as she said, "And I liked you too last year. Even two years ago."

He seemed pleased and surprised. "You did? But you left anyway."

"I didn't think you had any thoughts or feelings about me, except that I was just a grumpy neighbor." At that, he chuckled. She said, "You seemed to have a scowl on your face whenever I saw you. I thought I'd never convince you I was a fun person. Besides that, I didn't know anything about you, what you were like, what you believed, whether you were a nice guy or not."

"Glad we got that straight." He grinned, his face shadowed by the candlelight. "At least we both know we aren't as ornery as we thought the other was." They both laughed again, the soft sound intermingling with the music.

When the laughter faded their eyes remained locked together. Alex leaned forward and gently tilted her chin with his hand then kissed her. She leaned toward him, embracing the softness of his lips, the taste of wine, the faint but manly aroma of his cologne. He shifted closer to her on the couch and she folded neatly into his arms, surrounding her as their lips met again, more ardently this time.

She could feel his back muscles through the grainy cotton of his shirt under her fingertips. Sheltered in his arms, the minutes seemed to stop, suspended in another world that didn't touch them.

A hazy thought began to form far away, where conscious thought was still possible, buried beneath the waves of joy of the present moment. Maybe Alex was part of the big picture, why she returned to Larkspur, what gave reason to her confusion and fulfillment to her emptiness and thirst.

She'd think of that later or maybe not at all. She'd learned enough to understand that many answers were simply not within her reach and she'd have to accept the clarity alongside the fog. Soon both dissolved, chased away by the taste of peaches and tenderness in Alex's kiss.

Chapter Twenty

The rhythmic drumbeat of the looms met Hailey's ears as she passed through the vast space filled with machinery. The sound had always been a comfort to Hailey, a tempo of daily life. As a child she loved to watch the filmy strands join into solid rows that, with every passing second, resembled a piece of cloth. Now with many more looms, the sound was a fuller, richer symphony.

In each department she visited, she surveyed not only the machines, but the employees who operated them. Did they seem content, efficient, in their best role? She was vigilant for any signs of disgruntlement or conflict since the petition which, thankfully, had simply died away.

She entered the finishing department, relieved to escape the noisy army of looms, but instead heard a voice raised in anger. Daniel was speaking to a female employee, who cowered against the wall. She didn't know if she should intervene. Daniel would likely accuse her of meddling.

Hailey stayed out of sight until Daniel passed through the doorway in a brisk stride. She approached the woman, who she recognized as a relatively new employee named Claire. Claire didn't see Hailey approach. She reached up to swipe away a tear.

"Hello, Claire. Is everything okay?" Hailey kept her voice as gentle as she could, but loud enough to be heard over the blanket of machine noises.

Claire looked embarrassed and cast her eyes down.

"It's okay, you can tell me. Was Mr. Carlton upset with you about something?"

She hesitated. "I was coming back from break, just a minute or so late because I had to talk to my little girl. She's home sick. It won't happen again."

Hailey touched the young woman's shoulder gently. "Claire, I know you try to keep your break times, but you have a life too. If you need to check on your little girl, that's fine. Maybe Mr. Carlton didn't know about it."

"I told him, but he figgered I was lyin', so I could get a longer break. I don't do that, Miss Anderson. You can check with my old bosses. I was always on time for everything."

"I believe you, Claire. Does Mr. Carlton criticize you for other things?"

Claire looked down again and murmured, "When I see him coming I'm always sure that I'm doing everything right, 'cause I see him sometimes yelling at some of the other girls."

"He only yells at the girls?" Hailey frowned. "Does he ever yell at the guys too?"

She shrugged. "I don't know. Seems it's just the girls. There are a lot of us, but there's more of us to criticize too."

"Yes, I know you ladies do a lot of the work here. If you have any more problems with Mr. Carlton that you feel are unfair to you, you can come to my office upstairs and let me know. I'm giving you permission to do that, okay?"

The young woman's blue eyes widened, but she nodded.

Hailey stepped away to allow Clair to return to her work. Claire looked back over her shoulder once, a meek smile a brief nod toward Hailey.

Just beyond Claire, Hailey's gaze settled on a middle-aged man with dark hair who was staring at her intently as he stretched out a large piece of cloth on the tenter. Probably nothing but curiosity, but the fixedness of his stare made Hailey uncomfortable.

As she returned to the main lobby and mounted the stairs, the kindling of anger in her stomach began to smolder into a small flame. Daniel. He hadn't annoyed or undermined her in over a month. She thought he'd finally fallen into line, but this was different. This wasn't against Hailey's authority, which he'd apparently accepted, at least on the surface. This was his manner of dealing with employees, possibly targeting the women.

From now on she'd watch him even more closely than before. In her eyes he was less worthy than the dozens of people laid off months earlier, yet he enjoyed an authority and higher paycheck than even those who stayed. And everything he did grated on her.

Hailey's annoyance was jolted off course when she glanced down at her phone and saw a text message from Alex.

"I've been covered by dirt all morning, but my mind is far away, thinking of your green eyes. And lips."

She grinned and wrote back, "My green lips? You didn't tell me."

"Ha Ha, I meant ruby red and delicious."

"Sounds like one of your wine flavors. Sure it's me you're thinking of?"

"Absolutely, many times per day. Very distracting. Gotta go. I'll call you later."

Though they were both busy during the day, he often texted something romantic or fun, an inside joke or an ongoing conversation between them. They'd attended Nina's wedding together the previous weekend, so many of their friends knew they were now a couple.

She smiled, contentment flooding inside her, as she was drawn to Alex Moreno with compelling force she felt unable to resist.

Could she have felt anger just a few minutes ago? What a boomerang of emotion she was capable of these days. Often, she felt like she was floating two feet above the ground. Between their schedules they managed to see each other two or three times on a good week, but there were phone calls and messages between. Thoughts of him were her secret oasis, a hunger anticipating fulfillment in the face-to-face meeting.

When she crossed the threshold to her office she pulled her thoughts forcibly from Alex to Daniel. Should she confront Daniel? No, better to watch him and see if it was a pattern. He'd probably defend himself or accuse her of being soft with latecomers from break. She was building a mental dossier against him but was unsure yet what to do about it.

As if reading her thoughts Daniel materialized in her office as soon as she sat in her chair. She looked coolly up at him and back down. "Daniel." She acknowledged him then arranged her desk, as if he weren't there. When he didn't speak she looked up at him. "Do you need something?"

Daniel cast her a flaccid gaze through pale blue eyes, but his expression lacked his usual combative challenge. "No, just wanted to touch base, since we haven't talked in a couple of weeks." He still didn't know that Hailey arranged her schedule each week to avoid him whenever possible.

He shifted his weight, seeming lost for words. "Things are going smoothly on my end. I thought you'd want to know. Nothing to worry about there."

Hailey stared at him, uncertain what to make of his comment. Was he trying to keep her from learning something about his activities? She made a mental note to check into them.

"Oh. Well, that's good news." She nodded absently, thinking he'd leave. He didn't.

"Um, you look nice today. I mean, you do most days, but you look especially nice today. Sort of glowing."

She put down her pen and stared. "Are you okay? Is something wrong?" Maybe he was going to snap and run through the mill firing off a pistol. She'd heard of this happening with high-strung employees who began acting strangely.

He laughed awkwardly. "Is it strange if I tell you that you look nice? I mean, you do. I'm not your enemy."

Her mouth fell open slightly and she slammed it shut. "Well, Daniel, you can't really say you've been a team player since my arrival. Seems like you did everything you could to make my job harder. So, yes, I'm a bit surprised by the compliment."

"I'm sorry if it seemed that way to you. I've been under intense pressure from long before you got here, and I guess a change of leadership added even more. I reacted badly to the stress."

Hailey narrowed her eyes and leaned back in the chair, disoriented. Had she been wrong about him? Was there a reasonable explanation for his efforts to undermine her? For speaking negatively about his employer to the press? For treating the warehouse employees harshly? She couldn't think of one, even if he were doing the unexpected, admitting he'd behaved poorly.

"I understand the pressure. I left Anderson a year ago because of it. My dad had heart surgery because of it. I don't doubt that you were under stress, but it would surely have helped us both if you had supported me as I tried to do my best for the mill."

Daniel dropped his head and nodded. "Maybe I felt threatened too." A spark of honesty?

"Maybe you expected to be named interim president?" Hailey asked softly.

He grimaced and pressed his lips together. "Maybe. But I understand, you're his daughter, so you were the logical choice. He'll leave this whole place to you one day."

"That could have been what he was thinking. Along with the fact that I grew up in this mill and know quite a bit about it." Hailey shifted in her chair. "Don't take it personally, Daniel. He approved of you or you wouldn't still be here." *She* didn't approve of him, but he should know that already. He looked miserable, so she bestowed a small smile in his direction.

He didn't respond, but cast a glance around the room. "You've redecorated. Looks better." He turned a blank look back at her. "Well, I'll let you get back to work." Before she could respond he vanished from the office. She shook her head in bewilderment.

Maybe he was truly contrite over his attitude over the last seven months. Maybe he'd doubted her, but realized he'd been wrong. Or was he simply trying a new angle? In any case she would continue watching him.

It took her several minutes to realize that he hadn't apologized for anything.

ᆭ   ᆭ   ᆭ

Hailey parked in front of her father's brick colonial home. She scanned the flower beds and shrubs, noting her father's renewed care.

Another first in her relationship with her father, he'd invited her for dinner. Of course, she'd offered to bring a baked chicken and sweet potato fries from the deli, and he'd gladly accepted. She knew he didn't cook and was thankful for his gesture of inviting her.

"Thanks for bringing all this, Hailey," he told her as they settled into the big padded dining room chairs. "You know I don't cook a lot. I just thought it would be nice to have dinner together." He smoothed the napkin into his lap and reached for the pitcher of iced tea. He looked better each time she saw him, with a deeper tan and brighter eyes.

"Does Sharla still cook for you sometimes?"

"Oh, once in a while. She likes to make things in bulk to last me a few days. Little packages in the freezer. These vegetables are hers, the broccoli casserole and carrots. I like the way she does them."

"Things still going well with her?"

"Yes, just fine. Pass me the potatoes, please."

"I'd like to see her again sometime. I met her just briefly when I first got here, but it would be nice to talk with her one day."

"Hmm. Maybe you will one day."

Best to let the matter drop. He'd talk more about Sharla when he felt ready. Or not. Hailey reached out to the ample plates in front of her and served herself from each one. The warm companionship she longed for with her father still lagged behind her hopes, but by small degrees, a relationship was taking root.

Each time she crossed the threshold into the house, inhabited by filmy shards of memories, a chill still slipped into her bones. Unbidden, she recalled often feeling like an orphan among her own parents. It had been easy to push those years out of conscious thought as she embarked on a new life in the west. Now as she faced it by choice she was determined to forge new memories, but she couldn't rush it. At times she wondered if her previous life in Larkspur had been driven by her desire to matter—to someone. The same quest that then drove her to Colorado. Now it was new territory, but with the same old ghosts. She'd be deliberate this time in understanding how the past drove her.

"Things still going well over at the mill?" Her father sliced a leg quarter off the bird and slid it onto his plate.

"Yes, I'd say so. I think we're over the big drain and starting to get into the black again. I was able to hire a few people back from those laid off last spring."

"Oh, now, that's good news. When you can start hiring back, that's excellent. Maybe one day you'll be able to expand the staff beyond that number. Mmm, these potatoes are good, even if they do come from the grocery store deli."

"I remember Mom's sweet potatoes. She didn't make them like this, but hers were even better. Do you remember those?"

Her father shrugged. It wasn't as if they'd had frequent family meals, talking and laughing around the table, enjoying each others' company. "That was so long ago. I can hardly remember what I had for breakfast this morning."

"I used to wish we could sit together more often around the table, just taking our time, catching up on the day," Hailey ventured lightly. It was a feeble attempt to open up something deeper and find out how her father felt about the past, to learn if he, too, missed what had never been created.

"Life was such a whirlwind back then. Retirement is much better than all that."

A wave of disappointment fluttered by then disappeared. It was better to leave the past where it lay, at the bottom of a well of regrets. Her father seemed unable or unwilling to peer into that well. He, too, likely had regrets, but talking about them with his daughter was more than he could do. He was only beginning to talk to her about anything. How much more could she expect?

Could she expect him to remember that she had a birthday the following week? In the past he'd remembered because her mother had remembered. Since he'd been on his own, he hadn't. Some things had changed since her return to Larkspur. Some things had not. *Leave it alone, Hailey.*

"Dad, can I ask you something?" She saw her father tense, as if expecting another probing question. "Did you like Daniel Carlton and his work at the mill?"

He leaned back in his chair with a shrug that extended up to his face. "Not my favorite person, but for the job, he seemed adequate. He's been there, what, seven or so years? I figure he knows the business now. He came from some other mill before us, I forget where."

Hailey nodded. "Just curious. I have to say I don't really like him, as a person or as an employee. He and I don't share the same values. He wasn't supportive of me when I got there."

Her father turned a sharp eye to her. "But does he do his job? That's the important thing now, Hailey, not that he's your friend. He did his job well. I ignored his sissy ways. They don't concern me."

She almost laughed at her father's description of Daniel's mannerisms, but felt a deep thud at his response. "I'm not trying to be his friend. He just makes my job harder."

"As I said, he knows the business and he does the job. You need him now. I'm not saying you don't know what you're doing. I'm saying you need a right hand who has been there for a few years. At least for now when you're new. You can't run the place alone."

Hailey's shoulders sagged. Maybe her father was right. She needed Daniel's experience, despite her feelings about him. She could separate those, couldn't she, at least for a little while longer? And Daniel had taken a different attitude with her that day. She might be able to mend fences with him. "Maybe you're right. I don't see him all that much. We have our separate roles."

"There you go, you can avoid him on most days. Pick your battles. Daniel might end up being an ally."

What kind of ally? She hoped a true one. A sudden image flashed through her mind, that of a snake shedding his skin. She flinched. Was God trying to tell her something, or did it simply spring from her own distaste with the man? One thing was clear, her father wouldn't support her desire to get rid of Daniel Carlton.

"That was pretty good." Her father wiped the napkin slowly across his mouth. "Maybe next time it'll be homemade. You ready for some ice cream?"

Hailey nodded. While her father shuffled toward the kitchen to get the bowls and ice cream her eyes wandered around the room. Everything looked the same as when she was a child. If Sharla married her father and moved in one day, hopefully she'd change everything. Or maybe they'd move somewhere else. Or Hailey's memories would simply have to heal on their own, with nothing at all changing at the big colonial house.

Suddenly Hailey longed to be with Alex. He'd understand her web of feelings, her gratitude over her father's clumsy attempts at relationship, her stale memories triggered by the house, and her frustration over Daniel and how to handle him. She glanced at her watch. She could leave within a half hour and still have time to see Alex, or at least call. They hadn't made plans, since she'd already had a dinner date with her father.

Her father returned with two half gallons of ice cream, several spoons, and two bowls on a large tray. He set it before her on the table. "Chocolate or butter pecan. I can't remember the one you like."

Of course, you don't remember what I like. Hailey choked back the thought. Here was her father full of good gestures and all she could do was fault him for what he didn't do in the past. She smiled up at him with gratitude. "Great. I like both."

As they dug into their bowls of ice cream she ventured, "Did I tell you I'm dating someone? A guy who lives in my neighborhood."

Her father continued exploring his chocolate ice cream with his spoon. "That's nice, Hailey. Someone you just met?"

"I knew him before, but not very well. We've gotten to know each other since I've been back. His name is Alex." She bit back Alex's last name. Hailey had known her father to make disparaging comments about foreigners who had moved in large numbers to Larkspur. She'd tell him some day. Would he even care?

Hailey suddenly understood Alex's feelings of being judged without a fair chance. People like her father, good people, average people, did it every day in ignorance, unaware of the hurt they caused. She was almost doing it herself at that very moment. Shame flooded through her. Oh, Alex.

"What does he do?"

"He works at a vineyard. He's a botanist of sorts. He creates new wines."

"Hmm. That sounds interesting. He's like a migrant worker or something? Sure he's legal?"

Hailey bristled. "No, he's a *botanist*," she said again. "A scientist. He grew up right here in North Carolina. His dad was a doctor, but he always liked plants and growing grapes." She could imagine what her father was thinking. And she hated herself for trying to paint Alex in a better light for her father's sake. Alex was one of the finest people she'd ever known, and he didn't need her help in countering her father's bigotry.

As Hailey drove home, a barrage of conflicting emotions swirled around her. She almost missed her turn into the condo complex. She thought she'd changed, but still felt so desperate for her father's approval. She might have succeeded as president of Anderson Mill, but aside from that, had she grown at all?

If her father didn't approve of the man she loved—and she was certainly falling in love with Alex— it was his problem, wasn't it? She didn't need his approval for any decision she made. She'd waited a long time for even a hint of relationship with her father. If she went too far to protect it, she wondered what else she might be risking.

Chapter Twenty-One

Thanks to an early-morning visit from the plumber, Hailey was running thirty minutes late for work. Not the best way to start her birthday, but no one was aware of it anyway. It had always been so important to her, possibly linked to the rare attention she received from her parents on that day, as if she were a treasured daughter. She knew she was a treasured daughter to God, though it was mostly in her head. *Lord, show me I'm treasured to you. Always treasured, no matter what.*

A faint warmth took root. She'd tuck that neglected truth in her mind and try to nourish it, today in particular, because for her birthday, there would be nothing from anyone, except the favor she bestowed on herself. She'd buy herself a new bracelet or spend Saturday morning photographing the fall foliage. Maybe she'd get a call later from her mother. Hope would normally have called, singing Happy Birthday off-key, with Devon harmonizing or doing wolf calls in the background. Hailey wasn't taking anything for granted. She hadn't even told Alex that it was her birthday, but would do it that evening. He'd probably chide her for not telling him sooner. Her work at the mill had kept her there late several nights in the last two weeks, and they hadn't seen each other enough. Aside from wanting to spend her birthday with him, she missed seeing him.

Minutes later she pushed open the door to her office at Anderson Mill. When she turned on the lights she saw a vase filled with lilies and carnations in pastel colors. Alex. How had he known?

Hailey's despondency evaporated like dew on a hot day. Suddenly nothing else mattered, not her father's negligence or Hope's wounded distance. He'd remembered her passion for color. She must have spoken about it.

The barbeque. She'd told him then that she had a birthday in a couple of months and he must have remembered, though she still didn't know how he'd discerned the day. Didn't matter.

She sat back in her chair, still smiling. They'd have a proper birthday dinner that evening, probably a romantic one. She leaned forward and pulled the tiny card off of one of the blooms and eagerly opened it.

The grin slipped from Hailey's face and she fell back in her chair, as if pummeled by a lead ball. She read, "Just wanted to wish you a Happy Birthday. I hope we can start all over again and be friends. Yours, Daniel." Daniel Carlton gave her flowers for her birthday? Of all the people she'd want to remember, he wasn't on the list.

She preferred to ignore the gesture, so as not to give him any misdirected encouragement, but that would be rude. Hailey jotted a brief email of thanks and pushed 'send', hoping it wouldn't come up between them in an awkward way.

Just then her cell phone rang. When she saw Alex's name appear she frowned. She'd tell him it was her birthday and he'd probably feel hurt that she hadn't told him sooner. "Hi, Alex. We're still on tonight, right?"

"Yes, I certainly hope so." An unusual edge cut into his voice.

"Um . . . what do you mean?"

"We have plans, but if you end up having to work late again—"

"No, Alex. I'm leaving at five. No one will keep me here. No deadlines, emergencies, nothing. Are you okay? You sound kind of annoyed." She'd never heard that tone from him before.

He sighed. "No, I'm fine. I just feel like I've tried to cut back all the overtime so we could be together, but you're going in the opposite direction. Are you committed to this relationship, Hailey?"

A heavy weight fell down inside her. It was true, she'd made many excuses in the last two weeks, eager to see him, yet driven by deadlines and seemingly urgent projects. "Of course, Alex. You know I am. It's just the last few weeks that have been crazy. It will get back to normal, I promise." Hailey bit her lip. How could she tell him about her birthday now? It would only reinforce his doubt about her commitment to him. She'd tell him that evening. "I promise," she said again.

"Can't wait to see you tonight." The warmth had returned to his voice.

Hailey let out a breath of relief. "Me too. And you're right, I have been working too much lately. I will change that. I promise."

She hung up the phone and sat still for several moments, leaning back in the black leather chair. Had she slipped back, back to the days before Colorado? In those days, she'd sought her identity, her importance and value in what she could accomplish. She thought she'd learned by now. Maybe it was one of the lessons she'd have to learn repeatedly.

ભ   ભ   ભ

"Thanks for your time, Hailey." The pretty blond woman on Hailey's computer screen gave a final grin before she disappeared. A first for Hailey, being interviewed for Carolina Industry

Magazine. They'd wanted a profile of a struggling mill that had managed to make a come-back.

Hailey frequently asked herself if things were moving too fast. Although the mill was in significantly better shape than before, she needed a longer period of stability to know if it was, in fact, a success story.

A shadow in the hall caught her eye. Daniel. "You can come in, Daniel. I'm finished with my interview." She had difficulty looking at him and hoped he wouldn't mention the flowers.

Daniel's face looked blank, as if someone stretched his skin across his bones. "Um, here's the report you wanted." He set a stack of papers on her desk. She looked down at them. "Did you have a good birthday?"

"Yes, I did. Thank you for the flowers. That was nice of you." She hoped her voice sounded like his second-grade teacher.

Daniel shuffled his feet for a moment. "It's the least I could do."

Hailey frowned. How was she going to fire him now, when he was being so conciliatory? She looked up. "Was there something else?"

"I uh, wonder if you'd ever like to go have a drink after work one day. Maybe we can even become friends." He forced a chuckle.

Hailey's mouth opened but no words came out. Finally, she stammered, "Uh, I uh, well I never expected to hear that from you, Daniel."

When she saw his smile, she knew she'd said the wrong thing. "I mean, it's a nice thought, but I don't think it would be appropriate. I'm sure you understand."

"Why not? Colleagues go out for a beer, don't they?" A surly film covered over his smile.

"Yes, I suppose sometimes they do."

"Do you think you're too good to be seen with me?"

She stared at him. "You know very well I don't think that way. And if you don't, you aren't a very good observer. I don't really *want* to go out for a drink with you, Daniel. I'm seeing someone." She didn't want to give him any more personal details than absolutely necessary, but maybe he'd leave her alone if he knew that another man was in the picture.

"Oh, that Mexican guy. I knew him in high school, but can't remember his name."

Hailey stayed silent, her blank face belying the agitation just under the surface. How would Daniel know about Alex? Alex had never come to the mill before. Maybe Daniel had seen them together at a restaurant. A chill shivered up her spine. Had Daniel been spying on her?

"Seems like you'd have better taste than going out with him."

Hailey's agitation turned to a hot rage that roiled in her blood. In a tightly controlled tone she said, "I'd be careful about judging others, Daniel, since you're in no position to feel superior. Now, I have work to do. Please leave my office."

Daniel didn't move. Quietly he said, "We'd be good together, Hailey. We both have a passion for this place. We'd make a great team. You'd be better with me than with him."

She sighed and sat back. "Daniel, you had a chance to make a good team with me, professionally speaking, and you were against me. I'm not saying I'd never forgive you, but having a relationship outside of work is out of the question. As I said, I have work to do."

She threw him what she hoped was a cold expression of distain until he left the room. She rose and closed the door then returned to her chair, slumping as if all of the air had been released from her. She badly wanted to fire him for a host of reasons, but if she did it now he'd say it was because he had pursued her romantically. Could he have planned that? No, how could he know his days were numbered?

That is, if she had the courage to act.

Chapter Twenty-Two

The crisp bite of fall laced the morning air. Leaves on the oaks and crape myrtles were barely tinged with yellow and gold. By mid-morning the chill would be gone and the warmth of Indian Summer would erase the memory of it.

Hailey continued her covert observation of Daniel, which wasn't hard to do, since she made rounds once or twice daily in each department. She made certain he didn't see her. Twice she'd observed him treating an employee with impatience. Both times it was with a man. Apparently, his abrasive manner was no respecter of gender.

He hadn't been able to overcome her by intimidation, so he'd tried flirtation. As if she'd ever give *that* a moment's thought. Her mind traced back to her early months at the mill. What else might he have done that she hadn't even discovered yet?

Hailey pulled open a desk drawer and pulled out the crumpled petition. She had almost thrown it away, but had decided at the last minute to keep it. One person who had signed, Mona Munson, was an employee in the finishing department. Hailey had waited several weeks after the petition appeared under her door then sought out the employee. She wanted to show kindness to her. Although Hailey enjoyed showing kindness, she also wanted to win Mona's loyalty. She'd found Mona to be a timid young woman who might have been manipulated into signing the document.

219

Hailey phoned the supervisor of the finishing department, George Grant. "Hey, George. I'd like to speak with Mona Munson, but I need you to be discreet. She is not in any trouble and I don't want anyone talking about it. Can you do that for me?"

"Absolutely, Miss Anderson. She has a break in a couple minutes if you can wait."

"That will be fine. Just make sure she gets her full break afterwards, please."

"No worries, Ma'am."

A few minutes later Mona's frail form filled Hailey's doorway, her face pinched and pale. "Miss Anderson, you sent for me?"

Hailey gave the girl a wide smile. "Yes, come in. Please sit down. You look nervous, Mona. Didn't George tell you that you were not in any trouble?"

She nodded vigorously, brown curls bobbing. "Yes, Ma'am. He did."

Hailey kept a steady smile on her face in order to reassure the girl, who still looked like she was facing a predator. "I was curious about the petition that went around a few months back. Do you remember that?"

Mona shook her head quickly, keeping her eyes down. She kneaded her hands in her lap as she sat perched on the edge of the chair.

Hailey pushed the paper to the middle of the desk. "It has your signature on it, and of course I don't blame you for anything, Mona. Please understand. I wonder if someone *pressured* you to sign this."

Mona was nodding. "They was saying you was temporary and we should get someone else, that you wanted to lay a bunch of us off, except for just a few people."

Hailey lifted her brows. "Really? Who was saying that?"

"I can't rightly remember where it come from, but I know Mr. Carlton said there was more layoffs coming if we didn't get things put right."

Hailey nodded. "So, he wanted you to think that if people didn't sign a petition to have a new president, there would be even more layoffs?"

Mona nodded.

"And when did Mr. Carlton first speak of the layoffs? Before they were announced, or after? Or maybe it was after the layoffs happened."

"No, we didn't know nothing about it until he started saying things. Got us all scared."

"Well, I think we were all relieved that the layoffs were small." She smiled at Mona and watched the girl relax only slightly. "Please know that what you told me will not be shared with anyone. No trouble will happen because you talked to me today." She waited until Mona acknowledged her statement then added, "Is your mother doing well?"

Mona seemed surprised by the change of subject. "Yes, Ma'am, she's better. It's nice you knew about my mama. It took a couple of weeks, but she's nearly back to her old self now."

"I heard she'd been sick, but I'm so glad she's doing better. If anyone asks you why you were here, you can tell them I was asking about her, okay?"

Mona came close to smiling at that moment and nodded. "Thanks, Ma'am," she said. She rose and disappeared from the room.

Once she was again alone in her office, Hailey whispered, "No, thank *you*."

Paul Anderson must have been surprised by the unexpected phone call Hailey had made just before leaving the office. "It won't take a minute, Dad," she'd said. She needed some back-up right about now.

But once she was in front of his house, she hesitated. What if her father again disapproved of her desire to get rid of Daniel Carlton? Why did she feel the need to have his approval? She had sufficient evidence.

"My, Hailey, what is so urgent?" Her father sounded more weary than irritated. He closed the door behind her and shuffled in slippered feet back toward his favorite worn recliner, where he sank back with a sigh.

"Maybe I also wanted to see my old dad." Hailey perched on the edge of a nearby wingback chair that faced him and smiled.

He waved a dismissive gesture but smiled back. "Want something to drink? Should have asked you before."

"No, it won't take a minute. It's about Daniel. I've made some discoveries about him that aren't too pleasant. I've told you he didn't support my decisions and disagreed with me in front of employees, and I just found out that he instigated a petition to have me step down."

She waited for a look of shock from her father, but he stared at her as if waiting for the rest. "Don't you find that unbelievable?"

"Go on," he said.

"Well, I think that's plenty. But if you need more, I think he egged my car."

At this her father's bushy brows shot up. "He did *what*?"

Hailey nodded. "The same day that layoffs were announced someone egged my car. I didn't suspect him, but I saw someone who looked like him running across the parking lot shortly before it happened. I recognized his coat and stature."

"Unbelievable. What do you want to do, Hailey?"

"Fire him," she said without hesitation.

Her father leaned back in his arm chair and laced his fingers across his belly, which had gotten leaner since his operation. She mentally composed her retort to what he'd surely say about how much she needed Daniel at the mill.

"Well, what are you waiting for, then? Fire him. You're the president, Hailey, you don't need my permission."

Her mouth fell open. "Really? You agree with me, then?"

"Like I said, you don't need my permission."

"I wasn't really asking permission, more like advice. I think I have enough justification."

"I'll just caution you one thing. Think about who will replace him. You'll have to interview and that can take time. You'll be a man short for a while. Can you handle that?"

Hailey nodded vigorously. "Yes, I've already thought about that. It's not a problem."

"Go do it, then. It'll relieve your mind."

She leaped up and hugged her father's neck, something she'd rarely done in her life. He stiffened then relaxed. "Thanks, Dad."

She felt several pounds lighter as she drove home. She pulled into the condominium complex she scanned the street, as she often did, for Alex' jeep. When she saw it in his parking space, she turned her steering wheel toward his building.

The following day Hailey's buoyancy had vanished, replaced by a layer of dread. She only wanted the unpleasant meeting behind her, her ordeal with Daniel Carlton finally finished.

She called his office. "I need to speak with you sometime today, Daniel. It's not urgent, but sometime before the end of the day. When can you come?"

"Hmm, best for me would be early afternoon. Is that okay for you?"

"Yes, it's fine. About two o'clock?"

"Fine."

All day the minutes seemed to tick backward. Finally, hours later, Daniel was sitting across from her in her office. "Would you mind shutting the door, Daniel?"

He looked surprised but did as he was asked. He sat expectantly. "Is there a report due? I wasn't aware of one." His voice was cool. It had been his new stance with her since the day she'd rebuffed him.

"No, Daniel." Hailey leaned back in her chair, her heart pounding. She kept her face expressionless. *You're the president, Hailey. And this is long overdue.* "Daniel, we haven't had an easy time of it."

"No, but it's getting better, don't you think?"

"Um, on the surface, it is. But we have a fundamental problem. We're not a team. I've already spoken to you about not supporting me. It's water under the bridge. I know that you do your job. The problem is *how* you do it."

He shifted in his chair and chuckled. "Oh. I can work on that. Just tell me what you want me to change. I can be a team member."

"I want you to listen carefully to what I'm about to say. It's deeper than you think." Hailey stopped and drew in a breath. Daniel tensed like a caged animal. "In addition to being unsupportive, you talked to employees about layoffs *after* you and I had expressly agreed not to, for fear of spreading panic. Of course, people did panic, because you wanted them to panic in order to make me look bad. Then you instigated a petition asking me to step down." At this Daniel's eyes widened and Hailey thought she saw fear for the first time.

He opened his mouth to speak. She held up her hand. "I need you to listen until I'm finished. You have disagreed with me in front of employees on more than one occasion. You spoke to a local newspaper in a negative way about the mill, without my knowledge or permission. You are harsh and intolerant with our employees. Daniel, none of this fits with my way of running my business. You don't fit with me. I need someone I can count on, trust, and see things the same way. I am offering you the opportunity to resign instead of being fired."

Daniel had sat with what seemed like growing shock, which morphed into controlled rage while Hailey spoke. Red mottled fingers of blood seeped up into his otherwise pale face. When she finished, he exploded, "You can't do that! You don't have grounds to fire me. I've been a dedicated employee for the last seven years."

"Oh, but I do have grounds. All of the reasons I just gave you would have gotten you fired much sooner from another company. I wanted to believe the best about you, but this is quite a long list. I'll add one more: I believe you egged my car."

"That's ridiculous."

"I saw you running across the parking lot the day it happened. You were the only one out there. You will leave in two weeks, that's . . ." she leaned forward to look at her calendar. "That's the fifth of November. You will receive a month's pay, and that's generous considering what you've done."

"I was afraid you'd become a tyrant as soon as you became president. I was right," he spat.

Hailey's eyebrows went up. "A tyrant?" Despite the tension in the room, she laughed aloud. "Last spring you accused me of being too soft, because I wanted to avoid layoffs. Daniel, you've more or less committed treason against Anderson Mill, stirring up discord and vandalizing property. I should have fired you long ago. You were lucky that I was so flexible."

"Weak is more like it."

"You're right, I was weak. I saw red flags about you early on but I didn't fully trust my own judgment. I lacked the confidence I needed while I was only the interim president. But not anymore. That's all I have to say, Daniel. You will leave on the twenty-fifth, unless of course you wish to leave sooner. It makes no difference to me. I'll give you a standard reference without going into details on why you were fired. That's generous, too. And if you resign voluntarily, that'll look better for you. You can leave your resignation in a sealed envelope with Lenore."

Daniel rose to his feet, but had murder in his eyes. "You'll regret this, Hailey. You don't have any proof of these things."

"Oh, but I do. And I don't appreciate being threatened. That could go against you, too."

"You don't have the right. And you don't have proof."

Calmly and slowly Hailey shook her head and said, "I don't need it, Daniel. Now, please go, and shut the door behind you."

"I certainly won't be sticking around for two more weeks." He slammed the door so hard her ceramic vase rattled. Hailey found that she was trembling all over.

Slowly she rose and turned off the overhead florescent light. Only a table lamp glowed in the room, casting grotesquely distorted shadows that were strangely comforting. She settled back in her chair and breathed deeply. Calm trickled back in and replaced the tension. Daniel was gone. She'd done the right thing. Now there was one more thing she had to do.

Hailey dialed the number she knew by heart, after all the years. These phone calls had become the high point of her day, and this one would top them all. "Hi, Bill, I hope I'm not catching you at a bad time."

Bill Gatling cleared his throat. "Oh, hello, Hailey. I was just surprised to hear from you in the middle of the day. Hope nothing is the matter."

"No, not at all. I'm relieved to find you at home. I was afraid you'd found a job by now and I couldn't give you my good news."

"What good news is that? Are you all hiring again?"

"Just one position, and I hope you'll consider it. It's a different department than you are used to. Are you up for learning some new things?"

"You bet. But I've done just about everything over there. What else could there be I haven't done yet?" The older man chuckled.

"Assistant manager. Daniel Carlton is no longer employed with Anderson, and I'd like you to consider taking his role."

After a long pause Bill stammered, "You—you sure? You want me to take Mr. Carlton's position? I don't really have the credentials. I don't have college and all that. He was in top leadership, Hailey."

"As you will be. You'll be my right hand, working closely with me in all the operations of the mill. I have full confidence in you, Bill. As you said yourself, you know the mill better than most people, even me. That's a different kind of college. Your experience and skill would be a great support to me. I hope you'll consider it."

"Consider it! I'm so honored, Hailey, I don't know what to say. When would I start?"

"Come by my office tomorrow at eleven if you're available, and we can talk about the details. We'll get you in here by next week, if you want."

"Sure, I can come tomorrow. I have to say, this was the last thing I expected to happen today. It'll take a few minutes for it to sink in."

Hailey could hear his voice thicken with emotion even as her own heart swelled with joy. Finally, Bill would have a job where he could utilize his varied background, and she'd have a valuable assistant, instead of one who tried to trip her up at every turn. Finally, she'd have a team.

"I'm going to call Bonnie right now," he said. "This can't wait till she gets off work."

"Great idea. It'll be good to have you back, Bill."

•

Chapter Twenty-Three

"I'm sorry to bother you with this, Miss Anderson, but looks like the warps were cut on some of the looms." The gruff voice of Bert Shelton, supervisor of weaving, bit into the tranquility of Hailey's office.

"Cut?" Hailey sat back in her chair, phone in one hand. "Were the looms functioning normally?"

"Rich was down adjusting the tenters, so I just called him over to look at them. There were several where's been cut. I thought that was a bit unusual and wanted to let you know."

"How many beams are affected?"

"It looks like a few, maybe five, six. Shouldn't slow production too much."

"Thanks for letting me know, Bert. Please tell me what Rich thinks, if it was done deliberately or if the threads are breaking for some other reason."

Hailey hung up the phone. Warp threads had never been cut before, even though dozens of looms wove their crisscross pattern day after day. Maybe the new looms had faulty parts.

The following day her phone rang. When she heard Bert's voice again, she hoped for reassurance. "We got the looms set with new beams yesterday and they're running, but now there are five more down."

Hailey's eyes widened. "Five? Are any of these the looms we got from Downing Mill earlier this year?"

"No, none of them's the new ones. Or maybe just one of 'em. In any case, Rich assured me yesterday that the machines were functioning fine, except uh, it seems like to him and to me, um . . ."

"What is it, Bert?"

"It looks like to me someone might have done it deliberately, since the warp ends were cut at the same height. It wouldn't have required knowledge of the machine, just opportunity."

Hailey frowned. "That's what I was afraid of. That's ten or eleven in two days. More than a coincidence, I would say."

"Do you have any idea who would do such a thing?"

"I might. It could be someone who used to work here but has left angry."

"How would they get back in? Someone would've seen him, if it had happened yesterday or today in the middle of the work day."

"Unless it was done at night by someone who was able to get in," Hailey said. "Let me think about it. In the meantime, I'll have all the locks changed and we'll see if that helps."

Who would sabotage the looms? Daniel? He'd threatened her when he left, but that was over a month ago. He might still have access to the mill at night if he'd made copies of the keys.

Hailey called the locksmith and scheduled an appointment for later that week, though he wasn't able to come immediately. More damage could be done by then.

She redialed Bert's number. "It's Hailey again. Do all the weavers take break at the same time?"

"Not usually. About half of them go at a time and we work in shifts."

"Can you stagger them and make sure there aren't areas unattended during the day? Just in case it's someone who still works here. I'm covering my bases."

"Sure thing, Miss Anderson."

Dread slipped down over Hailey like a curtain. Sabotage. Whoever it was had direct access to the looms, but why? The newer looms were electronic and had many ways to be broken, ways that were expensive to fix. If someone meant to do damage, there was plenty of opportunity. It wouldn't take long for Anderson Mill's gains over the last months to be lost. She didn't know if Daniel Carlton would do such a thing. It was possible that he was already working for one of her competitors, but if he was still unemployed he might be angry enough to harm the machinery. His motivation, she could understand. But how was he getting in after hours? She was stumped.

Hailey slept poorly for two days following the sabotage, envisioning the consequences of more of it happening. Changing locks would incur a bill the mill couldn't afford, but if it kept the vandal away, it was worth it. On Thursday the locks were changed on all the entrances. As Hailey signed the locksmith's final paperwork she felt lighter, but only until she saw the grim face of the dye room supervisor.

"I hate to tell you this, Miss Anderson, but we've a whole batch that's been ruined. Got overcooked, because the controls have somehow been cut. It's messed up a batch of the new cotton we pulled off the tenters just this morning. Had to be someone familiar with the controls."

232

"We didn't get the locks changed soon enough," Hailey said grimly. Whoever wanted to harm the mill was dead serious.

ભ ભ ભ

Hailey leaned back in the passenger seat next to Alex as they drove toward Clemmons in the late afternoon on Christmas Eve. A humid chill framed the windshield with frost. Beyond it rumpled clouds like curdled cream hung low in the sky. Alex gently caressed Hailey's hand with his right thumb as they sat in comfortable silence. She'd made a deliberate effort in the last month to leave work at the normal time, so they could spend time together. As soon as she was with Alex she quickly forgot the pressure and deadlines, and felt increasingly close to him.

Another cause for relief, after the locks were changed no further sabotage occurred. During the Christmas holidays she tried to push it all from her mind and was partially successful. She wanted so badly to believe it was finished.

"I'm glad to finally meet your mom and your sister," she said into the silence. "I have such positive expectations, after what you've told me."

She turned her hand over to clasp his and watched his profile as he drove. She loved the strength and confidence she saw there, but increasingly perceived his gentle side as well. She wanted so much to be accepted by his family.

He glanced at her, smiling. "You won't be disappointed. They're both eager to meet you too."

"Have you've told your mom much about me?"

"What do you think?" He gave a short laugh. "If I didn't, she'd pester me with questions every time I called. She's impressed that you run a factory." He shot her another grin and drew her hand to his lips, pressing a kiss there. "I may be a guy, but I still like talking to my mom about the woman I love."

Hailey's mouth slipped open and a smile edged her lips outward. She blinked quickly. "I love the sound of that. You haven't said it before. I'm glad it's mutual, then." She watched his reaction. "Because I love you too, Alex. I have for a long time."

In the twilight of the jeep she could see a smile spread across his face. His voice was low and gruff as he said, "Too bad we said this while I'm driving. You know what would happen next."

Hailey chuckled. "Mmm. Sounds nice." She could almost feel his arms around her.

"We're here now, but we'll make up for it later." He winked at her then pulled the jeep into a subdivision lined with older homes. Well-tended yards sat beneath mature arching trees overhead. "I didn't grow up in this house. Mom has been here ever since Dad died. Her sister lives nearby, but she can't come tonight. My sister Adriana flew in from New York around noon today."

He parked along the curb in front of a two-story brick home with an elegant but bare crape myrtle trees centered in the front yard. A glow of warm light spilled out of each ground floor window onto the darkening yard.

Before Hailey could alight from the car an older woman emerged through the front door. Her hair was raven black, like Alex's, though streaked with gray. She clutched a fringed shawl around her shoulders and let it fall away as Alex swept her into an embrace. Hailey's throat tightened with emotion as she watched them. They pulled apart and the woman turned toward Hailey, a wide smile on her face.

"Hailey, I'm so happy to meet you," she called as she drew near. Before Hailey could decide if she should shake the woman's hand, Alex's mother enfolded Hailey in her arms. As she pulled away she said, "My name is Louisa." Her voice was tinged with a Spanish accent.

"It's so nice to meet you, too. Alex has told me so much about you. I just knew the woman who raised him must be very special."

Louisa's face brightened. "I'm so lucky to have such a fine son. He looks out for me, and doesn't get so caught up in his life he forgets about me. And now to meet his special lady. Come in, please."

Alex grinned and looped an arm around his mother's shoulders as they went inside. "I can tell you two are a team already."

Louisa continued to chat with Hailey, who nodded and smiled, enjoying the warmth and immediate acceptance.

When they entered the house, they were encircled by rich, spicy aromas. Louisa called in Spanish up the staircase then turned back to Hailey. "Adriana is on the phone with her boyfriend in New York, probably. But she'll be down soon. I must go check the food."

Knotty pine paneling gave the hallway and front room a cozy comfort. Hailey slipped out of her down jacket then paused in the hallway to look at photos of Alex as a high school athlete and as a college graduate. In one photo a man stood next to Alex and another boy stood on his other side. "Is this your dad and your brother, David?"

"Yes. David lives in Charlotte, but can't visit until New Years. His girlfriend's family will be there from the west coast. It's his first time meeting them."

"Big family meetings for all of us," Hailey murmured. They'd be eating Christmas dinner with her father the following day. She wanted the two men in her life to meet but dreaded it at the same time. Her background was so different from Alex's. Unable to paint her childhood in a warm and memorable light, she'd said little about it.

A thumping on the stairs grew louder until a stunning young woman appeared on the bottom step, curly black hair flowing over her shoulders like that of a gypsy dancer. "Hello, Hailey. I'm Adriana." A bright smile lit her olive complexion. Like Louisa, she threw her arms around Hailey for a tight hug. Hailey hugged back. Over Adriana's shoulder Alex grinned.

"Hey, where's mine?" he teased.

"Hailey was first, since she's new in the family. But I'm *so* glad to see you too, my dear wino brother." Alex embraced his sister with a bear hug and lifted her off the floor. She squealed and giggled like a young child.

New in the family, Adriana had said. Was she jumping to conclusions? In any case, Hailey liked the sound of it. At least she didn't have to worry about being accepted by the Moreno clan.

"I see, you are a fellow struggler in battle against curly hair," Adriana said, reaching out to touch Hailey's hair, which hung in thick loops down her back. "We can share our favorite methods for fighting frizz, can't we?"

Louisa called everyone to the table. Adriana linked her arm through Hailey's and led her toward the dining room. Hailey smiled, feeling like Adriana was the younger sister she never had, but quickly corrected herself. A friend, maybe. Not yet a sister.

Later they sat around a warmly festive table, covered with colorful, fragrant dishes, most of which were new to Hailey. Adriana spoke of her latest contacts in the music world as well as her part-time job waitressing. The warm aromas of garlic and chili pepper wafted toward Hailey from a tureen of pozole soup.

"Be careful of this." Alex leaned close to her. "It can be eaten as a meal but Mom serves it as an appetizer. If you eat too much you won't have room for anything else."

"Thanks for the warning," Hailey murmured back. "Looks like it'd be easy to eat too much."

"This dish is called bacalao," explained Louisa. "It's a traditional dish that I serve every Christmas. Alex knows how to make it."

"He's a wonderful cook." Hailey slid the tomato-garnished fish onto her plate. "This is such a feast." Nothing like the Mexican eatery she frequented in Larkspur.

Hailey turned to Adriana. "Alex told me you write your own music. What kinds of songs do you write?"

Adriana's dark eyes sparkled. "I don't follow a particular style, but just write what's in my heart, my impressions of the world."

"That's my approach to painting and drawing," Hailey said.

"I write about people. Everyone has different situations but the same needs and desires. I identify what's special about each person and write about it."

Though only twenty-five, Alex's younger sister seemed wise, sensitive, and sure of herself, the qualities Hailey herself longed to possess. "I'm sure your songs strike a chord in peoples' hearts."

"That's what I hope. I don't want to sing because I sing well. I want to touch people in a special way."

Adriana finished with a grin, as she realized that the rest of the conversation around the table had stopped. She glanced sheepishly at her mother. "Time for tamales?"

After an evening of heavy eating and laughter, the four of them sat in front of a popping fireplace, which bathed the room in cozy warmth. Louisa and Adriana told stories from Alex's childhood, painting vivid pictures of young Alex, unafraid to try anything.

"Mom, you're telling all my secrets. I'm not sure Hailey wants to hear all that."

"On the contrary. You'll probably never tell me all the good stories." Hailey leaned toward Louisa and Adriana. "One day you can tell me *everything*." She winked at Alex.

He shrugged with a modest smile. "I've got nothing to hide." To his mother, he said, "We'll need to hit the road, Mom. But this was wonderful." He slung one arm around his mother and the other around Adriana and squeezed them in a sideways hug.

Hailey said, "I enjoyed the wonderful food, Louisa, but the biggest treat is to finally meet both of you. I feel so at home here." In fact, she didn't want to leave. After her barren childhood, her soul eagerly lapped up the love and acceptance she found at Louisa's home.

Christmas morning dawned misty but warmer. Hailey belted her thick fleece robe then turned on the Christmas tree lights. Every year on Christmas morning her ritual was to turn on the tree lights and music and light every candle, almost before her eyes were fully open.

Soon the caramel aroma of flavored coffee filled the kitchen, woven with cinnamon and bread. The day before she'd baked a ham and made a pecan pie to take to her father's for Christmas dinner. The meal was scheduled at noon, but she'd share coffee and cinnamon rolls with Alex that morning.

She'd been disappointed to learn that Sharla could only come to her father's for dessert, since she'd see her own children and grandchildren that day. Hailey was looking forward to getting to know the woman better, but also thought her warmth would improve the atmosphere around the dinner table.

Hailey chided herself. *Give the old man a chance.* He'd changed in the last six months. Maybe he'd be cordial and welcoming. She told herself she hardly cared anymore, because Alex loved her, and she loved him.

Hailey eyed herself in the mirror and decided to pull her hair up. Alex liked it that way. He claimed it set off her green eyes and made her resemble a noblewoman from ancient Greece. A sage green cashmere sweater lit up her eyes even more.

The doorbell rang as Hailey reached the bottom stair. She opened the door and Alex pulled her into his arms. After a kiss from lips chilled by the morning air, he pulled back and sniffed the air. "Mmm, smells fabulous. Is that cinnamon?" He pulled off his down jacket then wandered into the kitchen.

"My Christmas morning specialty." Hailey followed him. "Coffee?"

"Absolutely."

They sat on Hailey's couch sipping coffee with the cinnamon rolls. Filled with contentment, Hailey rested her head on his shoulder. "I'm so thankful you came into my life."

He turned toward her and his lips brushed her forehead. "I'm thankful you came *back* into mine."

At twelve ten Hailey and Alex stood before her father's door, adorned with a festive wreath of pine branches and red metallic balls. The door opened and Hailey's father said, "Merry Christmas." He wore an understated smile, as well as pressed khaki pants and a fresh-looking button-down shirt. He stepped aside and allowed them to enter.

"Dad, this is Alex Moreno. Alex, Paul Anderson." The men shook hands.

"Glad to finally meet you, Alex," her father said. "Come in. Here, Hailey, I'll put these in the kitchen."

"I can do it, Dad." Hailey took the ham and pie to the kitchen and set them on the counter. A catered turkey sat on the sideboard and a pan of vegetables heated in the oven. She returned to the living room quickly, so as not to leave the men alone for too long.

"I would offer hors d'oeuvres, but I don't have any, so I guess we can go right to the table," her father said. "What do you think? Want some wine?"

"Oh, I almost forgot." Alex pulled a bottle from a canvas bag he'd set on the chair. "I work at a vineyard and this is one of our best wines. It's a Muscadine red with a splash of Catawba. Hope you like it."

"Thank you, Alex. I'll get the salad and we can sit down." He shuffled out of the room. Hailey exchanged a smile with Alex.

When they were seated Hailey's father said, "That must be interesting work, Alex. How long have you done this profession?" The table was set with china and glowing from taper candles.

"I grew up helping my grandfather during summers on his vineyard in Mexico, but as a profession, about ten years. I'm what they call an oenologist. I studied horticulture in undergrad, then did a masters in oenology and viticulture. That's the study of winemaking."

Hailey's father lifted whitened eyebrows. "Didn't know you could get a master's in wine-making. That's news to me. I figured it passed along from parents to sons in the family."

"Often times it does. But you'd be surprised at how many degree programs there are across the country for wine-making, particularly in wine-growing areas, like Sonoma in California. Many state universities, too."

"I guess the college kids get a taste of alcohol then figure it'd be a nice profession." Hailey's father chuckled.

Hailey glanced at Alex, not sure how he would take her father's comment, but Alex was grinning back at the older man. "Yes, I'm sure some of them get started that way. But they learn quickly that they can't drink up all the profits."

When both men laughed at once, Hailey relaxed. Maybe they'd get along.

"Did you grow up in Mexico, Alex?" Hailey's father reached for the salad dressing.

"No, my family settled in Durham when I was young."

"Did you already speak English when you came here? Your English is very good."

He smiled. "Thanks, I work on it." Hailey suppressed a snicker. "My mom taught me before we moved to the States. I was young and caught on quickly."

241

"You mother speaks English? And she taught you."

"She was a high school English teacher in Mexico until she had me. I'm the oldest of three. Then she stopped teaching."

A silence followed. Hailey observed that everyone had finished their salad. "Dad, do you want me to get anything from the kitchen?" Before he could answer she pushed her chair out.

"Thanks, Hailey." Her father looked relieved.

While she lifted the platter of turkey to bring it into the dining room Hailey scolded herself. *Relax, be in the moment. Don't worry about what he thinks.* The fist of tension flexed in her stomach and she realized it was too important to her. She wanted her father to approve of Alex, but if he didn't, it shouldn't matter. She'd break her addiction to her father's approval one way or another.

During the rest of the meal Hailey interjected questions and comments whenever the conversation began to wane, as it often did with her father. He'd done well, though, compared to the way he was during her childhood. He'd shown interest and conversed with Alex. Maybe being on his own had obligated him to make social efforts. He seemed to like Alex at least acceptably well. And he was being polite.

"That wasn't too bad for a store-bought turkey, I think," her father said. "The best one I remember was the time Joel was here. Do you remember, Hailey?"

Hailey's eyes widened. Why would her father mention her ex-boyfriend in Alex's presence? "I haven't thought of him for a long time, Dad." She hoped that would end his mental tangent about the man who had broken her heart three years earlier.

"He was a nice boy, all-American, you know, football star and all that." He nodded at Alex, who seemed unsure of how to respond.

"We don't need to talk about my ex-boyfriend right now, do we? Seems a bit out of place." Hailey wore a smile, but couldn't help wondering whether her father was sending a message about Alex's ethnicity or just oblivious to his own gaffe.

"Oh, yes, maybe. That was a long time ago. What do you hear from him these days?"

Hailey hardly hid her exasperation. "I told you I haven't even thought of him in ages, much less kept in touch. By the way, what time is Sharla coming?"

Her father glanced at the wall clock and seemed to be distracted. Hailey released her stiffened shoulders.

"Oh, any time now. She's bringing dessert."

"Hopefully she's coming soon, if she's got dessert," Alex said with a wide grin, graciously sliding past the previous exchange.

"And I brought a pecan pie, remember. I made it yesterday." Hailey sighed.

"I think I saw Sharla's car pull in just now, some lights through the front window."

"I sure hope so." Hailey looked up and then said brightly, "I'll clear the table to make space for both desserts and I'll make us a pot of decaf."

Alex pushed back his chair. "I'll help."

Two hours later Alex drove toward the condo complex. "I guess that went pretty well," murmured Hailey. "Don't you think?"

She heard his chuckle in the darkened car. "You worry a bit much, my Hailey. Doesn't matter how it went. He and I are just getting to know each other. I'm sure it will be fine. The first visit is always a tad awkward."

Hailey squeezed his hand. "I love that about you, Alex. You take things in just the right way, without making them into a drama like I tend to do. I need to be around you so it'll rub off. Not to mention that I really *love* being around you."

"Over the years I've just learned to take people as they are. I've been misjudged and treated with prejudice. I've also been warmly accepted, and everything in between. I just try to believe the best. I think that's what God would want me to do."

"I do love you," she whispered fiercely. At that moment it didn't matter what her father would ever say or think about Alex Moreno.

Chapter Twenty-Four

"Looks like the gate is unlocked." Hailey heaved open the metal gate of the empty parking lot at Anderson Mill which had been closed all week for Christmas. The darkened brick building rose up like a phantom castle in the mist.

"I always wondered what went on inside these places." Alex nodded toward the building. "They look so forbidding from the outside, with smoke stacks and fences." They returned to the car and drove through the gate to in front of the main building.

"Good place for a scary story, eh?" Hailey grinned and closed the car door. "There used to be four buildings, but now we just have two. We'll go straight to weaving. That'll be more interesting for you."

"I'm trying to imagine you running this place. Seems like an evil-looking man with a black handlebar mustache should be at the helm, not my sweet, beautiful Hailey."

"Oh, I can be pretty evil sometimes. Ooooahhhh." Hailey made a face.

Alex laughed. "I'd love to see that. I meant to tell you, you were a huge hit with my mom and sister. They keep talking about you. Adriana wanted to take you back to New York to become her new best friend."

"She's so sweet and smart. And wise about life, too, even so young."

Hailey unlocked the heavy door that led to the weaving department. A pale panel of winter light spilled down from high windows and lined the concrete floors between the rows of bulky metal looms, each one the size of an upright piano.

"Textile was the biggest industry in North Carolina for almost a hundred years, even bigger than tobacco." Hailey's voice and footsteps echoing through the hangar-sized room. "It influenced the development of the whole state, including banking and government buildings."

Alex raised his eyebrows. "I had no idea. I thought it was primarily tobacco and furniture that were the primary products here."

"They were important, but not like textiles. It was a major catastrophe when things starting falling apart back in the nineties and before. When Canon closed in 2003, nearly five thousand jobs were lost. The industry never fully recovered as before, but there are still many thriving mills today. They've had to do business differently."

"I guess every business has to do that sooner or later. Are these looms?" Alex fanned his hand out toward the identical machines lined up like soldiers.

"Yes. You should hear them when they're all running at once. Everyone who works here has to wear earplugs."

"I can imagine."

Hailey led him down darkened aisles and pointed to a long cylindrical beam on a loom. "This is called a loom beam. See all the threads? There are ten thousand of them."

"That's a lot. Do you spend much time in here?"

Hailey panned her gaze around the large room and gestured. "I walk through every department a couple of times a day, once to check on everything and at other times to talk to the shift supervisor and other employees. I'm in my office too, doing paperwork or talking to clients or sales reps."

Alex stopped and looked around then down at her. "Is it what you expected, being in charge? Do you enjoy coming each day?"

His question caught Hailey off guard. Did she enjoy it? Or was the enjoyment in the challenge of making it work?

She shrugged. "I—I guess it's what I expected, though harder. Now with the sabotage, and before that, with the layoffs. It's such a part of my life and identity, I never asked the question. Maybe I should. You enjoy your work, don't you?"

"I love my work. I'm lucky to be able to say that, because not everyone does. It's like painting for the artist, or design for the architect. Making wine and getting it just right, from the grape to the glass is art for me."

"You're blessed. And I'm happy you love it." Hailey tipped her head up and kissed him lightly. He drew her back for a longer embrace.

"Yes, I am blessed." He held her gaze for a long moment. "On many counts."

They resumed their stroll, their footsteps making a hollow clap on the concrete floors. "One thing that has changed all over textile is so many jobs are now automated," she said. "Mills have had to update their machinery, and you can imagine how expensive that is. It takes fewer people to run everything. See that huge machine over there?" Hailey pointed to a machine double the size of the loom.

"That's called a draw-in machine. It used to require ten to twenty women. Now there are only one or two operators."

"Why women?"

"Textiles have always employed a lot of women. They had the patience and coordination to sit for hours on end, entering ten thousand yarns into harness frames for the loom. Many of them were unskilled before working in textile. They can become good weavers and end up making pretty good money. That makes it harder when they're laid off, because they usually have to take a cut in pay anywhere else."

Hailey led him to a doorway and locked the door behind her. "Now we'll go into the finishing department. Depending on the type of fabric, there are different things that happen here. Cotton needs a lot more finishing than synthetics. For instance, cotton may have more impurities that need to be removed. Different treatments are used to make the fabric smoother, wrinkle-free, softer, mercerized, tested, pre-shrunk, whatever it needs. Dyeing also happens in the finishing department."

"Is the yarn dyed before or after weaving?"

"We can do both. There's another process called pigment pad dye, where the design is more or less painted onto the fabric. That's done a lot these days. You can tell because the design doesn't go through to the other side of the fabric."

When they entered the second building Hailey sniffed. Sniffed again. "Something's wrong here." She flipped on the florescent overhead lights and scanned the vast room, striding purposefully through the shadowy aisles, glancing left and right.

She sniffed again. Fire. "Something is burning."

"I hope we're catching it early." Alex was already peering up and down the aisles. "Imagine if we hadn't come today."

"Someone was imagining just that." Hailey gritted her teeth. "The smell is stronger as we walk toward the wall." Large bolts of multi-colored fabric sat piled high under the window overhead, almost haphazardly placed. A thin spire of blue-gray smoke snaked up from behind them.

Hailey's eyes followed the wall up to the window. It was ajar. Someone had made sure before the Christmas holidays that fabric was positioned under the window and the window was left open.

She dashed to the bolts of fabric with Alex at her side. They peered behind the stacks. "It's coming from back here. Let's try to pull these out."

They each grasped one edge of the stack and heaved it away from the wall. A faint flame licked at the base of the stack of bolts. The bottom bolts were singed in a long black line. Hailey stomped on the flame and waved away the smoke.

"The flame probably lost power on the way down from the window where it could have been tossed in from outside." Alex peered up toward the small open window.

If they hadn't passed by that day, the bolts could have caught and possibly the whole building would be in flames. Anderson Mill would be finished, after all Hailey had tried to do.

"This must be what was used." She held up the remains of a burned piece of twine clinging to a small rock. Tiny pieces of burned newsprint still stuck out from the wire. "Thrown through that upper window, that's my guess."

She coughed from the smoke.

"Maybe they brought a ladder to toss something that was already burning." Alex stared back at her. "Remember when we arrived? The gate was open. Is it usually locked?"

"During the week sometimes it's forgotten, but during Christmas it would be locked. I'll check to see if it was cut. Do you think we got everything?"

"We'll keep looking." Alex was already scanning a long row of shelves nearby.

Who would do this? Daniel? Hailey shook her head. "I just can't see Daniel doing this, but I can't imagine anyone else either."

"You might be surprised by Daniel." Alex glanced under shelves and among small hills of fabric searching for flames. "Vengeance can be a strong motivation. He was humiliated, and that can make people do unreasonable things. We should call the police and let them know what happened."

Hailey sat down on a small stack of fabric bolts. "I will. But even if the police get involved, this won't be over until we know who it is."

A lot of damage could be done before then.

ભ   ભ   ભ

It had been wishful thinking to hope the sabotage had ended. It wouldn't just stop for no reason, unless the perpetrator was preparing for a new and bigger attack at an unexpected moment.

Hailey didn't want to alarm the employees, but needed their eyes and ears. She also wanted to send a message to whoever was responsible that management was taking measures to be proactive. The department supervisors were soberly briefed in a closed-door meeting, told to watch the employees in their areas and leave no machines without surveillance. She instructed them to choose several trustworthy long-term employees to keep an eye on daily operations . . . and operators.

Though the locks had been changed, there were still ways to do harm, as she'd seen. Employees wore photo badges and Hailey hired a night watchman to stand guard in the long-abandoned guard tower near the front gate. She'd win this battle. She'd find out who had done this.

Don't forget to ask for God's help. Let Him win the battle. In the midst of panic, forgetting the most important part was too easy to do. *Lord, I need a quicker reflex toward You. The battle belongs to You.*

After a stressful week, Friday finally arrived. Hailey let out a belly-deep sigh of anxiety then relief when she saw the clock. She needed a break from the stress. Her spirits lightened when she locked her office and took the winding staircase to the front door. The cold, January air hit her face as she pushed through the front doors.

When she reached her car, she let out a cry. Her tires lay in a black heap of rubber strips. Broken egg traced a wide swath across her windshield. For the first time fear prickled her scalp. This was getting personal.

She called Alex but he didn't answer. "Please, please call me as soon as you can," she rasped into the phone. He called back ten minutes later, during which time she paced around the damaged car.

"Hailey, are you okay?" His voice held an edge of fear. "I'm in a meeting, so I can't talk very long."

"My tires were slashed. I'll get a cab home since you're tied up."

"You may be in danger, Hailey. I'm so sorry I can't come now." His voice lowered. "I'll be another forty-five minutes. Can you wait in your office for me?"

"No, it's fine. I need to be home. I'll call a cab and deal with this mess tomorrow." It wasn't the way she imagined her relaxed Saturday.

"I'll come as soon as I get off."

"I love you, Alex." Her voice broke, and she hung up without hearing his response.

Chapter Twenty-Five

Mixed with the usual mail, contracts, invoices, ads, was a smaller envelope which caught Hailey's eye. She stared at the unfamiliar handwriting.

An eerie chill prickled her scalp as she slit open the envelope. A crinkled sheet of lined paper fell out. She read the words and her eyes widened. Aloud she repeated them. "Your family will pay for what you have done. You're finished, Hailey Anderson and Anderson Mill. I will make sure of it."

Of course, no signature. Blank on the other side. A vague film of apprehension became a cool sweat on the back of her neck.

This wasn't Daniel. She was sure. Daniel might still be angry but he wouldn't do this.

What you have done. What did *that* mean? Giving employment to hundreds of people over four generations? Aside from an inevitable and limited layoff, she didn't know what could earn them the letter's predicted punishment.

The strange recent events at Anderson Mill were not accidents. The letter in her hands wiped clean any remaining doubt. Someone—an unknown, invisible enemy—wanted revenge for something. Her only guess was someone who'd been laid off and wanted a twisted sort of justice.

Hailey had reported the arson to the police the same day she and Alex had discovered it. The police did an investigation of the finishing department from one end to the other. Unfortunately, most of the bolts that had been near the window, even those that didn't catch fire, were infused with smoke odors and couldn't be used. That delayed the order of an important customer who'd threatened to send his business to another mill.

Now she had a direct threat clutched in her moist hand. The rules of the game had changed.

She glanced at the clock. It was no longer a relief to be able to drive home and cower inside her condo, since the fears and stress of new attacks only followed her there and haunted her at night. She called the officer who had done the arson investigation.

"Officer Graham, it's Hailey Anderson. I just received a written threat in today's mail."

She heard a weighty sigh on the line. "This guy means business. Save the letter and envelope. Can you bring them by the station today or tomorrow? If it's been handwritten, that may help us."

"I'll try to do it today. If not, tomorrow morning on my way in." Depended on if her nerves would allow her to make a stop or if she would compel her car to drive her home to hide.

"Be careful, Hailey. Be aware of everything going on around you. I'll send some plain-clothes officers to patrol the mill until we get this thing tied up."

"Thanks, Officer Graham." She was sure the officer could hear the fear and agitation in her voice. He was used to frightened people. Yet he sounded genuinely worried himself. Things like this just didn't happen in Larkspur.

She sat still for several minutes, thinking. The loom sabotage would have been most easily accomplished by a current employee who'd had unobserved access. The fire could have been set by either a current or former employee, or someone outside the mill entirely. The letter also could have been sent by anyone.

Hailey grimaced and shook her head. No pattern. A current employee would have been able to do all of these but would lack a motive. Why would an employee sabotage his own employer? And what was the grudge all about? None of it made any sense. She wished she had the ability to look at it all coolly from an objective distance instead of feeling like the bait in a sick-minded hunt.

She glanced again at the clock. Five more minutes. Never mind. She stood up and pulled her coat off of the hook and stuffed the letter and envelope into her purse. Stopping by the police station would take her ten minutes out of her way if she took the shortcut. Although she was dog-tired she would make the effort to drop off that letter. Every moment counted.

The sky hung heavy, metallic gray, backlit in patches by the dying winter sun. Though there was no wind, the chill bit into Hailey's face, reaching cold fingers under her collar and scarf. She couldn't get to her car fast enough, as if walking across the parking lot left her exposed to spying eyes and imminent danger. Her eyes darted around nervously but she saw no one. Most of the employees were still inside the building.

At the turnoff to the police station she was brutally tempted to keep going straight toward her condo, as fast as possible. The light blazed red and her mind chanted, *go straight, go right, go home, turn right, no, just go home.* She growled in frustration and turned right abruptly, cutting across the turn lane. There. She decided.

As soon as she turned she saw a car follow behind her, hardly visible in the muddy daylight. He'd forgotten to turn on his lights, as many people did when day turned to dusk.

She'd been to the station once before, a low unimpressive building that was easy to miss. Going the usual route would have planted her in rush hour traffic, but she'd discovered a shortcut through a small industrial park and a patch of wooded roadway.

A quick glance in her rear mirror told her that the car without headlights was still behind her. He seemed to have crept closer to her car, probably in a hurry to get home.

As Hailey approached the wooded area her fear spiked. What if her car broke down on this deserted stretch of road before she got to the station? She chided herself. Her car had been checked after the incident with her tires, and it was in good condition. She had, as Nina would say, a good case of the willies.

Nina. Hailey hadn't called her in a couple of weeks. Now she was the one neglecting her friend even though she'd been afraid that, once newly married, Nina would drift away. She'd call her when she got home. She hadn't even told her the latest in her drama.

A tap on her car jolted her from her reverie. The other car had lightly rammed her from behind. She could barely make out the face of the driver, but didn't recognize him. It was a man with a knit cap on. Maybe he wasn't paying attention, or was drunk.

He bumped her car again, harder this time. No question, this was deliberate. Hailey accelerated and tried to observe the make and model of the car. Ahead was the wooded area. She didn't want to get stuck there with a madman behind her. She wouldn't be found for a week. He rammed again. She pressed down the rising wave of panic. "Oh, God, help!"

Next thing she knew he was nearly beside her, almost forcing her off the road. If she went over the ravine he would come and find her, unless he decided to drive away. He tapped her side bumper again, then abruptly swung left up a cross road and disappeared.

Hailey drove too fast through the wooded area, emerged into the industrial park, then stopped the car, shaking all over. There was no sign of the other car. It was all connected, the threats, the sabotage, now this.

She wasn't sure how long she sat there. She looked up and two cars waited patiently behind her. She waved and drove the last half mile to the station, despite a nearly uncontrollable urge to keep going. She really *had* to go to the station now.

Officer Graham wasn't on duty so another officer took the letter from her. She told him about being nearly forced off the road and gave a description of the car.

"I left today about five minutes early," she told him. "Whoever it was must have been waiting for me outside the gates. All this time I thought it had to be someone who worked at the mill, but they get off at five and I left early."

"Maybe he left early then waited for you," the officer said. "Or someone from the outside could have waited for you to leave the building." Hailey shivered. In either case it was simply creepy.

The officer went outside to look at her car. He took pictures and paint samples left by the other car then sent a police escort to follow her home. She didn't know if she'd feel safe in her home or not. She no longer felt safe anywhere.

 C C C

Hailey pulled on her furry house socks and climbed into bed. Temperatures had dropped to single digits that week. Though no snow had fallen, rings of frost framed the windows. She unfolded the extra blanket across the bed. That should keep her toasty.

For the last week life had been a facsimile of normal. On the outside. Inside, anxiety gnawed at her every day and especially at night. During the darkest hours of night, she often woke up. It was then that her fears nearly overcame her. The first night after her car was almost driven off of the road she barely slept. At three a.m. her eyes were still wide open.

"Okay, Lord," she had said aloud into the darkened room. "I'm not big enough or brave enough for this thing, but you are. You're God, and I'm not."

She drew comfort from her own words, as if the message was being handed gently back to her. Since that night, when she awoke in the darkness to a shapeless mass of fear she spoke aloud similar words. "You are the God of heaven and earth. Nothing is too hard for you. You can take my fear and give me your peace."

That particular night as she snuggled into her extra blanket a small wave of fear skittered by then was replaced by calm assurance. Each time her thoughts drifted to the danger and the sabotage she shifted it to God's protection, to Alex's love, to the blessings that had already come. She'd get through this. God would help her. She drifted to sleep.

Hailey jolted awake, sure it was about two o'clock, the hour she usually awoke. She glanced at the clock. It was only midnight. Something had awakened her. She listened in the silence and heard a sound downstairs at the window or the door.

She slid out of bed and reached for the robe draped over the chair. She slipped it on and crept to the top of the stairs. Down in the living room all was still and dark, except for a stream of light from the streetlamp spilling onto the rug. She stilled and listened. Silence. Maybe she'd imagined it.

Then she heard it again. A rattle at the window. A bolt of terror shot through her. Someone was trying to get into her condo. Her heart pounded up into her throat as she molded her body against the wall, in case he looked through the small crack between the curtains and up the staircase. She slid back into her bedroom and grabbed her phone.

"Alex, I'm sorry to wake you up," she whispered. "Someone is trying to break into my house."

"Huh? Hailey? What, you're kidding." His groggy voice responded. "Do you see anyone?"

"I saw just a shadow and heard someone fiddling with the window as if to get in."

"Do you have an alarm?"

"No, I wish I did. I wouldn't have called you. I was just scared." Maybe she should have called the police first but Alex was the one who leaped into her mind.

"I'll come over if you want. At least the guy will know someone is looking out for you."

Hailey smiled in spite of her hammering heart and the wave of fear that engulfed her. He *had* looked out for her. Alex had driven her to and from work several times since her incident on the road.

"Do you mind?" she asked him. "You'd get here sooner than the police would, I think."

"Yeah, I'll be right over. I can stay on the couch if you want me to stay. Otherwise I'll stay till you feel better then come home."

"No, please stay. I promise I won't take advantage of you."

They laughed. A burden lifted. He was coming.

Several minutes later she heard a knock on her door. She saw him through the peep hole and pulled opened the door in a cloud of relief. His eyes crinkled with sleep and his hair stood up in spikes on the top of his head. She collapsed into his arms, which encircled her with a squeeze.

Hailey looked up at him. "Did you see anyone hanging around out there?"

He shook his head. "Not a soul. The guy picked a pretty cold night to try to break into your house."

"Your nose is red. You walked?"

He nodded then stepped back at arm's length. "You're pretty cute in your fuzzy bathrobe. I guessed that you probably would be."

She grinned at him. "Not just anyone can see me in my fuzzy robe. And slippers."

He looked down at her slippers, a grinning cat head flopped to one side. "Gotta say, no one can compete with that fashion."

Once his smile had faded he looked at her soberly and ran his palm gently along the side of her face, where it rested beneath her chin. "It's going to be okay, Hailey. You'll see. This is all temporary. God has it covered."

She nodded and fell against his chest as his arms circled around her. He held her with his cheek resting lightly on the top of her head. They stood quietly, peacefully, for a few minutes and she felt as though no harm could touch her again.

Finally, he pulled back and lifted her face with two fingers, brushing her lips gently with his, then pressing deeper. She circled her arms around his neck and responded eagerly, her fear far away, enveloped by safety and warmth and love.

Hailey slept soundly, knowing that Alex was just a floor below her. The next morning, she arose. She quickly checked her morning face in the mirror and pulled back her unruly slept-on hair.

She went downstairs and made coffee as usual, but was acutely conscious of Alex asleep on the couch. She shouldn't have let him stay, since he had his own work to prepare for that day. But she'd have been too afraid to stay by herself.

She planned to dash upstairs and shower before he awoke, but when the coffee machine began to sputter she heard his voice from the living room and saw his disheveled head rise up above the back of the couch. A band of morning beard smudged his chin. "I could get used to this." He grinned at her.

She smiled at him from the kitchen, feeling self-conscious in only her pajamas, fuzzy robe and slippers. "Me too," she said softly. "How'd you sleep?"

"Not bad. Didn't hear anything else." He pulled himself up to his full rumpled height, still rakishly handsome. "I'll share some of that coffee with you and scoot back to my own place, before the neighbors get to talking."

She poured the coffee and served him then sat down across the table. "Do you have a long day today?"

He nodded. "I was going to tell you it'll be hard for me to pick you up this afternoon."

She laid a hand on his arm. "No need. I'll be fine. God is with me, and it's all going to be fine."

"I won't let anything happen to you, Hailey," he said fiercely, his eyes dark. "Call me if you're afraid or if anything happens. Even at night. You should still call the police, though, after this."

She nodded. "Yes, I will. They can add that to my file. I'm sure it's getting rather thick." She gave him a wry smile. "It'll be interesting to see what will happen next. What hasn't he tried yet?"

Her smile fell and she swallowed a lump of fear, one that was spreading day by day, like a quickly metastasizing cancer. How long before it overcame her?

Chapter Twenty-Six

The February chill broke near the end of the month. In its place flowed mild breezes in the upper fifties. Hailey breathed in the nearly spring air in a deep gulp just before unlocking her condo door at the end of the work day. A faded wooden flowerbox hung on her window sill, forlorn and empty. Another few weeks and she'd refill it with flowers and fresh potting soil, and replant Gerber daisies in the terracotta pots to brighten up the front steps. Her mind had been far from such things in the preceding tense weeks but the softening in temperature reminded her of the gentler side of life.

Once inside, she pushed open the windows for the first time all winter, coaxing the timid breeze into the stuffy living room. She flung wide all of the curtains, which she'd kept shut since her incident with the midnight visitor. Muted afternoon light spilled into the room.

Despite the fear that still sat on her shoulders daily, a few drips of happiness seeped in when she thought of spring, and especially when she thought of Alex.

It was Tuesday. He normally played basketball at a local community gym but that day said he needed to stop by to talk to her about something. He didn't hint at the reason. Curiosity nipped at her as she put away her files from work. She'd invited him to stay for dinner, but he'd been uncharacteristically evasive. She'd rummage through the fridge, just in case. Wouldn't hurt to be prepared.

In the last several weeks there had been no new threats against her, on the road, by mail, or anywhere else. The police had interviewed several people at the mill but had gotten no leads. The absence of any clues made Hailey increasingly uncomfortable, since she was convinced the man would strike again. Was he simply trying to scare her, or was she in real danger? The lack of an answer to that question kept her on edge day and night. Even if he were only harassing her, she felt desperate for it to stop before she lost her mind.

Hailey hadn't told her father about the sabotage. He'd just worry and that might affect his healing process. An underlying reason, he might wonder if she was losing her grip on the mill, after he'd trusted her with it. These things had never happened before her arrival. Maybe the fact that she was a woman president gave someone the idea she could be frightened or intimidated.

She wished it hadn't worked.

Hailey took chili she'd made a few days earlier from the freezer. Once it thawed she'd heat it slowly in a saucepan, if Alex wanted to stay for dinner.

Why was he making an unscheduled stop at her condo tonight? Would he—no, it might be too early in the relationship for a marriage proposal, though she'd still welcome it. They seemed serious enough for it to have crossed his mind. Once in a while he made oblique references to their future, and a thrill would ripple up her spine. But if he wanted to propose, wouldn't he choose a more romantic setting, like a restaurant over candlelight? What else could he possibly want to discuss with her?

Maybe he was buying a house and wanted her advice. She knew he'd been thinking about it lately, feeling increasingly cramped in his small condo with a forest of potted trees and vegetables in his miniscule backyard. A few other possibilities flitted into Hailey's mind as she straightened the kitchen counters and poked the chili with a fork to break up the clumps of thawing meat.

She heard his knock and wiped her hands on a dish towel. When she opened the door, she noticed a drawn look on his face, though he gathered her into his arms as usual for a tight hug and kiss.

It would be bad news. Immediately she thought of his mother.

"Alex, is everything okay? You don't look normal. Is your mom okay?"

He stared at her a second too long then forced a tight smile. "Yes, she's fine. I just needed to talk to you about something important. I don't think I can stay for dinner, though."

"Is everything alright?" she asked again. "I'll get you something to drink. Water, or something else?"

"Water's fine."

She glanced at him and her tension ratcheted up several notches. He was sitting stiffly on the couch, looking like she'd never seen him before. Normally he'd lean back, long legs stuck out in Ls, knees spread wide, arms stretched along the back of the couch. That day, he looked like he was about to be fired, or worse.

She sat opposite the coffee table from him, a cold glass in her hands, and waited quietly. He looped his hands together and rested his forearms on his knees. "Do you remember last year when I spent about a month in California at a vineyard near Nappa?"

"Yes, I remember." She watched his face.

Alex blew out a puff of air. His eyes didn't meet hers. "Well, a few days ago they called me at home and offered me a job."

Hailey stilled. No, it couldn't be. Of course, he'd say he wasn't considering it. But then, if he wasn't, his demeanor would be different, wouldn't it? He'd probably laugh and tell her he was flattered but not tempted. He'd tell her he couldn't imagine living without her.

But he didn't. His eyes told her everything. She felt herself back into the cushion of the chair, as if to increase her distance from him.

His voice took on a pleading tone. "I've been agonizing about this since that day. I didn't want to say anything to you until I'd worked it out in my mind."

"You're—you're going?" Her voice sounded tinny and broken to her ears, as if coming through a pipe, but she could hardly hear it for the roaring, which crashed and hurtled miles below to a bottomless, soundless explosion inside her. Her breath became shallow and for a moment she wondered if she'd suffocate.

Alex was speaking. What was he saying? She tried to focus. "—and I don't consider that this changes our commitment to each other. It's a new experience, but it doesn't mean that you aren't important to me, Hailey. I hope you understand that. I love you, and you mean so much to me, but—"

"But I can't really compete with grapevines, can I?" Tears singed her eyes and blurred her vision. Her acrid words felt like ash in her mouth. She turned her head away from him and pressed her fingers against her lips.

"Hailey, please try to understand. I need to try this."

She looked back at him. "I understand everything, Alex. You criticized me for putting work before our relationship, but it didn't take much for you to default to the same thing." By this time tears were coursing down her face. Inside, all her organs seemed to seize up and knot together, creating waves of spasmodic pain. "You'll leave for California. Then what? We'll commute across the country to see each other? How long will that last, a year? No, my guess is that we'll be done within about four months. I know because I've been through it."

The silence that followed was louder than his words and more devastating. She arose to snatch a tissue from its colorful box on the console under a framed mirror. "When will you leave?" She kept her eyes on her hands, which trembled slightly.

"In about a week and a half. I wish it were further out, but they're testing a new product and want me there to begin learning their system. It's a far bigger vineyard than where I work now, with really advanced techniques and equipment."

"I'm happy for you," she said dully. As he spoke of the vineyard, the familiar lilt had returned to his voice, for just an instant. "I hope my stalker is caught by then, or else you might be reading about me in the California newspaper." It was a low blow, but anything felt legal just then.

She looked up in the mirror just in time to see his wince in the reflection.

"That was one reason I wanted to go later, to make sure you were going to be safe. But they need me there for the testing." He gave her a plaintive, pleading gaze, almost like a teenage boy who'd been grounded. "I'll worry about you every day."

"Well, don't worry. I'll take care of myself, like I always have." Her voice had become brittle. She didn't like it, didn't like herself with that voice. Not with Alex.

She crossed her arms, suddenly feeling cold. "I know this is good for your career, Alex." Her tears hadn't stopped and grief strangled her words. "I'm glad they like you so much. I hope you have a stunning career, since that has always been so important to you, to prove yourself. I hope your grape vines keep you warm at night." Her voice broke even as her words tumbled out unchecked. Of course, she was being ridiculous, immature. The outrage kept throbbing, like a series of lightning bolts sizzling through her skull.

Hailey breathed deeply and stared at him. He sat, still bent miserably on the couch, his face tinged with gray.

Her voice was quiet now. "What's this thing we've been doing for the last six months, this expendable relationship? What is it, that you can just walk away? *Who am I,* that you can walk away so easily?"

She turned and ran up the stairs, not looking back, though he called her name after her. Through blurry eyes she fumbled for the doorknob of her room and locked it behind her. He wouldn't come after her. There was nothing more to say. She'd have to apologize later for her bad behavior, but she couldn't think of that now, not with all of her nerves and sinews feeling stripped of skin and burning raw with pain.

Hailey fell down onto her bed and the torrent came. She knew it had been too good to be true. She'd been too happy. It couldn't last. She should have tempered her feelings, reigned in her joy. She wasn't meant to have it for long. Only a taste, before it was snatched away. Sobs shook her shoulders for several long minutes. She heard the front door as Alex let himself out.

What was it about her that was so easy to leave? Her sister Hope had left. Joel had left. Her parents had been indifferent to her. Now Alex, the man who supposedly loved her, found it so easy to walk away, for the sake of a job.

He'd said they were still together, but who was he kidding? He'd settle into his new life and she'd continue on at the mill, that is, if the mill continued. Or would it all fall apart, victim of sabotage?

Would the perpetrator finally hurt her? Would she lose the mill, or her life, or both?

What had been the point of this chapter of her life? She'd thought God had guided her. She thought part of the reason she'd returned to Larkspur was to meet Alex and build a life with him, as well as restore the mill to vibrancy.

She'd failed on both counts and was left holding nothing but wind in her hands, howling through the empty hole in her heart. Leaving Colorado had been a gamble, one with a huge price tag, her sister, Hope. Desperately wanting to make up her losses, Hailey had taken the bet and lost.

And the faceless madman was going to win.

Chapter Twenty-Seven

"Hailey, did you hear what I just said? Earth to Hailey."

Hailey's chin shot up. She smiled wanly at Nina, who sat across the table licking her dessert fork. Her friend's pale blue eyes crinkled with sympathy as she smiled back.

"I'm sorry, I'm not very good company, am I?" The lunch crowd at Sunny's, their favorite local diner, had ebbed away while they finished the brownie sundae, a treat for which Sunny's was locally famous.

"You're great company. I know of someone who is probably right now missing your great company, in fact."

"He's been calling every couple of days. Always enthusiastic, telling me how much I'd love it there. I wonder if he's subtly suggesting I move there."

Nina cocked her dark head to one side. "Unconsciously, maybe. I'm sure he wants you to be with him. The question is, would you want to go?"

Hailey shrugged. "I might. But I'd probably be just running away again. I've done that once and look where it got me. Back to square one." She twisted her straw wrapper between two fingers. "I feel less motivated to go to work. It's like the life got sucked right out of me and I'm only partly alive. It's Alex, but it's also the strain of this criminal who is probably watching my every move."

"That's an understandable feeling. I don't agree that you're at square one, though. You've grown." Nina paused. "Do you think God is anywhere in this picture?"

Hailey shrugged then nodded. "Good question. I figure He's waiting for me to surrender and not worry anymore. But I'm confused, even a bit angry. I shouldn't be." A sob escaped from her throat and her eyes stung with fresh tears.

Nina squeezed Hailey's wrist, her eyes filled with sadness.

"I get so confused about God's will," Hailey said. "If He's guiding us, shouldn't things be clearer? I mean, I wasn't one hundred percent sure when I moved to Colorado, although the handwriting seemed to be all over the walls. Then when I came back I was fairly sure, but still had small doubts. Can't we ever be certain of anything?"

"You've had losses in both places. That makes everything confusing." Nina leaned back and pushed her brownie plate away from her. "Sometimes I think that if I'm following God's will, everything will work out and there won't be any obstacles. But I don't think it works that way. Life is messy, but He leads us through it. And we grow more than if everything were easy."

Hailey lifted her face, which she was sure must be red and splotchy. "Is it possible that God's 'perfect will' doesn't exist? Maybe we're just supposed to follow the best we can as life unfolds and hope for the best." She sipped the melted ice in the bottom of her glass. The late afternoon sun spilled into the front window and painted the edge of the table in pale light.

"We follow the best we can." Nina stared intently at Hailey. "Then if the results aren't what we hoped, we respond in faith. It's a walk, not a revelation. Step by step."

Yes, that description fit what Hailey's last year had been like. "Like a walk with a flashlight that's low on batteries." Hailey sighed. "I'd love to have clear answers. So much of life is like this, though. Every day I just pray my decisions are good ones."

She stared down at her hands for a moment then looked back up at Nina. "You said you saw growth in me. Did you mean it?"

Nina's gaze was compassionate but direct. "In the past I've known you to be unsure of yourself, too eager to please people, especially your dad. Now you seem stronger in your own abilities. Your faith seems stronger to me, too."

"Lot of good it's done me," grumbled Hailey, though she felt a nudge of encouragement at Nina's words. "I did my best taking care of my dad and the mill. But Hope and Alex—" She squeezed here eyes shut, unwilling to start crying again.

"Hey," Nina whispered. "Where's my Hailey Warrior? The girl who is brave enough to take on a failing factory?"

"I don't know if there is a warrior in the vicinity. She just puts up a good front." Her eyes met Nina's. "I know I'm feeling sorry for myself. I don't like being like this."

"It's okay to indulge in a touch of self-pity, but not for too long." Nina leaned back in her chair and sat still for a moment. "How long has Alex been gone?"

"Three weeks. It's not getting easier, if that's what you're about to say."

Nina laughed softly. "No, I wasn't, though I do think it will get easier. I'm sure he misses you too."

"Doesn't sound that way. Anyway, let's change the subject. How is Justin? You just celebrated six months of marriage."

"Nearly six. Three more weeks. And he is fine. We're both worried about you in this mill business. I think you should have police protection at your house, patrolling your neighborhood."

Hailey frowned. "I live in fear of that he'll do something soon. He's already tried to burn down the mill, run me off the road, break into my house. What else can he do, put explosives in my car?"

"That's not funny."

"You don't see me smiling."

"Well, this can't go on. The police have to find something soon. You're welcome to stay with us anytime you feel afraid."

Two fresh tears squeezed out of Hailey's eyes and traced a hot path down her face, as she remembered Alex sleeping on her couch when she was afraid.

"You're thinking of Alex again, aren't you? Hailey, he said he loved you. He's not the kind of guy to say it, then walk away. It was a professional decision to go to California but it doesn't cancel out his love for you."

"I just miss him. I'm afraid of what will happen to us in the future, of course, but in the day to day, I miss hearing his voice and seeing his face. I wish I were stronger."

"It's okay to be weak and call out for help."

"I want to have more faith. I feel so demolished. But I am going to try to just give everything over to God and really believe. It sounds hollow, but I'm going to try."

And she would, despite being completely bankrupt of her usual grit and optimism. Faith seemed miles away, out of her reach. Yet she knew that her heart needed time to grieve in its own way. She couldn't hurry the process. She could, however, lean back into God's strong arms. At that point, she could do little else.

After hugging Nina goodbye, Hailey decided to walk around downtown Larkspur before returning home. Shoppers filled the sidewalks on that mild Saturday afternoon. It was the middle of March and buds had begun to push through the branches like delicate green lace. The sun licked at her shoulders with a layer of toasty warmth.

Nina's words rumbled in her mind. Life *was* messy and often so tangled, it was hard to see the purpose. There were periods of peacefulness and periods of confusion, but rarely would there be certainty. It required a quiet walk of faith, with only the guarantee of God's love and presence and His ability to work things out sooner or later. Maybe it was okay to not see the end of the road, or even more than two feet in front.

She walked alongside shops with colorful awnings and displays, occasionally stopping to peer into the windows. It was as though everything in the city had emerged from a long winter sleep, as people milled about and bins of flowers, clothing, and house wares lined the sidewalks.

On one shop windows hung a few posters, boasting restaurants, exhibits and other local happenings. Hailey stepped closer to skim them. One announced an art festival two weeks later in the central square of town. If she'd kept up with her artwork she might have had enough to exhibit at the art festival. She'd let so much go in recent months.

Hailey turned away then felt drawn back to the window. It wasn't the poster that attracted her as much as the concept behind it. A festival. If she held a festival or carnival at Anderson Mill, it might smoke out the criminal who wanted to destroy her and the company. He had lain low for several weeks and was likely waiting for the perfect opportunity to strike again. What better moment to create havoc than a company-sponsored event? At the same time, the carnival would build good relationships with the town residents and provide a day of family entertainment and solidarity for the employees.

"Okay, Lord," she murmured aloud. "Here's one more risk, but you can handle it. Even if I can't." She forced a small smile, as a tiny filament of fresh hope needled through the fog around her heart.

Back home, Hailey stopped by the mailbox. Letters, flyers, and bills jammed the narrow crevice. She carried them inside and, still standing, sorted through them at her coffee table.

One card had no return address but was post-marked New York. Might be one of the sales reps or Judith, though she didn't recognize the handwriting. She tore the letter open and skimmed the first lines. It was from Adriana, Alex's sister.

"Hi, Hailey", she had written. "I guess this letter is a bit late, since I met you over two months ago, but I wanted to say I was really happy to meet you and I am so glad Alex is dating you. I know he's in California, and I'm sure that makes you both pretty sad, but when there's real love it all works out." Hailey smiled and briefly held the letter against her chest, though her eyes stung.

She blinked and continued reading, "I wrote some lyrics to a song the other day. It wasn't really written with you in mind, but for some reason with one particular verse, you kept coming into my thoughts. I figured I was supposed to send that verse to you. This is just a rough draft, but here goes. Hope you like it."

Hailey's curiosity was piqued. Adriana was keenly aware of people around her and very thoughtful. Hailey read the words,

You're remarkable. You're unique in all the earth.

Unmistakable. There's no limit to your worth.

Some people will not see, some of them will even leave

Even you will doubt sometimes

It won't erase the treasure inside

How sweet. Surely these lyrics would touch someone. Hailey sank down onto the couch and read the simple lines again, then a third time. A stirring began inside and sent warm waves slowly through the layer of clouds that had accompanied her for weeks. Moisture pricked her eyes.

How had Adriana known what she so needed to hear? What had compelled Alex's sister to send part of an unfinished song? Was it God? Its simple truth tunneled through and flickered feebly through Hailey's hopelessness.

A few tears tracked down her cheeks. "Father, You see me, don't You? You think I'm unique and remarkable," she whispered. "I guess You always have, even when people leave me. I don't know why You chose to tell me through this song that I'm not invisible to You, but thank You."

She hadn't been hidden from Him, like she was to her father or all of the people who so easily walked out of her life.

Hailey finished reading Adriana's note through blurry eyes. "Well, Hailey, I guess that says it all. Hope that encourages you today. Love, Adriana."

It certainly did. More than Adriana could know.

ଓ ଓ ଓ

Hailey scrutinized her clipboard and checked off each item. She surveyed the east parking lot, which had been transformed by rows of booths in various sizes all covered with vinyl tarps. The following day the booths would display crafts and artwork . . . jewelry, pottery, paintings, hand-made purses and scarves, all made by employees and local artists. At other booths visitors could buy home-baked goods, drinks, sandwiches, and ice cream.

To the west, several rides overshadowed the patchwork of covered booths. The mill couldn't afford a full-scale carnival, but she'd have at least a sampling of rides as well as musicians and costumed mascots roaming around.

Hailey prayed for good weather and a good turnout, but an even more fervently for her stalker to show up, either tonight or tomorrow, and the nightmare to end. She wanted to be able to walk around town, go home, go to work each day without looking over her shoulder wondering what would happen to her next.

Since the mill would soon launch some new products online, Hailey took advantage of the expectation of a crowd by leaving stacks of brochures scattered at booths around the grounds. With rides and concessions, maybe they'd even make a small profit, or at least offset the costs of the carnival. Her heart may be breaking, but she could still be a businesswoman when necessary.

When she'd first spoken to Officer Graham about the carnival idea a few weeks earlier, he'd shown enthusiasm, since he lacked any real leads in the case.

"What can it hurt? It sounds like fun, too, Hailey," he'd said. "And maybe your hunch will prove right, that this guy can't resist a chance to mess up a nice event. And that's when we'll get him."

"And no one who visits, aside from a few carefully selected employees, will ever know it's actually a sting operation," Hailey had added with a grin.

The police department had agreed to supply plain-clothes officers for that night and a larger team the following day, in order to watch for mischief and protect the public.

Would he come tonight? Tomorrow? Would he come at all? She now believed that the suspect was a current employee. How else would he or she have had access to the equipment or known her movements? Yet she was still clueless about the motive.

Dusk fell. Hailey huddled inside an empty booth with a tarp hanging over the front, which helped block out the chilly evening air. She scanned the parking lot through a space in the tarp. All was quiet.

The police officers were hidden in scattered booths, watching and listening. A few unmarked police cars remained in the lot on the other side of the building. She had driven with one of the officers so that her car couldn't be identified, just in case the stalker checked. She was leaving nothing to chance.

Two hours later Hailey pulled a sandwich from her canvas tote bag and ate it, still watching. Another hour passed. Then a sound jolted Hailey out of a drowsy stupor. Every sense was alerted and her heart pounded. She lifted the corner of the tarp just enough to see out. Someone was there close by, but she saw only his back. He turned and she jumped back in fright.

"Bill," she whispered, once she recognized him. "What are you doing here?" Bill Gatling stood there wearing a white baseball cap.

"Hi, Hailey. I wanted to let you know that about eight of us are here to help out. Only those who know what's going on, of course. Then in about three hours another group will take the next shift. All of us are wearing something white, either a scarf or a hat, so that the guy we're trying to catch can be distinguished from all of us."

"What a good idea. Thanks for coming, Bill."

"Of course, I'd be here. I feel as much responsibility for this place as you do. And all these folks feel the same way." He jerked his head but Hailey saw no one. "We weren't about to miss out on the chance to bring this clown to justice."

She looked out across the aisle and saw a white scarf. Its owner, Nora from finishing, waved at her. Two booths over, more white hats and scarves. Fred from the warehouse crossed himself then clasped his hands. They were fighting alongside her, for the mill and for her. She wasn't alone. That understanding gave her a surge of strength.

Another hour ebbed by. Hailey shivered and did several knee-bends to warm up and stay alert. She didn't know how long they should stay. Maybe she should have come later, but her arrival in the middle of the operation might ruin the whole thing. She couldn't leave until it was accomplished. She'd stay as long as she had to.

Around ten fifteen a movement near the fence caught Hailey's eye. A dark figure moved through the silent parking lot among the empty booths. Hailey craned her neck for a better look. There was a man wearing a knit hat. She recognized him as the same man who had tried to run her off the road. He was carrying a black bag, maybe a tool bag, and headed toward the rides. Apparently, he wanted to harm, not only Anderson Mill, but the people of Larkspur, by tampering with the rides. Hailey shuddered.

She caught a glimpse of one of the plain-clothes officers, but he wasn't looking in her direction. As he turned she waved at him. Too late. The stalker looked at her just as she lowered her hand. He changed direction and started running toward her.

She managed to scoot out of the booth and dash behind another one. Her heart pounded and sweat prickled her back and neck. The man wasn't far behind. When she heard silence, her fear spiked. She couldn't move unless she was sure he wouldn't see her. But she couldn't afford to look in order to make sure. What if he crept around the other side and grabbed her from behind? There must be thirteen other people out there. Why didn't anyone see him?

On impulse Hailey made a dash to the next booth. The man shouted something and she kept running. "Help!" she cried. "He's here, he's here!" No need now to keep quiet. He was on her heels. She didn't know how long she could run.

She felt a hand grab at her jacket and heard an unfamiliar voice rasp, "Got you now, President Anderson."

Chapter Twenty-Eight

Hailey struggled to squirm out of her jacket but the zipper had snagged the folds of fabric. Several people began shouting at once. Flashlights panned across the grounds like strobe lights through the darkness. "Stop, police!"

Relief washed over Hailey as the grip release her jacket. She heard a thump and a groan. Turning, she saw a pile of Anderson employees stacked five deep. On the bottom of the pile was the man with the knit hat.

Shouts spun up into the night. "We got 'im!"

"Who is it?"

"Oh, my gosh, it's Michael Sweeny. Michael, what are you doing here?" Vera's voice was sharp. As the employees held Michael down, the police came running from the four corners of the parking lot where they'd been hiding.

"Who is Michael Sweeny?" Bill asked. Hailey had the same question shouting in her head.

The employees struggled to pull themselves out of the pile. One of the officers handcuffed the man, who was still lying face-down against the pavement. As the officer drew him to his feet he shouted toward Hailey, "You killed my grandfather! You people are all the same, you think you're above the law."

"Pipe down, Mr. Sweeny. You can tell all this to the judge at your sentencing," snarled one of the officers. Just before they led him back to the waiting patrol car the man turned and stared at Hailey. From an unfamiliar face, black hate-filled eyes bored into her.

"Why, Michael? Why?" she asked, shaking her head.

He narrowed his eyes and muttered, "Just ask your father. *He* knows why."

ભ ભ ભ

Hailey's gaze panned across the colorful, milling crowd scattered in all directions across the carnival grounds. The balmy March air was laden with the sugary smell of cotton candy, blending with the acrid one of fire-roasted hot dogs, and the tang of chili and barbeque sandwiches. When the gates opened at ten that morning, Larkspur residents trickled in and eagerly fanned out, to sample the food and peruse the craft stands. Others made a beeline for the rides.

Though the noise and activity around her was constant, Hailey felt like she was floating through a dream, disconnected from reality. The stress of the last five months had left her feeling like a thin, porcelain doll. The ache from missing Alex was a constant layer in the background of the trauma.

Her nightmare was over, but there were still so many loose ends. For starters, understanding why. She'd wanted to call her father first thing in the morning, but went to the mill early to oversee the launch of the carnival. She finally reached him at eleven-thirty and told him she'd stop by around three. He sounded alarmed when she told him it was urgent. She'd protected him long enough. If he had a clue to this tangled mystery, it was time for him to tell her.

Her phone rang and she fished it out of her leather purse. "Hailey, it's Officer Graham. I told you I'd touch base with you today to give you an update."

"Yes, thanks, Officer. Has he talked yet?"

"He keeps rambling about his grandfather and your grandfather, but we can't make heads or tails of it. Kind of like irrational babble. It's obvious to us that he's mentally unstable. Turns out he was the guy who tried to run you off the road, and he nearly admitted trying to breaking into your house, only to scare you."

Hailey lifted her brows. "Huh, that's not what his little love note said. He was out for revenge."

"I'm thankful that you're alright, and that he was caught before any more harm was done."

Hailey rocked back on her heels, mentally avoiding a possible next move for Michael Sweeny, had he not been caught. "I'll be speaking with my father later on today, so maybe that will shed light on the whole weird story. I'll let you know."

"Please do. Thanks, Hailey. And thanks for your help in this. The carnival was a good idea, and your employees were impressive. They helped us catch Sweeny."

Hailey smiled then. "Yes, they're loyal and dedicated. In fact, I'm not Anderson Mill, they are."

When she hung up an older couple was waiting to speak with her. The woman, with kind blue eyes and dark graying hair, said, "Hailey, you might not remember us, but we knew your dad years ago. We're the Stevens. We learned last year that you had taken your dad's place. We're so pleased with what you're doing here. For a while we were afraid that the mill would just close, like so many others."

Hailey smiled in gratitude. They didn't know about the roller coaster of the previous year, leading all the way up to last night.

"We're proud of Anderson Mill, and proud of our town." Her husband smiled. "Thanks for all you've done."

"Thank you both for saying that," Hailey said with sincerity. "It hasn't been an easy year, but we're pleased to have gotten through the worst of it. The employees have really pulled us through."

"With your good leadership, I might add," said Mr. Stevens.

Mrs. Stevens laid a hand on Hailey's arm and said, "And I'm happy things will be available for consumers directly through the internet. That's such a convenience and, I believe, a step in the right direction." The woman gave Hailey another smile before the couple wandered back into the crowd.

Hailey hoped their statements reflected the attitude of Larkspur residents. Many of the brochures at each booth had been taken. Standing near an art booth, she wistfully observed a watercolor in soothing colors. Now that her life was calming down, she'd need something therapeutic to help her begin to heal. "These are very nice," she said to the artist behind the counter.

As Hailey turned, Vera from the finishing department stood behind her. "I need to tell you something, Miss Anderson," she said.

"Sure, Vera, what is it?"

"Even though Michael Sweeny was the one breaking machines, when you first got here he didn't do anything. He was a good worker and no one complained about him. I do know that Daniel Carlton was unhappy that you had taken your Dad's place, and I think he wanted to discourage you. He seemed to want to stir up fear among everybody. He even started a petition one time."

"I know about the petition. I suspected that he was against me all along."

"But all the while there was a meaner one in the shadows." Vera nodded solemnly, her eyes round. "But Sweeny didn't make his move until *after* Mr. Daniel left. Maybe he thought Mr. Daniel would be blamed for everything?"

"It's a very good guess. Thanks for telling me about Daniel."

All along she had had two enemies instead of just one. Daniel was jealous and plotted to drive her away. Michael, on the other hand, was probably mentally ill.

Hailey corrected herself. She'd actually had three enemies. Along with Daniel and Michael, she had frequently been her own enemy, with chronic self-doubt. And she'd left God out too many times, trying on her own to prove herself.

"I still don't know why Michael did those things." Vera shook her head and crossed her arms tightly in front of her.

"I don't either," Hailey said. "But I'll find out very soon."

Just after three o'clock Hailey left the festivities, which were due to end at four. For the first time in months she walked across the parking lot toward her car without fear of being watched, followed or attacked. She thought she'd feel more joyful once the crisis was resolved. Instead, she felt empty. Relieved, but empty.

True, she was content with what she'd accomplished at Anderson Mill in the last year. She saw it emerge from the brink of trouble to achieve financial stability, as well as pushing forward with creativity and innovation. She'd been able to test some of the dreams and ideas she'd had over a year ago, when she'd tried to convince her father to be more forward-thinking. But it had come at a cost, namely her relationship with Hope. Had she made the wrong choice? And Alex, if she lost him—well, she wasn't ready to think of that just yet. One adjustment at a time.

Maybe her job at Anderson Mill was done. Maybe she had finished her mission, getting the mill on its feet again, and she needed to move on. Bill Gatling was a knowledgeable and efficient associate manager. He was trusted and liked by the employees, since he'd risen from among them and understood them. Yet he also had a keen sense of what it took to run a textile mill. He might be able to one day take her place, or she could hire a new president from outside the family.

Hailey sighed as she turned the corner and drove into her father's neighborhood. Was she ready to move again, whether to California, to join Alex, or back to Colorado? She shook her head. She was probably just reeling from everything that had happened, and would soon regain her enthusiasm for the mill. Probably.

As she approached her father's front door she prayed for clarity in the Michael Sweeny story, as well as a nudge that told her she hadn't made a mistake coming back to Larkspur.

"Hailey, you worried me." Her father ushered her in. "Sounds so serious. Here, let's talk on the back porch, since it's warm out. I'll get us some tea."

She watched him as he shuffled toward the kitchen. It had been almost two months since she'd been to her father's house. She hadn't meant to neglect him, but fearing for her life had been mentally consuming. As she glanced around the room she saw that he had gotten rid of a few pieces of furniture and replaced the drapes. The room looked brighter and less cluttered.

"I'm sorry I haven't been here in a while, Dad," she told him after they sat down on the screened-in porch in back of the house. "When I tell you what has been happening, you'll understand why."

She sat back and breathed deeply. Where to begin? "In the last several months someone from inside the mill has been sabotaging looms and dye vats, and over Christmas someone set fire to the finishing room."

Her father's face paled. "Who, why? Was he caught? Hailey, you didn't tell me anything."

"Well, that's not all. After Christmas someone tried to break into my condo, and tried to run my car off the road into a ditch over by Newell Street."

As she spoke a strange look came over her father's face. His eyes reddened and brimmed with tears. "Oh, Hailey—" He turned his head away, as if to keep her from seeing his emotions. Then he stood up and in an instant was beside her on the wicker couch, his arms encircling her shoulders. She sat stiffly for a moment, then slid her arms around his waist. Her dad was crying? Hugging her? When had this ever happened?

"I'm so glad you're alright. I don't know what I'd do if something happened to you." He'd pulled back but his voice was still muffled. She had the strange sensation of being with a total stranger instead of her father, yet at the same time, her thirsty heart was nourished by his words.

"Really?" was all she could think of to say. "I'm okay, Dad."

He returned awkwardly to his chair across the room and sniffed several times. "You never said anything."

"I didn't want to worry you, you know, with your heart." She blinked rapidly, as the tears stung her eyes and emotion flooded up from a well of longing.

"Did they catch him? Who would do such a thing and why? Someone who'd been fired?" Her father's voice returned to his usual dry distance, yet a softness remained.

"It was a man named Michael Sweeny. He's been working at the mill for almost a year with no prior problems, but when they caught him he kept shouting something about his grandfather and my grandfather. He said I should ask you. So, Dad, I'm asking. Who is Michael Sweeny and why would he want to destroy the mill and hurt me?"

"Michael Sweeny?" Her father's voice was incredulous. "I thought that situation was long buried and forgotten. I don't know Michael Sweeny personally, but I assume he's a relative of Ted Sweeny, who was a poker opponent of my father's." He let out a long sigh and shut his eyes briefly, as if unwilling to remember.

He reopened his eyes and saw her watching him, waiting for his explanation. His voice emerged as a thin strand and his eyes had become dull. "As you know, my father, Benjamin Anderson, was president of Anderson Mill and I was working as his assistant. But the mill had big ups and downs because my father had gambling and drinking problems. Nearly drove my mother crazy. She kept trying to convince him to stop, but he was addicted to gambling. She lived in fear that we'd lose everything and be on the street. And it wasn't an irrational fear, either."

He took a long sip of iced tea and paused. "Finally, my father made a very foolish wager. A man in town, Ted Sweeny, owned a little hardware store that wasn't doing too well. He always envied my father with the mill. One night they played cards late into the night, both drinking heavily. They ran out of money. My father bet the mill, and lost."

Hailey gasped. "He lost? What happened?"

"My dad came home and was ashamed to tell my mother. He didn't tell her right away, but she knew something bad had happened. I think my dad was thinking of committing suicide. There were little signs of that. Then the strangest thing. Ted Sweeny dropped over of a heart attack before he had the chance to claim his winnings and take over the mill."

Hailey's mouth fell open. "What? He died? A fluke?"

Her father nodded. "Yes, a lucky one for my dad. At first everyone who knew about it thought my dad had had him bumped off. He was questioned by the police several times, but the medical examiner ruled it a long-standing heart problem that would have killed him sooner or later. The timing was uncanny, though."

"I'll say." Hailey leaned forward on her knees, riveted. "What happened next?"

"People looked at my father with distrust for a while and rumors flew around. My mom couldn't take it, the stigma on them and the mill, and she was angry that Dad had gambled their livelihood. That's when she left him, moved to Florida."

"Ah, I wondered about that. When I was a child you never talked about them. I figured there was nothing much to say."

"No, there was too much to say, all of it painful." His expression was grim, his pallor gray. "Eventually, it all died down, but my father died about a year or so after that. You know that story. I found him dead in his office and I took over the mill."

"How tragic. He died suddenly, just like Ted Sweeny. But what about Michael Sweeny? He's only about fifty-something. Was Ted Sweeny his grandfather?"

"Yes, he was. They were very close. Michael's father was a drunk. Used to beat the poor kid, but his grandfather was his idol. When the old man died, poor Michael never really recovered."

Hailey sat for a long moment as the swirling pieces began to make sense. Michael Sweeny wanted revenge from the ancestors of Benjamin Anderson for what had happened to his grandfather years earlier. "I wonder what Michael Sweeny has been doing for the last thirty years, as he waited to get revenge."

"I think he's been in and out of jobs, in and out of jails, and maybe hospitals too. I have heard he's a troubled man."

"No doubt about that. I'm relieved he's been caught and we understand his motives."

"I'm sorry I never told you. It was so long ago, I didn't think there was any use talking about it. It was a sad, dark story better left untold. I don't know if I've ever recovered from it either."

"So, you tried all those years to erase the stain from Anderson Mill." Hailey swallowed the lump forming in her throat.

Her father simply nodded, the story of regret, fatigue, and sadness etched on his face.

Hailey stood and went to sit in the chair next to her father. She laid a hand on his arm. "It wasn't your fault, you know. You just had to bear the consequences. I often wondered why you worked so much and didn't seem to do things with us that other fathers did, but you were running from your demons, so to speak."

He covered her hand with his own, such an unfamiliar gesture that he seemed hesitant. "It wasn't worth the price of losing my family. I lost all of you, your mother, Hope, and then you. And I lost the time I could have been a good father to you both. You came back, and I didn't deserve that. I'm thankful you came. It helped me to get something back that I'd lost. It wasn't just about the mill, you know."

Hailey nodded, not trusting herself to speak. "On the way over here, I was wondering if it had been a good thing for me to come back, but hearing you say that makes me really glad I did."

"Of course, it's a good thing you came. For the mill, clearly, but for me too. That next heart attack might have been the final one."

"With all the baggage you were carrying, I wouldn't be surprised. Now that all this is out in the open, we need to really let it go. New chapter."

"You should come over more often, Hailey. Bring that young man, the Mexican boy who came to Christmas."

Hailey felt impaled by pain that almost took her breath away. "He's—he's out of town for a while, working on the west coast."

"Oh. Well, when he comes back, then. He seemed like a nice young man, smart and well-bred, and all."

"Yes, he is all of those things." Hailey's voice came out in a whisper. She wanted to leave quickly, to be alone to think.

No, she should do the same thing she had told her father to do. She needed to turn the page to begin a new chapter. She took a deep swallow and prayed for the strength to do it.

Chapter Twenty-Nine

Announcements echoed through the layer of noise at the Piedmont Triad Airport. Hailey glanced at her watch and scrutinized the arrivals board. The flight had landed. Any second and she would see Hope's face.

This was a moment, among many in recent history, that Hailey could never have anticipated. Weeks earlier, after she'd heard the story about her grandfather, Benjamin Anderson, a message awaited her on her answering machine at home.

"Hi, Hailey. It's Hope. Devon and I have decided to come see you and Dad over spring break. We really miss you and it's been a year, so . . ." Her voice had trailed off, then an unexpected duet of giggles from both Hope and Devon followed. When Hailey had called back, Hope sounded almost the same as she had before their year of distance.

Now they would spend five days catching up, rebuilding. Engulfed by gratitude, Hailey felt it was one more confirmation that she was where she needed to be, at least for now. Following the devastating revelation about her grandfather, Hailey's relationship with her father had become closer, almost as if a frozen dam had finally broken down and melted. The burden he'd carried for decades had been lifted.

And finally, a chance to knit a new relationship with her sister, after the hurt and distance of the last year. "Thank you, Lord," she

292

murmured even as her eyes scanned the river of people spilling out of the corridor leading to the waiting area.

Then she saw them, Hope's dark bobbed haircut, Devon's contrasting blond strands, swinging to cover her face. It felt like ten years since she'd seen them. In an instant, she was in Hope's arms.

They held each other tightly for several seconds, as Hailey's tears began. When she drew away, she saw that Hope, too, had wet tracks on cheeks. "You're finally here." Another hug for Devon then they linked arms and headed toward baggage claim.

"Well, I couldn't let my little sis just drive off into the sunset, could I? I had to come. Okay, I admit it's been too many years since I've been here. I've even lost count. No, don't remind me." Hailey had missed Hope's rambling banter, which was like music she thought she'd never hear again.

Standing at baggage claim with her sister and niece, Hailey was almost in heaven. Only Alex was missing, a piece of her heart that would never heal. He'd been relieved when she told him that Michael Sweeny had been apprehended, and shocked when he heard the story of her grandfather. But it wasn't the same as telling him face to face, seeing his expressions, feeling his arms around her as he expressed his relief. It wasn't like walking along the lake and chatting about work, about dreams and goals. Not like holding hands, enjoying a stolen kiss, watching for his car, absorbing his dark gaze that said so much to her . . .

He still cared, he still called. But she knew it was only a matter of time when he'd call less frequently, then rarely, then not at all. She knew how these things went.

But she wouldn't think of it now. She had pure joy in her life at that moment, healing of her heart bond with Hope, Hope's presence right here in Larkspur. It felt almost miraculous, after the splintered, bitter year they'd endured.

The suitcases trundled around the baggage conveyor as Hailey listened to Devon recount her latest soccer triumph in granular detail.

"Not even a doting aunt wants to hear all of that information, Devon." Hope chided her daughter lightly. "How many times do I have to tell you to *summarize*?"

"I talk just like you, Mom." Devon's braces sparkled with her mischievous smile. Hope and Hailey burst into laughter.

"She's got you there, Hope." Hailey pulled Hope close for another hug. Hard to believe they were there. In Larkspur.

"I have so much to tell you," Hailey told her. "It beats any thriller you've seen at the movies. It'll have to wait until after we see Dad, though."

Hope's eyes widened with intrigued curiosity. After plucking the suitcases from the conveyor, they returned to the parking deck, chatting all the way, sometimes all three at once.

"We have to go see Dad," Hailey told them, "but first we need girl time. He understands this. Let's run by the house and drop off your things, then we'll head out to The Scoop, if you want some ice cream."

"You remembered." Hope's smile was soft, as if fueled by memories.

Once at Hailey's condo, Devon threw herself down on the couch as she waited for the sisters to be ready to leave.

"Is this your man?" Hope peered at a framed photo of Hailey and Alex on the telephone table. "You haven't told me much about him."

In the photo, Alex's arms were wrapped around Hailey from behind, like a loving wreath. Hailey had kept the frame there, even though it caused her pain. They were still together, after all, just separated for the moment. For just how long was anyone's guess.

"Yes, that's Alex. He, uh, he left for a job in California almost three months ago."

"Ouch. That's gotta be hard. Is he coming back?" Hope continued to examine the photo. "He's cute."

Hailey let out a long sigh and blinked away the sudden tears. "I don't know. He seems to like the new job, so I'm not sure where that leaves us."

Hope shot Hailey a compassionate look.

A voice from the couch, "Let's go! I want some ice cream."

Hope lowered her eyes at Hailey with the familiar big-sister protectiveness she hadn't seen in a long time. "I want to hear more about him later. Think he's the one?"

Hailey nodded, with fresh tears squeezing out of the corners of her eyes. "Or I thought so."

"I don't want to make you sad, so we'll change the subject. Talk to me whenever you need to, just like old times."

"Yes, just like old times." Despite her burning eyes, Hailey smiled at Hope. She had her sister back.

Two hours later they stood at their father's front door. "I'm nervous, Hailey. I haven't seen him but once since I left in a huff twelve years ago, when Devon was three."

"It'll be okay, you'll see. He's changed. And you've made this step, so that means a lot, regardless of how he responds."

"True. I made the step for loads of reasons." Hope squeezed Hailey's hand.

"What are you guys talking about?" asked Devon, just as the door opened.

"You're here," their father exclaimed, with an understated smile of welcome. "Come in, let me look at you, Hope, Devon." He ushered the three of them in and after an awkward second or two he wrapped stiff arms around Hope then pulled her into an embrace. Over his shoulder she made round eyes of surprise at Hailey, who simply grinned.

He turned to Devon, who didn't wait to be invited into her grandfather's arms. "Hi Gramps. It's been a looong time."

He chuckled before releasing her. "Yes, Devon. Much too long. We'll have to change all that, won't we?"

"Yes, absolutely," Hope said. "I'm sorry it's been so long, Dad. Life just has this way of happening. But then you have to step in sometimes and make decisions. I'm glad you're okay. I was worried about you."

Their father waved dismissively. "Oh, you can't keep an old coot like me down too long. I'm feeling better. And Hailey saved the mill. If she hadn't come back, who knows what would have happened to it?"

"Oh, who cares about the mill, it's you I was worried about," Hope said.

"It's the family business, isn't it?" asked Devon. "That's important, even though I don't care about fabric and stuff."

They sat down in the living room. On the inlaid wood coffee table, a tray of iced tea and store-bought cookies awaited them. Hope looked impressed. "You've developed hospitality, Dad. These look great."

He looked embarrassed for a moment. "Sit down, please. Hailey came back at the worst time, when layoffs were just about to happen. They were inevitable, but of course, she got the blame. But mostly the employees love her and think she's doing a great job."

Hailey's mouth dropped open. Was this her father, Paul Anderson, singing her praises, unprompted? He continued. "Then she modernized the processes, started doing all kinds of online products. And all the while, there was this lunatic—"

"I haven't told her about the lunatic, yet, Dad. I'm saving that as my scary story before bedtime," Hailey broke in, then winked at Devon.

"I can't wait to hear, but Hailey wanted to wait to tell us about that. Build the suspense, I guess." Hope reached for a cookie.

"So, are you retired now, Gramps? What do you do all day?" asked Devon. Hope shot her a frown.

He chuckled, a new sound Hailey was enjoying getting used to, and said, "Since Hailey took over the mill, I was able to fully retire. Now I golf, I work in my garden. I have even started growing a few vegetables out there, the ones the deer don't eat, that is. And the squirrels. Big problem around here."

"Dad also has a lady friend, Sharla," Hailey added. She looked at her father. "Hope it was okay that I told on you."

He rolled his eyes. "Too late now. Yes, it's fine. My friend Sharla comes over sometimes, or we go out. You'll meet her while you're here. Nice lady. She's going to make us all a big, southern dinner tomorrow night, with all the fixings."

"Is it okay if I sit next to you, Gramps? I haven't had a grandpa in so long, I just want to enjoy it while I can." Devon settled next to him on the loveseat before he had a chance to respond.

He laughed and hesitated, then slipped an arm around her shoulders. "And I haven't had a granddaughter in a long time." He looked up at Hope. "Or a daughter, but now I have everything I want, right here."

℞   ℞   ℞

"I can't believe all of that happened in the last year. You were almost killed!" Hope shook her head and reached for a slice of pizza. "I almost lost both you *and* Dad. Makes me even more thankful that we came on this trip. Sometimes you don't realize how important family is until you almost lose them. That's what happened with Dad. I'd sort of written him out of my life, thinking, he doesn't approve of me, well, I don't need him either. But I do still need him, and there's a time to let things go."

Hailey smiled. "Yes, that's so wise. Some things aren't worth hanging onto, and you did see, didn't you, how he's changed?"

"Oh, yes. He's kind of approachable now. What a far cry from before." Hope's voice bubbled the same way it had in Hailey's memory. "But what a weird story. I had no idea about Grandpa gambling the mill. That's unbelievable."

"I'm just glad it's all over. It's no fun living in fear every day." Hailey pushed away her plate. "I've had enough. You guys are forcing me off my diet, with pizza and ice cream."

"You set the menu, so it's your fault." Devon grinned, displaying tomato trapped in her braces.

Hailey's cell phone rang. She glanced at it. "It's Alex. I'll be right back." She walked to the entrance of the restaurant, where it was quieter. "Hi, Alex."

"Hey, Hailey. Has Hope arrived?" His voice was warm, like melted brown sugar coating her heart.

"Yes, we're eating pizza. It's a celebration meal. We went this afternoon to see Dad, and that went really well. Seems like lots of things are healing these days."

As usual when she heard his voice, her insides ached a little bit. One day, maybe they wouldn't anymore, and she'd be able to keep her sadness reigned in. She hadn't gotten there yet. In an animated voice he told her about what he was learning at the vineyard, about a new type of grape they'd brought in from Europe. It was the same Alex, but the world had changed.

There was a silence on the other end of the line. Then his voice was sober, soft. "Hailey, I really miss you."

His words hit her like a well-aimed bullet. She squeezed her eyes shut as a trickle of tears wound down her cheek. She tried to make her voice normal, but it still cracked. "I miss you too. A lot."

"Don't let go of me yet. I promise we're not over. Please, be patient."

Patient for what? She didn't know. "I will." It was all she could say.

"I'll be able to come visit soon. I had to get through the training period, but I'll come in early summer. I really want to see you."

"Me too."

When they'd hung up she stood near the doorway to the restaurant, head bowed, arms folded over one another as she shuddered quietly with sobs. With all the wonderful things that were happening in her life, his voice still had the power to reduce her to a miserable wail, which she usually held inside, except when she was alone in her house. She hoped she'd heal sooner or later. Probably much later, if ever. Would he really come for a visit? Was he just trying to placate her? If he came to visit, he'd just have to leave all over again. That might be harder than the first time.

When she returned to the table Hope's eyes grew round. "Hailey, are you okay? What did he say?"

"That he missed me. He wants to visit. No, we didn't break up. But I miss him so much, sometimes I just want to curl up and die. It's crazy, everything else in my life is falling into place. You, Dad, the mill. But it's like someone tore my heart out and I'm left with this hole. How do I enjoy all the blessings when this hurts so much?"

Her shoulders shook with a fresh wave of sobs. Finally, she took the tissue Hope proffered, and mopped her face. "I'll be okay. I'm sorry to put a pall of sadness on our festive dinner. I'm fine." She forced a cheery smile and reached for another tissue.

"Hey, don't do the happy face on our account. We're real, remember? Hailey, have you ever considered moving to California to be with him?" Hope stared at her until she squirmed. "You might love it, and of course you'll love being with him."

"And it's closer to Colorado," Devon added.

"Yes, I have. I've been thinking about it for a few days now. The only problem is, he hasn't asked me to."

"He probably doesn't dare. He knows he'd be asking you to leave the mill and North Carolina."

Hailey shrugged. "People in a committed relationship do it all the time. I could find another president for the mill. It's not like we'd be selling it to some other family. And—well, I'm less defined by the mill, like I was all my life as an Anderson. And even more so, with this Michael Sweeny crisis. I—I could move."

Hope leaned forward on her elbows and cocked her head. "It's worth thinking about, rather than losing Alex, if you really love each other."

Sure seemed like love while he was here, when he'd hint about their future. It sure looked like love when he was out of his mind with worry, accompanying her home from the mill every day. All of it bore a striking resemblance to love . . . up to the time when he boarded a plane and left her life.

"I have thought about it, even worked out the steps of finding a new president, streamlining the processes, or even doing some managing from a distance. So many things are done remotely these days, with outsourcing and virtual everything. I could do staff meetings through video conferencing. That's possible. In this modern age, there are options."

"The modern romance," Hope said dryly. "All that sounds kind of temporary, though. You'd need to make a decision sooner or later, to go there, for him to come back here, or to end. Hate to say it that way."

"Yeah, I hate to hear it." Hailey grimaced, then looked up brightly at Hope and Devon. "I would offer ice cream for dessert, but we've already had that. Maybe we should just go home and pile on the couch in our pajamas, like old times."

"Yay! Let's watch a video together," suggested Devon.

When they stood up Hope circled the table and wrapped her arms around Hailey, holding her tightly for several seconds. "My little Sis, everything is going to be fine. I'm not the believer in the group, but I just have faith about that."

301

Hailey felt a wave of shame. *She* should be the one with faith. But for now, she'd let Hope's love *and* faith carry her.

Ca   Ca   Ca

The porch chair creaked as Hope sat back on it. She crossed her arms and let out a contented sigh. "It's been a great visit, Hailey. It went by too fast, though. But you know where we live."

Yes, it had been a good visit, which had gently rubbed a nourishing balm into Hailey's emotional exhaustion. She had her sister back. "I won't hesitate to show up on your doorstep, you know that."

"During the last year you probably thought I was nursing my anger at you for leaving. I was, some, but I was just so sad that you weren't there anymore. I think I was depressed all year. It was like my arm had been cut off, or rather, my head."

Hailey laughed softly. "So *that's* the reason."

Hope grinned. "I just couldn't believe you'd bring such happiness and tear it away so fast, and for *him*. Dad didn't seem worth that sacrifice at the time. I guess I see the big picture now, with your commitment to the mill, with Dad's health concerns, all that. You had a mission to accomplish, and you did it. I'm proud of you."

"Thanks for saying that. I'm glad you have a new understanding of what the mill has meant to our family. Not that I'll never leave it, but it's important, going way back."

"I'm so glad we did a tour there. I don't think I've ever seen every building, and all the employees like bees in a busy hive. Made me kind of proud to be an Anderson. I never felt that way about the mill before. It was always this curse, the one that broke up our family. And now we know that the curse goes back further than we thought. I'm glad you're there." Hope leaned back, linking her fingers together over her waist. She shot a glance at Hailey. "That doesn't mean that you can't leave, though, if you decide to do that."

"I know. I'm still thinking about that. I'd like to hear Alex say he wants me to come. Then I'll give it more serious consideration."

"I think it'd be hard for you to leave North Carolina. Am I right about that?"

Hailey nodded. "I rushed out of here last year and almost never wanted to see the place again. But roots were still there, and when I came back, I felt like I belonged. It's my place. I won't say I'll never live anywhere else, but it gave me a context and a history."

"Me too, believe it or not. During this visit I've been surprised at how much I enjoyed being here. There's that southern culture, along with the progress in the town, and the people who have been part of our lives since we were born."

Hailey nodded. Hope understood how she herself had come to feel.

Devon pushed through the front door. "What are you guys doing out here?"

"Come join us. We're just summarizing the blessings of life."

Devon sat on the step and gave Hailey a quizzical stare.

"I was just getting philosophical, Devon. For a change." Hope rubbed the top of her daughter's head. "I realized it's good to have an original home, as well as an adopted one. Colorado is our adopted home, but this is our original one. You don't remember a lot because you were three when we left. But this is where you were born and where your gramps lives."

"And your Aunt Hailey," added Hailey.

"Yes, and your Aunt Hailey." Hope looked back at Hailey. "You're the only sister I have and Dad is the only dad I have. Life's too short to let petty things separate us from the people we love. Right?"

"Right," shouted Devon. She looked up at Hailey. "I guess if you're going to stay here from now on, we'll have to visit more often."

Hope and Hailey exchanged a long glance. "I'd love for you to visit more often." Even if she wasn't sure where she would be in a year.

Chapter 30

"As soon as you know the dates of your visit, let me know." Hailey pressed her foot to the brake as the light turned yellow. She shifted the phone to the other ear. "I'll take off a few days from work." Maybe this time Alex's visit would materialize. It had been over two months and, for a variety of reasons, he'd been unable to get away. Her heart grew heavier, her hopes more fragile with each unfulfilled plan.

His warm voice filled the phone. "I'll remind Geoff to confirm my dates before the end of the week. If nothing else, I'll come for a long weekend. I need to see you. *Soon.* I'm cravin' Hailey!"

Hailey laughed. She was glad he'd used the word *need*. She really needed to see him too, and had begun despairing that he'd ever visit.

The light turned green and she waited for the car in front of her to move. "I have a lot to tell you when I see you," Alex said. "Some things can wait until then."

"Oh? That sounds hopeful. Maybe you'll really come, then." She hoped her voice sounded teasing and not petulant, but doubted she'd pulled it off.

"My Hailey. I'll come, don't you worry. I have to go now but I'll call in a couple of days. I love you."

"I love you, too."

Since his departure, Alex had been consistent in his verbal commitment to her, and his promise to visit one day in the undetermined future. A filament of hope flickered inside as she pulled into her parking space and pulled her canvas tote and a plastic bag of emergency groceries from the back seat. April temperatures had climbed into the low sixties and a soft breeze made it difficult to go inside the condo.

As soon as Hailey deposited her things onto the couch and poured a cold glass of water, she returned to the bench on the front porch. The chimes jingled with each wave of breeze, reminding her of the first day she'd sat there with Alex so long ago.

She'd come to a decision. She'd tell Alex during his visit that she would resign from the mill and join him in California, if he wanted her to. She'd been mulling it over anyway, ever since her conversation with Hope a month earlier. Why didn't he bring up that option? Maybe, as Hope had suggested, he didn't dare, knowing it would require her to move again, as well as give up her position at the mill.

Such passion for his work drove him, one that absorbed his days in fascinating tasks. At times she resented that passion. It was hard not to, when the empty cavern inside ached for him daily. She lacked his passion and intensity in her own work, she knew. An emergency had led her back to Larkspur. She didn't know if she'd answered the challenge as one more bid to matter, to make a difference. Or was it God's call on her life?

Since her youth she'd identified herself with Anderson Mill. Now the events with Michael Sweeney and the secret she'd learned about her grandfather confused her, and scattered doubt across her future. It wasn't just her desire to be with Alex, but her desire to be where God wanted her, where she fit. She still wasn't sure where that elusive place was, at the mill or elsewhere.

Hailey downed the last sip of cold water and set the glass on the stoop in front of her. As she did, she saw a man approaching her. Her scalp prickled with a chill and she sat straighter. It couldn't be Michael Sweeney, who was behind bars. Nor could it be Alex. She'd just spoken with him. This man wore a baseball cap. As he approached, his features came clearer and she gasped. It was Daniel Carlton.

He mounted the steps and stood two feet in front of her, hands shoved deep into the pockets of a light jacket, his face an inscrutable mask. She kept her voice calm, cold. "What are you doing here, Daniel?"

"I have something to discuss with you."

"I have nothing to say to you." She started to get up from the bench. Anything to get away from him, but he was standing close enough to touch her, blocking her path to her front door. She glanced at her car, but realized she'd left her keys inside her condo. She kept her voice gritty. "This is private property."

"Sit down." A harsh edge in his voice stilled her. She swallowed and sank back to the bench, thankful that they were in public, in broad daylight. Her heart thumped in her chest. She kept her face blank.

He said, "This will just take a couple of minutes."

"What do you want?"

Dispassionate but hard hazel eyes bore into her. "We both know that the Anderson family doesn't have a legitimate right to Anderson Mill."

A heavy weight thudded in Hailey's stomach. How had he known about this? "What are you talking about? It's been in my family for four generations."

"I know the story, Hailey. Lots of people do. I have all the facts of what happened thirty years ago, from Michael Sweeney himself."

"Michael is mentally ill. You must know that."

"Yes, he is. But he was able to give me the general facts, and Willis Brewster filled in the rest."

"Who is Willis Brewster?"

Daniel took a step forward. Hailey pressed back against the bench cushion.

"He is the only living witness to the bet that was made thirty years ago and Ted Sweeney's death afterward. He's eighty years old now and lives outside of town."

"So, what do you want? Revenge?"

"At first I did. Michael had the same goal, after losing his rightful inheritance. So, we were going to figure out a plan together. But then he took matters into his own hands, sabotaged the machinery, and got himself caught. So, I had to think of plan B. Now my goal has changed. I haven't been able to find another job and I liked my job at Anderson, so here's what you're going to do. You'll resign as president and name me general manager. You'll tell everyone it was a mistake, or better still, say I didn't like whatever new job I got, so you agreed to reinstate me." A brittle laugh shot out. "And tell everyone how fortunate you think Anderson Mills is that I agreed to come back."

"You're crazy."

"If you don't, I'll go to the Larkspur Sentinel and tell them everything. Everyone in town will be interested to hear how the Andersons cheated a man from his winnings in a fair bet. After all your efforts to turn everything around, the world will know you're a fraud. And once word gets around . . ." He finished with a shrug, a sardonic half-smile frozen in place.

Hailey's mouth went dry. Her mind darted like a trapped sparrow. She maintained a calm face despite the fluttering inside and the drops of perspiration that trickled down her back. "Okay, Daniel. I'll consider your proposal, but I need time. Three days, then I'll let you know my answer. I—I'd have to consider the current operations to see how it would be to re-integrate you."

"Forty-eight hours, no more. I'll be back here at the same time. Friday."

Before she could respond Daniel turned and walked briskly back to his car. Hailey watched him as he drove down her street and out through the gate. She let out her breath.

After all that had happened, Anderson Mill was still under a shadow. A curse.

Hailey went inside and groped in her purse for her phone. "Dad, I need to see you right now."

Ten minutes later she stood at his door. He pulled the door open as he muttered, "My goodness, Hailey, what could it possibly be *now*? Is it something at the mill?"

Hailey waved away his offer of iced tea and sat in the chair opposite his. "Daniel came by just a while ago and is blackmailing me."

Her father's face paled as he leaned backward in his recliner. "How? And why? To get money? Or get his job back? It's been months since he left Anderson."

"Yes, that's true, but he hasn't found another job. He and Michael Sweeney were working together to bring down the mill.

They both had a motive. Michael did the sabotage on his own, not Daniel. Now Daniel wants me gone, and a job for himself as general manager, or he'll go to the Sentinel about what happened thirty years ago."

Paul Anderson stayed silent for a moment. Hailey knew to let him alone to process. And she was relieved not to have to bear the decision by herself.

He moistened his lips. His hands clenched, loosened. "A lot of people already know what happened, the older generation anyway. Back then I asked them never to say anything to you girls."

"Oh." Hailey nodded slowly. "I wondered why I'd never heard the story, and why no one seemed willing to talk about it."

"I didn't want you two bothered by something that happened before you were born. It speaks so poorly of my father. I didn't want you thinking of him that way, even though you didn't know him."

"Is there any chance that if the story got out, it could lead to us losing the mill? There might be a copy of the transaction somewhere."

Paul shook his head. "No, it was never recorded before Sweeney died, apparently. That would be the only way the family could get it now, thirty years later. Then, so much time has gone by. Statute of limitations, or something like that."

Hailey was still perched on the edge of the chair. Would the Anderson Mill tribulations ever end? "What should we do? We certainly can't give into Daniel's demands."

"We could call his bluff. Tell him to go to the papers if he wants to. Lots of people don't care."

"Or . . ." she crossed her arms and leaned them against her knees. "What do you think if we went to the Sentinel ourselves? If you're right that some people already know and others wouldn't care, it might work. We could let them know that Daniel will be coming to them with a story. It's risky, maybe." She paused. "Wait, I know just the person to talk to."

As she spoke, Hailey reached for her purse, rummaging through for her phone. "Brigit Fleming. I still have her contact information. She's a journalist who interviewed me for an article a few months ago, not long after I came. If I remember correctly, she made a reference to my grandfather that day, which means she must already know the story." Hailey stared at her father. "I'll set up an appointment with her, if you agree."

"If Daniel gives them the story, we'll have gotten there first."

"We don't have much time." Hailey clasped her moist hands, then unclasped them. "Daniel is coming back Friday at the same time to get my answer. I'll have to call Brigit first thing tomorrow, since it's after five now. We can sleep on it. And pray."

"Yes, we'll do both."

A gentle breeze flowed into the small office at the Larkspur Sentinel through an open window. Around a desk piled with papers and folders, Brigit Fleming sat with Hailey and her father.

"Of course, I'd heard the story," the woman said. "At the time, it seemed like one of those legends of a small town. But it's blown over by now. The only people who would care would be the ancestors of the man who died."

Hailey exchanged a glance with her father.

She leaned forward toward the desk. "This is a desperate measure by Daniel Carlton to get his old job back. How would you or your staff respond to him, if he were to come here with that story? Would anyone want to print it?"

Brigit leveled a stare at Hailey. "Hailey, I told you what I think of Anderson Mill. And what many people in this city think of it. They're behind you. You represent *them*. What happened in the past won't interest them. Well, it might for some, but for most it won't matter at all. It's just interesting folklore. Gossip, you might say."

"But would you print the story?" Paul Anderson sat up a bit straighter.

Brigit shrugged. "No, I don't think we would. I'm not the editor in chief, but I can certainly speak with her about it. Tell her this is a blackmail situation and we don't want any part of it. Ask her to keep it to herself. What do you think?"

Hailey's shoulders relaxed. "That would be great."

"Then if Mr. Carlton shows up, we'll lead him to the door." Brigit grinned wide then, her eyes sparkling with mischief behind her wire-rim glasses.

Minutes later Hailey and her father returned to her car and got inside. She reached for her keys.

"Let's just sit a moment. Don't start the car just yet."

She turned to her father. "Are you okay?"

"Yes, I'm fine. Just want to have a minute. I guess this ends the whole darn story, finally."

"Yes, it does. We can put it all behind us. I'll talk to Daniel tomorrow and tell him we've spoken to the Sentinel, but he's free to talk to them if he wants to."

Hailey's father was silent for a moment. He looked over at her and said, "Hailey, there's something I have been thinking about, that I want to tell you. You came back here and did a wonderful job, got the mill out trouble and onto strong footing financially. Then I turned it all over to you, assuming that is what you'd want. But if you feel like you want to do something else, you should do it. You're not married to the mill, regardless of your being president, and regardless of your being an Anderson. We can always name Bill Gatling as the general manager. The mill doesn't need a president and an associate manager both."

Hailey cocked her head. He was always surprising her these days. Her voice was soft. "Why are you saying this, Dad?" Had he read her recent thoughts?

"Well, even though you're doing a good job running the company," he shrugged, "maybe you'd like to do something else. I don't know, something artistic. You have a talent in art and always have. I'm just telling you this so that you won't feel like I would mind if you went somewhere else." He paused and stared back at her, eyebrows raised. "Okay?"

Hailey smiled at him and nodded. "Thanks for saying that. It means a lot. Especially now, since Alex is in California and I'm not sure if I should go there or not. But don't worry, it wouldn't be immediately, if I go."

"Just so you know you are free to do what you're meant to do, as soon as you figure out what that is."

She nodded slowly, staring through the front windshield. "I'm starting to figure it out."

Chapter Thirty-One

Hailey pushed the glass door of The Grounds coffee shop and scanned the booths and tables for a middle-aged woman with light blonde hair, according to the description she'd gotten over the phone. The nutty smell of ground beans blended with fresh pastry. Her stomach growled, but it could wait until her mission was accomplished.

She approached a table where she saw a blond woman glancing around her, fidgeting with her purse handle.

Hailey touched the table and leaned toward the woman. "Excuse me, are you Marion Sweeney?"

The woman lifted pale, creased eyes to Hailey. A haunted shadow lurked behind her gaze. "Yes, I am. Hello, Hailey. Please sit down."

Hailey pulled out the wooden chair with a scrape and slid into it, suddenly feeling awkward.

The woman spoke first. "I want to apologize to you for all that my husband did." She shook her head and cast her eyes toward the table. "He must'a cost you all a lot of money, and I know he threatened you too. I'm—I'm so sorry about all of that."

Hailey laid a hand on the woman's arm. "Mrs. Sweeney— Marion— It's over now. That's not why I wanted to meet with you today. I want to offer you something."

314

The woman's eyes widened and her mouth opened slightly. "Why would you want to do that?"

Hailey smiled and lowered her voice. "I'm sure you know what happened thirty years ago with your husband's grandfather. It was a fluke that he died just days after winning Anderson Mill in a bet. With his death and my grandfather's, all of it was eventually forgotten, which was good for my family, but not for Michael's."

Marion nodded. "Michael never really got over it. I think it was more losing his granddad than the mill, but for him it was all wrapped up together. He's been very confused and angry for years."

"I only learned about the whole situation after Michael was caught." Hailey paused. "Your son's name is Robby, right?"

The woman nodded. "He's sixteen now. And he's real hurt by what happened, and angry at his dad."

"I would like to set up a trust fund for Robby to help him with his future, if he wants to go to college or go into business. It would be a special fund for him from Anderson Mill, sort of a secret fund. Would that be okay with you?"

Marion Sweeney gasped and tears pooled in her eyes before Hailey finished speaking. Several of them spilled over and splashed on the table top. "I—yes, we'll accept that gratefully. Thank you, Hailey. With Michael in jail now, things are going to be hard for Robby and me. Knowing there's something to help him in his future will be a blessing for both of us."

Hailey reached out and took both of Marion's hands. They felt rough and cool but the grasp she returned was strong. "It's been an ugly situation, Marion, but there's no reason we can't bring good out of it for at least one of the Sweeneys."

ભ્ર   ભ્ર   ભ્ર

He was right on time. As she parked she saw him sitting on her porch steps. A chill of dread rippled down her spine but at least she'd resolved the matter in her own mind. She felt strengthened by her father's support and by frequent prayers throughout the day. Parked nearby, Justin and Hal sat and surveyed, in case things got ugly.

Hailey approached her porch slowly, inwardly recoiling at Daniel's presence on the threshold of her home. She hoped it would be over quickly. His face was shadowed by the same baseball cap he'd worn two days earlier. She avoided his eyes and stood beside him. She wouldn't cower now.

"You've come to a decision? To preserve the integrity of Anderson Mill?" His words came out in a derisive sneer.

"I'm not worried about Anderson Mill's integrity, Daniel. The mistake of one weak man years ago doesn't tear down the integrity and strength of an institution that bolsters the economy of this town. But—why am I telling you this? It doesn't matter. My answer to you is no, I won't step down for your sake. As for going to the Sentinel, do whatever you want. I happen to know they aren't going to care about your story, which is very old news." She shrugged. "But you can try. See if they'll listen. In your place I would look for textile jobs in other parts of the country."

His eyes narrowed and one corner of his thin lips pulled upward. "You're so sure they won't care. And you're willing to risk everything." A harsh laugh emerged like a bullet.

"I'm sure because I've spoken to them already. That's what they told me."

His face closed, brows furrowed, eyes murderous. "You're lying."

Hailey gave him a soft smile emerging from a place she'd recently discovered in herself. "No, Daniel. I'm not lying. My father and I spoke to Brigit Fleming, who you've met, and that's what she told me. She also doesn't want to be part of a blackmail scheme, for which, by the way, you could be arrested. Just saying." Her voice stayed calm, though her heart pummeled against her ribs.

Daniel's face became pale and he seemed at a loss for words. Finally, he blustered, "Now I know you're bluffing."

"Try me. Blackmail is a federal offense, but feel free to check with a law enforcement officer or even the internet if you don't believe me."

He continued to stare at her, his face twisted into a frown, his eyes squinting.

Hailey added, "Like I said, you'd be wise to look for work in another state. Good luck, Daniel." She walked past him and pulled out her keys, trembling, knowing he could ambush her from behind. She glanced behind her shoulders and he was walking back to his car, his head bent forward and hands thrust deeply into his pockets.

Chapter Thirty-Two

The comforting whirring of dozens of looms filled Hailey's head, even through earplugs, as she crossed through the weaving department following a meeting in Bill Gatling's office. He was doing such a fine job, he should have been promoted to associate manager long ago.

From the outside, it seemed as though no particular crisis had occurred at the mill in recent months. Production was up, morale among employees seemed higher than ever, and the new line of online products was striking a chord with the public in Larkspur, as well as across the country. She'd been able to hire back most of the employees laid off last summer, those who still wished to return, and hire new people to fill orders for products.

Few employees knew about the incident with Michael Sweeny. Those in his department knew he'd been let go, but didn't know why. Those who'd helped capture him agreed not to speak of it to anyone, including the press. She'd asked the police to keep the details of the case quiet as well. Thankfully there'd been no media coverage. No sense in stirring up the past yet again.

Alex hadn't called since the day she encountered Daniel, and she hadn't even told him about it. When he finally came to visit—whenever that was—they'd catch up on everything. He was still being vague about the dates, as if he wasn't sure when he could get away.

Hailey walked to her car at the end of the day wearing a light sweater. April and May had been fragrant and mild. June was starting out the same way, but would likely heat up quickly. She breathed deeply the mild afternoon breeze. Full summer foliage clung to the trees, forming a heavy, green canopy overhead.

What a relief that no one would egg her car or slash her tires. In fact, she'd bought a new lightly used car the week before, to replace the car she'd gotten in Colorado and driven back across the country. She was eager to exchange the negative memories for new ones, including with the car she drove every day.

Hailey drove through downtown Larkspur into the bustle of a Friday afternoon. She could have circled around the congested area, but needed to do a couple of errands. Besides, she enjoyed driving into the center of things, feeling a part of her town. Occasionally she saw people she knew on the sidewalks or in their cars, and waved at them.

Once inside the pharmacy, she stopped to chat with a couple of women she'd known for years, and the same thing happened in the grocery store, so that her errands took much longer than usual. She didn't mind. No one was waiting for her at home and the connection with other Larkspur residents filled her with the comfort of having roots, as Hope had remarked just before leaving.

She wondered if she'd miss the town if she joined Alex in California. If she moved, Hailey would surely miss her father, with their newly close relationship, after all they'd been through in the last year. She had never expected to one day feel that way.

At home in her kitchen, she put away the few groceries she'd bought. Suddenly she disliked her condo. It had always felt impersonal to her, a temporary dwelling that didn't fit, a sterile cage without personality. The idea of buying a house had swirled around in her mind several times in the last couple of weeks. If she stayed in Larkspur she'd get out of this rental and pick a home that suited her, one where she'd have room for art and plants, her friends, and family. Maybe she'd even get a dog or a cat. She'd been on the verge of buying that house in Colorado. Maybe now was the time.

That is, if she didn't move to California.

They weren't kids anymore. She should just come out and ask Alex on the phone if he wanted her to come or not. She wouldn't wait for his visit to ask him, even if it put him on the spot. At least she'd know and could plan the next step of her life, here or there. What if he preferred to end their relationship? She swallowed, pressing down the gush of grief evoked by the thought.

Cool tea on the porch would be refreshing after a long week. She fixed a tall, cold glass, frosty against her fingers and loaded with lemon wedges, and carried it toward the front door. She looked up and saw a shadow in the doorway through the upper window. Her heart seized up in fear and she almost dropped her glass in the floor. Daniel again? Suddenly an opposite emotion, which flowed in on a tidal wave. She recognized the dark hair, barely visible through the window.

"Alex!"

She set down her glass of tea and yanked at the door, forgetting she'd locked it. She fumbled with the bolts and flung the door open. He stood before her, grinning. Time and distance dropped away and there was only Alex.

"Thought I'd surprise you," he said simply, moving toward her, his dark eyes latching onto hers. An early tan colored his neck and face. She flew into his arms, which wrapped tightly around her like a rope. They clung and swayed then his lips covered her cheeks, her neck and finally her mouth. She kissed him as if her life depended on it, clinging in longing and need, aching for him. His lips explored hers for long, luxuriant minutes. Several times he nearly released his grip then renewed his ardor, clinging even tighter to her.

Finally, she leaned against him, with his arms still about her shoulders and his head resting on the top of hers. "Hailey, Hailey. I missed you so much. Every day for the last three months I considered getting on a plane and coming back here."

She looked up at him and gently touched the strong curve of his jaw. "You could have fooled me. You sounded ecstatic out there. Made me wonder if you missed me at all." She knew she sounded petulant but she was being honest. She'd often wondered if she'd faded in his heart once he got to the west coast. But his lips had shown her otherwise.

He lifted her chin so he could look into her eyes. "Oh, Hailey. How could you doubt me? I told you I love you. I still love you, nothing has changed. Let's sit on the porch together, like we did that first time we talked. Can I have some tea or water?"

Hailey grinned. "Of course. I may want to jump all over you, but I still have some manners, I think."

He hovered behind her in the kitchen, kissing her neck as she prepared his tea. "I don't know how this will taste, with you distracting me like that," she said.

"Doesn't matter. I'm only tasting you." He made a sound in his throat and nuzzled her ear. She giggled. Could she afford to get used to this again, when he'd be leaving in a few more days? Could her heart stand another round at the airport? She thrust the thought away.

They sat down on the porch chairs, their thighs touching. It wasn't possible to get too close to him, so starved had she been for his presence during the last three months. "When you first left I thought you'd be back sooner for a visit."

"I thought so too. I kept trying to schedule a long weekend. Over and over there were meetings, projects, training, it just never seemed to stop."

"How did you get away? Did they mind?"

"They wouldn't have minded a visit, but they didn't like it too much when I told them I was leaving for good." He turned his head to face her. "I'm back for good."

Hailey's mouth dropped open as she sat up straighter and stared at him. "Alex, is it true? You've come back?" She clasped her hands over her heart, afraid he'd simply vanish in front of her.

In response he leaned toward her and cupped her face in his hands. "I can't be happy out there without you, Hailey. I thought we'd somehow be able to make our relationship work. I wanted both, but I was miserable without you. I loved the work, for a while, and I liked that area of the country, but it just wasn't the same. Work is just work. I love my job, but when the day is done, I wanted to be with you, and you weren't there. It just wasn't going to work for me." He leaned toward her and kissed her deeply, a long, languorous kiss.

When he pulled back Hailey said, "I—I was thinking about moving out there so I could be with you, you know, getting someone else to run the mill."

"No need to cross the country. Our place is here." He leaned back, took a deep gulp of tea, and looked around her porch, as if to remind himself he was really there. "I loved parts of the job there, but it's such a big company that I only worked in one or two areas. When I was here at the vineyard, we did everything. We grew the grapes, tested the product, adjusted the sweetness, added other varietals, everything. We bottled and distributed, too. Out there, everyone has their specific job, and that's all you do. It got a bit like working on an assembly line. It wasn't for me. And already I was going crazy without you, so it wasn't a hard decision."

"What will you do?"

A smile spread across his lips and his eyebrows twitched upward. "I have a plan. First, I got my old job back, but they know it's just temporary, until I can find a vineyard to buy. I've been looking, and there is one I'm very interested in, which isn't on the market just yet, but it's perfect. I'll tell you more about that. I'd like to start my own label. I learned some techniques in Napa that I can use in my own vineyard. And I always wanted to work for myself."

"That's wonderful, Alex. I can really see you doing that."

"I have a network of contacts here, so that's always an advantage in getting started. I'd never have had that out there. First, I was new and didn't know anyone, and I would have had stiff competition in Napa. Here I can find some colleagues and friends who'll come work with me once I get set up."

Hailey leaned against him, smiling in contentment. That was her Alex. It was hard to see him doing only one thing at a large winery, far away from the vines and the grapes, and the soil and the sun.

"Where will you be living now, since you rented your condo? You're in the same position as I am, renting a place while someone else rents *your* place." Hailey chuckled at the irony of it.

"I found a little place nearby on a short-term lease. It's not in this complex, unfortunately, but I'm not far. And there's more to my plan I haven't told you yet." He gave her an inviting and sensual smile and added softly, "This part involves you."

She lifted her eyebrows, returning his smile in anticipation.

"I'd like to buy a house. The house and vineyard could be on the same property or two separate places, but I'll need a house with some space, room for my plants and all. And I need *you* to help me pick it out."

"Oh, okay," she said warily. Was he interested in her taste, her opinion?

"I want you to help me," he was speaking deliberately, watching her face, "because I'd want you to like it too." He paused.

Her heart started beating faster. "Because . . ."

"Because it won't only be my home, it will be yours too, if you're willing to live there with me. As my wife." His smile had seeped away but his dark eyes didn't waver from hers. Softly he added, "Forever, Hailey."

"Oh, Alex." Tears leaped into her eyes. She blinked rapidly. "I've never wanted anything more than to be with you forever, regardless of where we live."

"So, that's a 'yes'?"

"Yes, it's a yes!"

"I told my mom I was going to ask you and boy, was she excited. Adriana, even more so. She told me she knew you were going to be her sister, since she first met you."

"Really? I'd like to say I knew the same thing, but I thought I was rushing, when you hadn't asked me yet. And then with the separation . . ."

"She's very sharp, my sis. I guess you picked that up. Often she sees things in advance." Hailey just grinned and shook her head. Alex had no idea how much his little sister saw.

When Hailey thrust back into his arms, he buried his face in her neck and murmured, "Never again, we won't be separated ever again." He covered her lips again, moving hungrily against her until she felt breathless. "My Hailey," he whispered against her curls as his arms tightened around her.

He pulled back. "There's something else I need to tell you. Maybe I should have said this before."

"What is it? Nothing can take away from the joy I feel now." She grinned at him and wiped a tear from the corner of her eye.

"I found an ideal vineyard to buy, like I said. It'll go on the market in a few months. There's only one thing."

She tilted her head and looked at him quizzically.

"It's in McDowell County, about seventy miles west of here. So, uh . . ."

"I'd have to leave Anderson Mill."

He nodded. "Eventually. But I can keep looking. There are vineyards for sale in other parts of the state, some closer to Larkspur."

"Alex, when I came back to Anderson Mill, I came to prove something to myself. I came so I could matter, so I could prove to my dad I could make a difference. But by the time I finally *did* make a difference at the mill, I'd realized that I already do matter, to God and to myself. It just wasn't a need anymore. I'm ready to be where you are, wherever that is. California, McDowell County, wherever. My place is with you."

He stared at her and blinked once, twice, then drew her into his arms and squeezed her with an intensity that cut her breath. Then he planted a kiss on her brow and whispered, "What about your dad?"

She grinned. "I think he'll understand."

Alex nodded. "Well, we'll see what happens first, which vineyard God wants us to buy."

He held her for several moments as he stoked her hair, neither of them speaking. Finally, he pulled back from her. He searched her face and stared solemnly into her eyes. "We're back where we belong, aren't we?"

She felt giddy, almost lightheaded, with an overwhelming and jubilant desire to laugh. Why had she doubted? Why had her faith taken a detour? Why hadn't she known everything would fall into place?

"Yes," she answered, eyes searching his face. "Yes, we certainly are."

The End

Hope you enjoyed reading *Circle Back Around*. If you did, please consider leaving a review on Amazon and/or Goodreads for me. It would help other readers discover my books and be encouraged by their inspiring truths. You can also sign up to receive updates about new books at www.Kyle-Hunter.com

More inspiring (and romantic) stories that take you places with *Love on the Move*

One December

Is there any way to recapture what happened under a Christmas moon one December, when Mike and Nikki see each other for the first time in three years? Find out how their paths take unexpected travels (including Paris!) and turns in *One December*.

Prodigals in Provence

Bree is the stressed-out owner of Le Bon Voyage, a tour company specializing in trips to Provence, France. Travis is a prodigal who hides his wounds behind a successful career as a travel journalist.

As Bree and Travis lock horns amidst the stunning backdrop of Provence, they find they have more in common than they thought.

Read Chapter One of both books at www.Kyle-Hunter.com

Kyle Hunter writes inspirational romance and women's fiction that sometimes take her characters to faraway places. She lived in France for thirteen years. Currently she lives in North Carolina where she writes fiction, non-fiction (under the pen name K. B. Oliver), and teaches French.

www.ingramcontent.com/pod-product-compliance
Lightning Source LLC
Chambersburg PA
CBHW060517180626
46817CB00002B/390